ALSO BY SANDRA NOVACK

PRECIOUS

For Boo

Everyone but You

Dearest Sue,

Everyone but You

STORIES

Sat Nam!

Sandra Novack

With Much Love,
Sandy Novack

RANDOM HOUSE
NEW YORK

Copyright © 2011 by Sandra Novack

All rights reserved.

Published in the United States by Random House, an imprint of The Random House Publishing Group, a division of Random House, Inc., New York.

RANDOM HOUSE and colophon are registered trademarks of Random House, Inc.

The following stories that appear in this work have been previously published:

"Rilke" in *The Baltimore Review;* "Fireflies" in *The Chattahoochee Review;* "White Trees in Summer" in *The Gettysburg Review;* "Memphis" in *Gulf Coast;* "Hunk" in *The Iowa Review;* "Ants" in *Northwest Review;* "My Father's Mahogany Leg" in *Paterson Literary Review;* "Please, If You Love Me, You Should Know What to Do" in *Palo Alto Review;* "A Good Woman's Love" in *South Carolina Review.*

LIBRARY OF CONGRESS CATALOGING-IN-PUBLICATION DATA
Novack, Sandra.
Everyone but you: stories / by Sandra Novack.
p.   cm.
ISBN 978-1-4000-6681-0
eBook ISBN 978-0-679-64397-5
I. Title.
PS3614.O925E94 2011   813'.6—dc22   2010053002

Printed in the United States of America on acid-free paper

www.atrandom.com

2 4 6 8 9 7 5 3 1

First Edition

Book design by Liz Cosgrove

We are not really at home in our interpreted world.

—*Rainer Maria Rilke,* Duino Elegies

CONTENTS

Everyone but You

FIREFLIES

<hr/>

The night I met Lola was the same night Floyd's Used Cars seethed into an inferno. She leaned against a truck, picking pieces of cigarette filter from her tongue while firefighters ran past her, unleashing their coiled hoses and shouting to one another from under insulated coats and oxygen masks. The flames had already consumed the cars on the showroom floor, the chairs, and the rows of flakeboard desks before making an ascent, pushing through the roof and into the night air. Heavy plumes of smoke bloomed against the darkness. It was a dry August. The trees next to the car lot crackled and hissed. Brittle leaves ignited and then floated down around Lola like fireflies.

I felt the heat—intense, raw—I smelled the smoke adrift in the moonless sky, I sensed the possibilities. So when Lola drifted across the car lot to where I stood watching, when she breezily ran her hand over my crotch and said, "I've always loved a quick blaze, Lucius," I said, "Yes."

I guessed Lola was no more than twenty. In the firelight, her eyes appeared turquoise green, pale like smooth sea glass. Chunks of red hair framed her face and stopped short of her shoulders. Red hair on a girl sends me into a particular meltdown. Pleased with her self-assured groping of a stranger, pleased by my dick's affirmative response, she smiled and then looked around, finally, at the burgeoning crowd, at the people who walked out from their monotonous half-double homes across the street. A gas tank exploded. Smoke mushroomed up into the air and seemed to reflect the illusion of everything: Nothing was substantial and nothing lasted. My hands crawled along Lola's ribs. I kissed her neck—salty, hot from our proximity to the flames. A group of frat boys lingered behind Lola and me, their drink-induced laughter rising in the air as they gave each other high fives. One of the guys, a big, dumb jock, yelled, "Bring it on. Let's see if you really got it in you."

Lola seemed to be weighing her possibilities. She stopped my wandering hands for a moment, holding them briefly before letting them climb to her breasts. This acquiescence made most of the frat boys whoop and holler and curse in what amounted to a real scene, the kind of full-throttled force that said anything might happen on a night like this, when a fire blazes out of control and when the city is set to unpredictable motion. Lola searched my face for something familiar. I am not a bad-looking guy. I have a beer gut, yes, but my calves and arms are rock hard. I've been told by my old girlfriend, Sheila, that my dark eyelashes and blue eyes send women into a frenzy. I have two years of community college under my belt, and for someone twenty-six years old, I am aware, almost painfully so, of the larger world around me, which is more than I can say about the other guys I work with at Red Robin. I have a large Adam's apple and am perhaps too tall and (short of the gut) lanky, but Lola was also tall, and slouchy. I considered this fortuitous at the time, a meeting of the heads, lips, and middles.

My name, by the way, is Harold.

Lola turned and stared off into the flames. Fire, it breathes, moves. Smoke suspended in the air above us, and seized my lungs. My eyes burned, watered. Sirens blazed. The windows of Floyd's cracked and buckled. I swooned from the heat and from the close proximity of Lola. She said, "So you want a girlfriend, Lucius?"

"Not really," I said. "Not on a full-time basis. But tonight we can pretend anything goes. Tonight I'll be your Lucius. Tonight I already love you." Lola looked at me strangely, and then I delighted in the burnt smell that radiated from her skin. She had small tits, but her T-shirt clung to them. She wore white shorts that showed off her legs and the rounded curve of her ass. You tell yourself it's all about that—the ass, the tits, a certain measure of a girl that suggests she'll be good in bed and not too much of a hassle, eating you out of house and home and taking over your bathroom, adding to the general thrust of entropy in your life. I said, "Who is Lucius, anyway?"

"I thought you said you'd be," she told me. With a horrific boom, another gas tank exploded. Someone, I don't know who, shouted for backup. I was not fanatical about cars—I rode a bicycle to work and told the guys at Red Robin that for Christ's sake they should *think* about emissions—but a car on fire was still something to see. Metal covered by flames, paint crackling in the heat, and the effluvious vapor of oil and gas in the air caused an almost pleasant high.

"Okay," I said finally. "I'll be your boyfriend, and I'll be this Lucius fellow, but only for the night." I stayed as collected as I could, made it about what she wanted, what I wanted. I whispered to her. I said, "It's mostly because you have great tits."

"Please, Lucius," she said, whispering back. "Call them breasts. And, please, call me *Lola*."

AT MY APARTMENT there was frantic motion as Lola breathed, "Yes." I laid her across the bed and undressed her quickly, taking pleasure in the smoky heat that rose from her clothes and skin. Lola had an earthy smell—cumin, exotic spice—and her red hairs curled in wild, moist circles. A tattoo of a Phoenix rose up—wings spread, head twisted back—and stopped just below the mole on her belly button. I kissed every inch of her. I flipped her around to behold her, but she said *wait* and pulled out a condom from her purse. After that things moved so quickly I felt dizzy. The world accelerated and Lola was the reason for speed—Lola and the fire—and all I could think to do to slow down was hum the *Ride of the Valkyries*.

"You're kidding me," Lola said, laughing between squeals. I hummed more. Lola pulled from me, turned over, and then brought me close to her again. Afterward, she got up and made her way, naked, to the bathroom. The air felt hot and sticky with our sex, with everything about us that seemed to fill the small room.

I lived a few blocks from Floyd's, on the first floor of a decaying building. Pipes leaked and clanged throughout the night because the landlord, some Indian guy named Gopald Dusvehma, didn't, as he said, fix things that weren't broken. It was a one-bedroom efficiency with a small kitchenette. The walls were painted the color of canned peas. I'd covered the ratty sofa with an afghan in an attempt to make things homier, but the place was really something of a shithole, and I knew it. Still, after sex, Lola stood naked, looked around, and then walked over to my bookshelf and took down a picture of my mother and father. She commented on my associate's degree in English, tacked up on the wall. "Why didn't you go all the way?" she asked, turning around to face me. Her nipples were rock hard, pointed like rubber nubs on a pencil. Her hip bones protruded slightly, in a pleasing way. Her body, I decided, was beautiful.

"School?" I said, shrugging. I got up, pulled on my jeans. A part of me was hoping she'd take this as a sign to leave. Nice and simple, I thought. In my experience, too much history, too much talk, and things start to go downhill. Soon she'd be asking about my parents. "I don't know. Lazy, I guess. I got tired."

"Interesting," she said. She ran her hand over my collection of books. Then she placed her hands on her hips. "You know what I'm thinking?" she asked.

"I'm no mind reader."

"I'm thinking that even in a shithole like this, Lucius, there are always possibilities."

Did I love her then? I loved the look of her, the contours of her body—the two dimples above her ass, the line of her backbone, the unending supply of freckles that spotted her body. I could even say I loved the way the room felt with Lola in it, which is to say surprising, bright.

Lola came back to bed. She lay naked atop the covers. "Got any pot?"

"Hell, yes," I told her.

"I figured," she said. "I'm a very good judge of character."

I pulled my stash of pot out from the bedside table. Lola

flicked on the television and we smoked some dope together. I was pretty supportive of *that* shit, I'll tell you—the strange, pleasant feeling that only dope can give, coupled with that sense of wonder and amazement and, yes, even love. Lola inhaled. She smiled widely. The pipes clanged. She said, "What is it with your pipes, anyway?"

"Gopald Dusvehma says they aren't broken, so what's the problem?"

Lola snorted. She couldn't help it. She snorted again. When she stopped, we watched the Weather Channel, the swirls of precipitation that appeared on the Doppler radar. *That* was something to see.

She said, "That's something else. Quite a fire, too. All those explosions."

"It was good for me."

"It was fate."

"I don't believe in fate."

"You will," she said. "After you're done with me you will."

"Oh, I'm *sure* I will."

Lola slapped me gently before passing me the joint. She leaned back, yawned. "Listen, I need a place to crash," she said. "Are you hearing me? Stop laughing, because this is a serious query. Lucius, listen, will you? I need a place to *crash,* and after I've sucked your dick, I think it's the least you can do."

"Crash and burn," I said, snickering. I was going to tell her all the reasons she couldn't stay at my apartment. I was going to tell her I had a girlfriend, or tell her the place was infested, the latter of which was at least probably true. Instead I inhaled slowly and thought too long about all this, and Lola took that pause to be an affirmation. She lifted a long, thin leg, stared at her thigh, and stroked it. "Great," she said. "It's settled. I could use a new boyfriend, anyway. My last one turned out to be a real dud after everyone thought he was promising. The right people always end up being wrong."

I exhaled. I passed her the joint. "And the wrong people?"

"Beats me," she said. "I never tried one out before. Anyway, that's part of the reason I need a place to crash—old boyfriends and the like who are jealous, practically lunatics, really. And *stupid*, Lucius. You have no idea how incredibly stupid some men can be. So just tonight, I'll stay. Maybe a few days. Definitely not longer than a week, okay?"

The pot had made me mellow. "Lola," I said. "Maybe we shouldn't."

"I'm harmless," she told me. She held up an imaginary gun and squeezed the trigger. "Or do I look like Annie Oakley to you?"

"I don't know," I confessed.

"Look, it's just that my last boyfriend was a real fucker, Lucius. He messed around with my best friend, my *roommate*," she said. Her eyes narrowed. "She was a real fucker, too. I needed a change of pace after that, let me tell you. I needed a way out of that dorm room."

My legs felt heavy, like doused wood. I wanted Lola to leave. When you tell yourself it's about sex and the sheer presence of a girl, you don't leave room for conversation in the equation because conversation is frequently a mood killer. You certainly don't expect to hear about ex-lovers. It was all a bit alarming, but the alarm was still distant, like sirens making their way across the city. *Danger is near,* the sirens announce. You sense it, too, the faint alarm it stirs in you. But it's not in your home, in your bed, *your* place isn't in flames yet, and in that regard it's still okay. I cupped my hands behind my head and stared at the watermarks that spotted the stucco ceiling like a huge question mark. "We were getting along, Lola," I said.

She inhaled deeply, allowing herself time to calculate a response. "Good, then," she said. "It's settled. I'll stay."

Somewhere during the course of two hours she had gotten the upper hand. That much was clear. I said nothing. There were practical considerations to Lola entering my life so easily. Even Sheila, my last girlfriend, didn't stay overnight on most nights we slept together, and certainly not even until a few weeks into things. This was Lola's and my first meeting, our first fuck. There were modern-day discretionary boundaries, I felt, that were being quickly toppled, and I felt unnerved at the prospect of Lola spending the night in close proximity. If you give a girl enough leeway, she'll take over like wildfire, like Sheila eventually did. It took only a few weeks before Sheila acted as though she owned me. *What are you doing, Harold?* Sheila would ask when she called from the office. *Are you thinking about me? Have you thought about other women? Do you want to fuck someone else, Harold? Do you?*

Et cetera. Sharing fluid was one thing, but sharing an apartment was an altogether different matter. What if Lola peed voluminously? Hung her clothes from the curtain rod? Lined the medicine cabinet with condoms and tampons? Worse, what if Lola was a lunatic? I hadn't indulged the thought before that moment, but as the pot took a stronger hold over my thoughts I wondered: *What if Lola was the one who set the fire?* I had often heard that criminals hung around the scene, which made sense, and in Lola's case certainly would have been true. Deviance of the criminal kind was definitely something I couldn't handle in my life. This was what I thought in the amount of time it took

Lola to hand me the joint, get up again, and go to the bathroom and pee voluminously.

When she came back, I said, "We were getting along so well, just with the impromptu fucking. Why go and ruin things?"

"The first Lucius said the exact same thing. What is it with Luciuses?" she asked, biting her lip. "I've *got* to try out a new name."

"Not that it matters," I said. "But my name is actually Harold."

"Harold?" She made a face. Then she cackled. "That's not much of a name. It's a little outdated."

"It's my mother's father's name."

"Does that make it right? What, does your mother hate you or something?"

"No."

"You might not think so," she told me. "But with a name like that I bet she does."

So, good, I thought. *Sex with a mysterious stranger! Bodies slapping together! Raging climaxes!* But Lola wasn't some dumb chick you could easily fuck and then discount. In the four months we were together, in that hazy time I've come to think on as our *relationship,* I learned that, on the contrary, she had big plans and ambitions that for a time stretched outward to include yours truly. She had *aspirations.* She had a bank account. I spent my days scrubbing down toilet seats, vacuuming rugs, scraping caramelized soda from tables, and placing signs about the specials in the windows at Red Robin—Ninety-nine cent burger! All you can eat buffet! Free Coke with meal purchase! Advertise, advertise, advertise. I was barely getting by riding a beat-up bike to work and earning three bucks above minimum wage, a salary enhanced thanks to my associate's degree. It turned out Lola was a sophomore in college part of the day and the other part of the day she spent balled up on a couch at the Barnes and Squat downtown. She drank cappuccinos. She read Voltaire and Salinger and thought the world of literature would, in her words, *rise again!* She gave me a copy of *The Catcher in the Rye* and told me I could stand to learn a thing or two. "Here's a dictionary," she said one day after I came home from work. She had checked out an *actual* dictionary from the library. She said, "Now use it, will you?" This, all while she was contributing so little to the apartment, or the refrigerator. It was as if her sense of responsibility was both grand on the one hand and totally lax on the other. She aspired to the greats in art and literature, but she also seemed to think that the orange juice she so loved would just magically appear for her consumption every morning. Voltaire didn't think about buying orange juice, she told me once as we sat eating breakfast, so why should she?

There are certain differences in people that stem down the line of generations, certain things you cannot overlook that should be factored into relationship equations. For example, star-crossed fantasy aside, children of doctors generally end up finding well-to-do, well-groomed, and well-mannered mates. Or, as another example, people who hate eating meat don't generally end up marrying a butcher. Things like that. As for Lola and me, my mother was very old-school about things and probably wouldn't have approved of the way Lola introduced herself, if she ever found out. Also, my mother and father didn't have a lot of money. They were middle class, which translated to pretty damn poor and fucked in America. My father worked as a cashier at a retail store. My mother worked at a dentist's office, filing papers. She crocheted at night while my father went hunting on fall weekends and spent the rest of his time watching CNN and complaining about taxes. It turned out Lola's parents, whom I never met, lived in an entirely different state: Connecticut. Her father was a doctor and made something like a zillion bucks a year. Lola's mother didn't work at all. She volunteered at the church shop and served meals to the homeless. She dressed in designer clothing and read to the elderly on weekends. They were good, Christian people, who, through the mystery of genetics, still managed to crank out a hellion like Lola. They were *Republicans.* They spent their summers in France. France, for Christ's sake. Lola spoke three languages, while I was struggling to master the nuances of one.

I'M GETTING AHEAD of myself. It happens sometimes, looking back at things from a distance, that the time line of love becomes obscured; things meld together. How did I even come to wonder or to care about Lola's background? How did we cross that mystical line, where *she and I* became an *us*?

In the week following the fire and our first, fateful encounter, Lola showed up each night at my apartment, even though I hadn't committed, in any overt way, to letting her room with me. I'd be bone-tired after work, and she'd be standing there at the door, waiting, dressed in cut-off jean shorts, a top that clung to her. Sometimes she'd have on bohemian-type bracelets and long earrings. She'd look red hot. "Hey, we should probably get some ice cream tonight before bed," she'd say, matter-of-factly. Or, "I brought Scrabble and a copy of *Backdraft,* in honor of our meeting." Or, "Baby, we've got to stop running into each other like this." She'd reach out and squeeze my arm, bite her lip, and give me a rebellious, mischievous look. After sex I'd resist having her stay the night. I told her, like a lot of guys my age, I didn't necessarily want a girlfriend or a roommate; I pretty much just wanted to get laid. I explained that sex was one of the great motivating forces in life. "Sex and food," I said. "Just watch *Animal Planet* sometime and you'll see what I mean."

She thought I was joking. She said, "Don't tell me I'm not the best thing that's happened to you all year." She was right. By the end of the first week, she was cleaning out my closets and moving in her things. By the second week she had keys and was painting the walls because she claimed to be allergic to drab surroundings. Every night when I came home from work she'd make dinner and light candles. My professed need for only sex and food aside, it was hard to deny the benefits of Lola's entrance into my life. The place began to feel like a home. She even brought her goldfish, Boo, over from the dorm room. "Boo isn't safe with that lunatic fucker of an ex-roommate of mine," she said. She wanted to know how I reacted to animals. She tapped her finger on the glass bowl. "I learned in my psychology class that most deviant people don't relate well to pets," she said. "Can you please tell me your thoughts on that?"

"It's not a pet," I told her. "It's a goldfish."

"Uh-huh," she said, like she was noting this. "Having a fish is no different than having a dog or a cat or a new boyfriend or girlfriend, you know. If you're not going to learn how to take care of them, if you're not going to give them the proper conditions in which they can thrive, then you don't have any business having them in the first place. In that case you might as well be

like my ex-roommate or boyfriend, both of which are some serious fuck-ups, Lucius."

"I started out alone," I remind her. "Happily."

"Didn't we all start out alone?" she said. "Happily?"

I tried to be reasonable about all this. I stopped asking her to
leave when it became clear she had no intention of leaving anyway. I stopped resisting her affections when it was clear that re-
sistance only made her desire stronger. That's the kind of girl
Lola was. I pushed her away but she persisted and hung on and
made me love her.

I'd heard that romances were sometimes born under extreme, hostile conditions, which I suppose is how things went
with Lola. After Floyd's, and in those weeks when Lola and I
were reconfiguring our boundaries, fires sprang up all across
the city. The blazes were set in the dead hours of night. The police began referring to the culprit as the "Lunar Pyro," since the
person set the fires during those occasions when the moon was
full and beamed down and grew diffuse amid the artificial lights
of the city, those same nights when crime in general rose and
sirens sounded in urgent ways.

Lola and I followed the story. One night in September we sat
and listened to the latest news report on the Pyro's antics out on
Third Street, where a small Mexican restaurant had been set
ablaze. Hearing this, Lola shook her head in disbelief and bit
into the apple she was holding. She tucked her legs under her
and turned to face me. "Lunar Pyro," she said. "It really doesn't
have much pizzazz, does it?"

I agreed in an absent way, thinking how good Lola looked
eating an apple, how in her hands and against her full lips an
apple became a thing of beauty. "You know the type Lunar Pyro

is?" she continued, chewing. "He's probably your average Joe, the type you'd never expect, seemingly pleasant, oh sure, but a man who holds a grudge against not just a single person, but against the entire world."

"Hm," I said. "Can I have a bite?"

"Get your own."

I went to the kitchen and retrieved an apple. When I came back to the couch, Lola turned off the TV and tossed the remote on the table. She gave me a curious expression. She said, "Why do you ride a bike, anyway, Lucius? That's what I want to know."

"Harold, Lola. I've told you before to call me Harold."

"Okay, *Harold*. So why the bike?"

"Environmental protest."

She raised her wonderfully expressive eyebrows. "Really."

"Somewhat," I said. "Also I don't have a ton of cash. Do you know what gas costs these days?"

"Next question," she said. "Have you ever been in love? I mean, before me."

"Well, there was Sheila," I said. "She was pretty hot."

Lola studied me intently. She waited.

"Anyway," I told her, "I've never been in love."

"I believe you, because it's very obvious. My last boyfriend was in love *all the time*. He was what we'd call a romantic. But you, you're different. You're terrified of real love. Trust me, I know it when I see it. It's like looking in the mirror."

"Okay." I bit my apple.

"But the thing is, everyone should at least have some sort of story. Love, unrequited love, broken love, the search for love, recovery efforts, you know, stuff like that. And if you don't have it, well, then, you've got to make shit up because the world requires conflict and heartache."

What was I to say? I shrugged.

"You know what I think? You set the fires. You, Lucius, are the Lunar Pyro."

"Get out of here," I said. "I'm not a pyromaniac. I'm a comic-maniac, maybe."

"True," she said. "But let's pretend anyway. You set the fires because your girlfriend—let's name her Bertha—the light of your life, the fire of your loins, broke your heart, and when she left, something deep within you died. It's the fires that make the pain go away for a time. Think of it, Lucius, the blaze, the energy, the excitement of it all. It makes you forget that you're heartbroken."

I turned toward her. "So what's Bertha like?" I asked. "Is she at least a hottie?"

Lola rolled her eyes. "What does it matter?" She thought for a while, before continuing. "Fine. Bertha Copeland, twenty-one, blond hair, short legs, a little stocky—frankly, Lucius, I'm surprised at you—but generally soft-spoken, lacking backbone. It's a wonder she had the nerve to break up with you in the first place, the few prospects that she has. She's really rather quite homely, now that I think about it, but her ugliness has fostered in her a good soul, a kind disposition, and that's what you loved."

"I did?"

"Yes, you did. Pay attention."

"Was she good in bed?"

"Hardly. But she had a way of looking at you after sex, you know, a meeting of the souls or something like that."

"Interesting," I said. "I'm starting to get horny. Can I call you Bertha?"

Lola flushed with embarrassment. She shook her head. She

picked up the dictionary from the coffee table and opened to a random page: "Effluvious," she said.

"Effluvious," I said.

"It's wonderful when you do that."

"What?" I asked.

"Play along."

AFTER THAT I STARTED taking Lola out on bona fide dates. Movies, art shows held on campus, dinners at the Red Robin. By mid-October she was officially my girlfriend and I'd begun, for the first time in my life, to think of a life with Lola that spanned out beyond our exultant fucking. I realized that in Lola's presence I was becoming a better person. It began to feel that our meeting was fated. I talked about going back to school. I thought eventually I could get a better job, and Lola and I might even get a small place with a yard and a dog. In actual conversation, though, I limited the scope of such thinking. I talked about what we might do for a New Year's celebration, or how the following summer we might go to the beach for the weekend. When I discussed these things, I tried to ignore the look that overcame Lola, as well as the certain phlegmatic "maybe" she issued in response.

"So what's the status update on us?" I asked one rainy day while we sat together at the Red Robin, sharing a sundae. Lola looked out the window to the dreary cityscape. "I mean," I added, "do you have plans to take off to France anytime soon, get on the right side of the tracks?"

She glanced back at me then, picked up her spoon, and dug into the sundae. "'Us,'" she said. "Weren't you the one opposed to the notion of an 'us'?"

"Initially," I said. "But then I started working to support your orange juice cravings."

"Okay," she agreed too easily. "So there's an us; but remember, two beings can't share the same space at the same time. We're not fused together or anything, Lucius. This isn't like *Harold and Maude,* after all."

"For the twentieth time, Lola, my name *is* Harold."

She shifted. She pushed the sundae forward, toward my side of the table. "Lucius adds some distance to things," she said. "Sometimes I find I require it."

"Oh, you *require* distance? I thought you wanted a real boyfriend."

"I wanted a place to crash initially," she said. "Then it got complicated."

"Right. Like your girlfriend begins evasive maneuvering just when you agree to care. Isn't that always the way it is?"

She thought for a while. "Fine, *Harold,*" she said. "I'll be your Maude. Still, a girl's got to protect her heart, regardless."

"Huh," I said. I looked out the window. I waited.

She rummaged around in her purse, pulled out her keys. She got up. She left the bill, leaned in, and kissed me. "See you later, gator. I've got a date with Voltaire."

"OH, YOUNG LOVE!" my mother exclaimed when I called and told her I didn't understand women. It was probably then, at the moment I solicited the advice of an elder, that I should have known I was undeniably screwed.

"Because sometimes she seems distant," I explained. "What's up with that?"

"Look, Harold," my mother said in an affectionate, doting

way. "I think you've got a good thing going here, so don't over-think it. She's in college and she's smart—just like you, except she's currently enrolled in classes."

"Don't push it, Mom," I said.

She sighed. "On the subject of women and distance, buy her something nice. That's what your father always did when I got distracted. Flowers. Cards. It's the little things."

"That's it?" I asked. "That's the solution to women?"

"Don't knock it until you've tried it," she said.

The next day, I bought Lola red roses from the corner store. Lola beamed. "Harold!" she said.

"It was my mother's idea," I confessed

Lola asked if she could call my mother. They talked for an hour, mostly about what I wasn't doing with my life. Lola said, "He's signing up for a night class in spring."

I could hear my mother's relief flood the wires. When Lola got off the phone, I said, "You're joking, right? About the class?"

Lola rummaged under the sink for a vase. She set the flowers in water. "I'm going to pay for a class. You can consider it my share of rent or groceries. You could try an English class, maybe creative writing. You know, improve your vocabulary."

"Lola," I protested.

"*Lucius*," she said. "No arguments. I don't like to argue. It makes me feel tense."

"No arguments," I said. "But thanks."

She said, "Don't say that, either."

After that my mother stopped by on a regular basis, which was something she never did pre-Lola. She'd show up after work, dressed in a long skirt and ruffled blouse, her heels traded in at the end of the day for bobby socks and sneakers. She'd bury Lola in a wall of flesh. They'd sit and chat. My mother even crocheted Lola a pair of mittens. "For winter, to keep you warm," my mother explained. "You're so skinny," she added, patting Lola's shoulder. "Where's your family, dear? Tell me, are you on your own?"

ON A COLD DAY in December, when the light filtered through the tree branches and the sun hung low and birds darted overhead, Lola and I stood once again in front of Floyd's. Lola had been somber for a few days—I realize this now—and she suggested we walk there. The wind whipped through her hair, and she shivered. She wore mittens my mother had made her. She reached and took my hand. "You know the thing about people with criminal hearts?" she asked. "They always return to the scene of a crime. It's usually guilt that drives them. And look," she said, waving with her free hand at the dilapidated structure, the boarded-up window frames, the demolition trucks parked in the lot next to piles of salvaged, blackened wood, "ruins."

Did I smell death in the air? Transformation? Probably not. It started innocently enough. She said, "Bertha worked here, didn't she? I mean, this was the first fire you set, after all. You've kept the police on their toes for months now. Still, you can't hide the truth forever."

"Oh good," I said, squeezing her hand. "I like this game. As I recall, Bertha is a hottie."

Lola said nothing. She inhaled and waited. "Lucius was here that night."

"Of course I was."

"Not *you*, Harold. The real Lucius. He was here with his stupid frat brothers," she said. "It's been bothering me that I never told you. Lucius Lee—what a stuck-up name, right? It was a dare," she said. "A stupid frat dare. He didn't even care that I slept with you. He said he wasn't in charge of my body."

I let go of Lola's hand. I remembered the big jock who shouted *Let's see if you've got it in you,* but I said nothing. Something closed in me. I balled my first. It was all a show, and Lola had staged it. "You used me," I said.

"*Use* is a relative term," she told me. "You didn't mind. You enjoyed it." She smoothed her hair. She shivered and pulled her coat closer.

"You lied."

"You know I take umbrage at that. Most people I know are pretty much serial liars. My parents, for example. They pretend to be happy, and everyone knows my mother is fucking her shrink. My roommate was doing it with Lucius, and I just smiled, pretending—lying, really—that it was all okay."

"Were you fucking him still?" I asked. "After us?"

Lola fell silent.

"Jesus," I said.

"Twice. Only twice. We haven't really spoken in a while."

I inhaled deeply, smelled the rank trash from the Dumpster next to the building. I stared at the wreck that was Floyd's—the ashen, ruined quality of it. I wanted to destroy everything. I wanted to smash my fists against Lola. I saw myself as Lola saw me, dousing the building with gasoline, igniting a spark, watching everything burn. I was that incredibly jealous, angry man whose girlfriend had dumped him. I wanted revenge. Then, in an even stranger moment, I saw Lola and me in those flames, burning to ash and cinder.

I yanked her around, hard, and she jerked away. "Have you lied about everything?" I yelled. "Do you even know what it means to be real?"

Lola looked as if I'd slapped her. Her face was red, blotchy. She was on the verge of tears, and so was I. I didn't understand what Lola's tears meant, and I didn't care, frankly, because I was still pretty pissed off about the Lucius revelation. I walked away from her, left her to her burned-down building. "I'm going home," I said. "Maybe you should go sell your bullshit to your last boyfriend."

IT WAS AFTER MIDNIGHT when Lola came back to our apartment. I don't know where she went after our fight or what she did during those long hours. Perhaps she went to the library or the Barnes and Squat. Perhaps she went to see her old boyfriend. Women, I've found, can be impossible to know.

She threw her keys on the kitchen table and took off her coat. Her eyes were bloodshot and puffy. She pulled her hair back into a small ponytail, undressed, and turned off the light. When she slipped into bed, I said, "So, did you go and fuck the first Lucius? That would be just like you, I bet."

"I'm exhausted," she said. "So please don't start."

"You have no idea."

She lay there for a moment. "At some point it stopped being a game," she said. "Do you really think I don't know how to be real? Do you think all I do is lie?"

"I don't know," I told her. That was the truth. "You tell me."

"I don't want to be with Lucius," she said. "I mean, *that* Lucius. If you don't know that, then you don't know me."

"No kidding," I said. "Really."

She didn't speak for an hour. I don't know what Lola was thinking about. Eventually I got up, went over to the couch, and drifted off to sleep. I dreamed of Lola. In my dreams, I held her close, saying, "Lola, Lola, my firefly."

THE NEXT DAY LOLA dressed and left for class. When I came home from work later that night all her drawers were empty, the bathroom was stripped bare, and Lola was gone. That was it. Sometimes even when you sense the end, you expect that it will be drawn out and painful, but the truth is a lot of times people surprise you. They simply leave. There is that sort of ending, too.

The only thing she left was Boo, who swam mournfully around his fishbowl. I sat on my bed. I thought some troubling things as I sat there, things I'd never thought about before that moment. I thought: Eventually people just quit and leave you, whether you want them to or not. Maybe they don't even really want to leave—who knows?—but they leave just the same. I wasn't angry, but a quiet terror filled me.

I searched for Lola in the weeks afterward. I'd ride my bike to campus and wait while a flood of students poured out of the Arts and Science Building. I started to worry. I texted her at least a hundred times, but she didn't answer. I thought, Even in this day and age, if people want to disappear, they can. A few weeks later, I finally caught sight of her. She was wearing jeans and a wool coat and high-heeled boots. I called to her, and, when she ignored me, I rode my bike behind her, pleading until she stopped.

"Lola," I said. "We've got to talk."

She repositioned her backpack. "I'm a liar, remember? A user? A bad person?"

"What did you want me to say?"

"You meant it," she said, raising her voice. Some students stopped, some turned around. "And it was a mean thing to say, but that wasn't the worst part. The worst part is it's true."

"Come on," I said. "We'll talk in private."

"No," she said. "That's it. End of story."

WAS MY LIFE so bereft before Lola entered it, before we agreed, for a time, to play along with each other, and pretend? I can hardly remember now, and yet, a year later, I still think about her with a fondness that is unmatched by any other. I'm telling you all this because, see, the thing that happens is you forget over time. I mean you remember this and that happened, you have a vague sense of events, but the feelings become blurred and foggy. I don't remember the exact moment I needed Lola, and I don't remember the exact moment of love and how it came to exist as its own force, in its own complicated proportions. But I know that I felt these things; I know Lola and I had *potential*. I don't question that love exists, but I do sometimes question the mechanisms of it. Maybe love simply happens when someone steps into your life and opens up your imagination, and you can see yourself in new ways. I think it's at least a possibility. But what the hell do I know? My name is Harold and I ride a bike to work, and in twenty-six years I really haven't learned a lot, that's the goddamn truth.

Last week was the anniversary of the first blaze, the one set at Floyd's. The networks covered it on what was an otherwise off night. They recapped the months of havoc, the Lunar Pyro's path of destruction. Eventually the guy got caught. Turns out he was a disgruntled employee, so Lola was almost right. I wondered what she thought of it all and what she would say.

She must have been thinking along the same lines of completion because today the post office forwarded a letter—a letter!—to my new address. It was a fat envelope, taped shut, my name clearly printed on the outside with no return address. When I saw the handwriting, my hands shook. Thirty pages—I shit you not—written in the small loopy handwriting that was Lola's. I will not bore you with all the details, but one part stood out:

You were right, you know. I touch my skin and know there's flesh. I look in the mirror and see my face and it is a confirmation of something, I suppose. I exist in this world. I breathe and eat and fuck and learn things and forget and remember. But I almost never feel real. Do you know what I mean? Can you hear me? Because there's no sense in writing if you don't.

I'm sorry I left like I did, Harold. You probably deserved more of an explanation, which is just that I was suddenly very horribly afraid of sharing the bed another night because there was no place to hide anymore. It's not you. It's me, really. I end things as easily as I begin them. I've been doing that for as long as I can remember. If I were capable of love, I might have loved you. I can say without a doubt that I liked you. I liked you quite a lot, even if your apartment did smell a little funny and your pipes cranked and cranked. You need to believe me, by the time I wanted to stop pretending there were too many lies to undo. It sort of put a kink in things, really, but I guess that's what lying does.

In other news, I've discovered a true passion and have enrolled in a creative writing class. I am writing about fires and a lonely man who keeps a goldfish. I've been having difficulty with the overall flow of events and I am plagued—absolutely plagued, Harold—with questions of point of view. I have tried writing it from the fish's perspective, but it didn't work out so well. My instructor has told me that in ten years I might have a story, but certainly not even then if I keep writing about animals. I swear they pay these people to be miserable, but I will persevere.

So, why am I telling you all this, anyway? Because I hope you will listen, really. Because this all has some pertinence to us, you and me. I know what you are thinking, that you are the lonely man with the fish. And partly that is true. But the strange thing is that when I'm writing, the man is also me. We are one in our aloneness.

Is that love, Harold? It's real, I think. I can't quite touch it, but it's real just the same. For that, I owe you thanks.

Please give my best to Boo.

Sincerely,

Bertha McKern (your Lola)

I sat on the bed and read Lola's letter again. I thought, My darling, skinny Lola had a fat girl's name. I just couldn't get over that. I took Lola's note to the kitchen. I burned the first page of it. The fire consumed it. The paper folded in on itself and smoked and burned before becoming black and breaking into pieces at the bottom of the trash can. I burned another page, then another and another. I burned it all. It was a small gesture on my part, a gift to Lola, one required to complete a story.

ATTACK OF THE POD PEOPLE

———

Beginning at midnight, you watch a twenty-four-hour marathon of macabre movies like *The Thing* and *Die, Monster, Die!* Your boyfriend, who loves horror movies, has two days off before his unit ships out to some country that you know we're fighting. You've decided on a sick day tomorrow, which you feel certain you will need and which he justifies by saying that you have too much sick time accrued anyway, so why not stay in bed? Is it your fault you're resilient, he asks? Smile and say, *Yeah, right.* Thank him for his support, but tell him he doesn't have to tell *you* twice.

He supplies the popcorn with extra butter. You supply the quilts and comfy pillows, which you will hog during the scary scenes. Share one of your pillows with Chance, your dog, though, because you recognize that, being a pound mutt, Chance has already had a raw deal in life. You try to wean him from his nasty temper with offerings of bad people food like popcorn. He gobbles pieces from your hands, and, if you are not careful, you could lose a few fingers.

After the dog licks your fingers clean, he goes to the kitchen and laps up water. You say, Too much salt, and rub your own belly. You lie down with your boyfriend on the bed, feel the water ripple under your bare limbs, bouncing the two of you, you and him, up, then down, knocking your knees together. You draw the quilt up to your chin in anticipation of anything frightening.

Invasion of the Body Snatchers comes on and he, your boyfriend, says, Oh, I love this one. You don't bother to tell him this one is a remake, that the original commented more on communism and the Red Scare while this one, with Donald Sutherland, supposedly comments on relationships in the seventies. He will not care anyway. On TV, there's a distinct absence of pods and snatchers. You ease the grip on your quilt and say, Hey, maybe this won't be so bad. Everything seems innocuous, a world filled with dewy, peach-colored flowers and rain. What could be nicer? Oh, look, you say, that woman plucked one. You call her a plant murderer.

Just wait, he tells you and smiles. Then he rubs his hands and says, Oh, yeah, so loudly that Chance, back from the kitchen, growls before he hops up and settles down at the undulating bottom of the waterbed.

You give your boyfriend the bowl of popcorn, offer it as a gesture, a sign that you want to be close. Then you make a grunting sound and hold your stomach. Chance growls again, this time at your noisy belly.

Your boyfriend says: It's a shame you can't ship that dog out to the Middle East.

Remind your boyfriend that that would mean the dog would be with him.

He asks why you ever picked a dog like Chance in the first place.

You pretend not to hear. The truth is Chance had a sorry-looking face and was scheduled for the old heave-ho at the pound. You are a sucker for cases like Chance.

You touch your boyfriend's arm. On TV, people are beginning to act suspiciously, without feelings or emotions. They do not laugh at work. They cannot appreciate a joke. Sex? Forget it. What do they care? You think of earlier that night, when you and your boyfriend had sex, how he didn't look at you, how he looked out the bedroom window instead, how, when you washed afterward, you had a red welt blossoming on your thigh. You think: This must be a bunker mentality, all aggression. No fear, no emotion. *Just the facts, ma'am. Just spread 'em wide.*

It turns out the Chinese woman at the dry cleaner is an alien. Her husband just knows something is wrong but no one will listen: She won't make love, won't look him in the eyes, won't iron and steam his shirts. You feel bad about all this and say to your boyfriend: What is it with these movies? You tell him that whoever you pin your hopes on meets the enemy. You say: Isn't that the way it always is?

He says he never pins his hopes on anything, so why should you?

Remind him about Chance. Chance perks up his ears. You say to both of them, Yes, there's always hope, isn't there? When you say this, you make baby-talk noises.

Work crews lug thousands of pods off overseas boats in an effort to create a world without hate or love, war, fear, joy, or anger. Not even bagpipes playing "Amazing Grace" can stop them. A man and a dog sleep too closely together. When they wake up, they have turned into a mutant.

You say, Come here, Chance, but when Chance doesn't listen, when he only raises his head and stares at you as though you are a stranger, a stranger with no food offerings, you inch toward your boyfriend instead. You take some small amount of strategic care not to let him know you are doing this, that you crave his skin, some knowledge of him there. You snuggle deeper under the covers and watch Donald Sutherland run into darkness, trying desperately to escape from what can only be inevitable doom.

How can a person keep their eyes open for days, months on end? you ask. They can't not sleep, you say. *That's* obvious. You are nearing delirium yourself, after watching this marathon of movies.

Sutherland leaves his lover to see if there might be an escape. He, your boyfriend, sees this scene and smiles knowingly. Here's the good part, he tells you. You grab one of his pillows and hold it over your face. If you're a puss, they get you, he says.

They're already here, you say. Aliens. You tell him you are certain Chance is one. We're all monsters, you propose, changed slowly from the inside out until we're unrecognizable. You remind him of sex earlier that evening but do not mention the welt on your thigh. You tell him only that his hands were a bit rough.

He laughs and kisses your cheek. He tells you he thought it was supposed to be a fun night. Then he tells you that you're acting like a prude, just like the woman at the dry cleaner.

You don't argue the point. Fine, you say. Let's just watch the movie.

He tells you he's *trying* to watch the movie, that he thought the idea was to have a good time before he left. He says this as if you didn't hear him the first time. You think: It must just be you, that you are the one who feels strange, who registers an alien difference.

On the screen, Donald Sutherland tries desperately to wake his lover, but the pod people have gotten her, and now, in his arms, her face and body crumble. Behind her, a look-alike emerges, sheltered in the grass. She is nude, though it is unlikely that, being an alien, she will perform sexual favors.

Your boyfriend whistles. He sits up, and Chance, in no mood for the undulating mattress, starts a yapping fit until your boyfriend throws a pillow at him, a little too hard.

You don't say anything about his offense toward your dog, about his ogling the alien enemy while lying in your bed, or about the welt that throbs on your thigh, because you don't want to fight before he leaves. You'd rather strike out, in little ways, against the thing that you can't name. And if you can't do that, you push and clamp down on it forever.

Trapped under a grate, Donald Sutherland prays. When next he appears, he is already transformed. You see him walking in unison with other alien people, resuming his duties, not joking about sex, staring off to some distant focal point, devoid of all feeling.

All's well that ends well, you say. Aliens rule the earth.

He wasn't strong enough to cut it, your boyfriend tells you. His mistake was leaving his troops; that's how they get you, when you're alone. Luckily, he tells you, he has his men, and they stick together.

You tell him you need a change of pace, that you've had enough alien action for one evening.

Your boyfriend says, What's wrong?

Oh, I don't know, you say. The world?

You coax Chance into the living room with a pillow and a trail of popcorn. Once on the couch, you find an old movie, *The Sound of Music*. As you watch Julie Andrews run across the mountains and spread her arms wide as if she could envelop the whole world in them, when you hear her sing that the hills are alive, you decide you have no choice but to take it on faith, to reach deep and bury all the dogs within you that bite.

CERULEAN SKIES

━━━━━━━━━━

Sylvia flops down on the love seat—the one item Raulp didn't relocate after he turned their small sunroom into a studio—and pulls away green, knobby pills from the cushions. Around her, canvases litter the room, some stacked up against the walls, others lying on paint-spattered tarps that cover the carpet. Soon Raulp will have his eye on renovating the sunroom, too, she thinks irritably, using it to store spare supplies and abandoned projects, and before she even knows it the whole house will be a testimony to broken dreams and outlandish aspirations. And then where will they be?

Still, she assesses: Where they are is in the sunroom/studio, on an otherwise pleasant and bright Saturday morning in May. Raulp stands amid a clutter of Folgers cans filled with flat brushes that spread out like miniature fans. "Hello, husband," she says good-naturedly, but Raulp's c-o-n-c-e-n-t-r-a-t-i-n-g.

He's been concentrating so much lately, in fact, that he's finally mastered the age-old art of tuning her out. He's also getting absentminded about things like showering in the morning or remembering to take lunch and sometimes dinner, and while other women might worry that both neglect and weight loss in a middle-aged man points to an affair, Sylvia knows better: Raulp is simply self-absorbed. He looks lean and careless in his slumping khakis and a black T-shirt that hangs out over his belt. A bohemian goatee has replaced his once fastidiously shaved face, and instead of looking like the businessman he once was, he now resembles a Beat poet, or a more muscular, hairier version of Bob Dylan, both of which aren't entirely disagreeable to Sylvia, but neither of which she would want as a husband, either.

As she pulls at the cushions, Sylvia traces, for the umpteenth time, the path of Raulp's midlife crisis and subsequent lunacy: First, there was the layoff from the bank, recent downturns, the housing-industry debacle and ensuing credit mayhem, followed by his prolonged use of the word *undervalued,* and his rather bizarre idea that fate had somehow saved him, at age thirty-nine, from a life of mediocrity and pushing through loan applications for newlyweds and pregnant couples. Then there came his decision to cash in stocks, take an evening class at the college, and paint again. Sometimes now when the mood strikes him he even speaks in French, talking about his *tour de force* and his *succès d'estime.*

It's all sheer and utter madness. Sylvia misses the times when she could practically chart Raulp's moods in accordance with the Dow Jones and the near sorcery-like predictions of Warren Buffett, but after years of marriage it is no longer so easy to figure out Raulp. She watches as Raulp tucks a wisp of graying hair behind his ear and runs his hands over the blank canvas. A mercurial expression spreads across his face, and Sylvia becomes aware, once again, of the changeability of his moods.

"Oh, look," she says, picking up the classified section of the paper. "Job listings."

"Sylv," he says distractedly. "You have your job at the bookstore, and I have a job doing this."

"You have unemployment benefits, a retirement fund, and a hobby," she tells him gently. Then, when he frowns, she adds, "Just kidding! Of course you have a job, sweetie. Of course!" She says all this in an animated, too-bright way, because, Jesus Christ, she reasons, she should at least try to be cheerful. Raulp is her husband, the man she loves, after all. And he's dedicated himself to his art again. He has! She has watched his formal considerations change over the course of class, marked how his field of vision, once bent on abject realism, has grown to add new weight and shape, more irregular patterns, less repetition. She's commended him on his earnest study because, she reasons, she should be supportive. And mostly she has been.

She stares out the window to fields lined with rickety fences and sagging wires. A familiar uneasiness settles in her, a familiar boredom. They live in Lancaster County, next to a dairy farm. "All that grass," she once told Raulp, after he was transferred from the city to work as manager at the local bank in town. "Who needs so much lawn unless you have twenty children?" It's the openness of the landscape that often leaves her strangely somber—a feeling she attributes to the region as a whole—but today, considering the unmowed grass shot through with dandelions and milkweed, she feels a crusty annoyance as well.

"Our yard looks like *Wild Kingdom*," she says. "I know you're busy with your art and everything, but I feel I'm waiting for the cows to come and graze."

Raulp opens a tube of burnt sienna and smears it over his palette. He dips a camel-hair brush into the paint and makes a solitary stroke that looks to Sylvia like the start of a landscape, the jagged line of earth as it hits the sky.

"Hey," she says. "I've got an idea. Maybe you could paint cows mowing the grass."

Raulp swirls his paintbrush in deft, short strokes. "Sure," he says absently. "Why not."

ON WEDNESDAY EVENING, Raulp comes home from art class and stands in the kitchen, his yellow slicker still dripping rain. He announces that for his final portfolio he has decided to paint a nude. "I think it'll really stretch my imagination," he says. "I mean, what's more complicated than the human form?"

A slight alarm shoots through Sylvia as she scrapes the last bits of lo mein from her dinner plate and into the trash. "What happened to the landscapes?" she ventures. "You know, cows, caribous, whatever. Look around you. Inspiration abounds in cow country. It's so serene my brain frequently wants to split open, and oh my God, the smells! I'm throwing you zinger suggestions here, guaranteed A's in class, and you're talking nudity. It's obscene."

Raulp takes off his slicker, hangs it on the back of the door. He grabs a beer and sits down at the table. "I just feel like I need something new, Sylv. I'm landscaped out, and that's the truth."

"I'm landscaped out, too, but nudity is nothing new. Nudity is the oldest thing in the book. Have you read the Bible lately?"

He nods in a way that lets Sylvia know he's simultaneously acknowledging and dismissing her arguments. "Crenshaw suggested something in the style of Ingres. He told me my landscapes are stiff and limited."

"He said that—'stiff and limited'?" She waves this off with her hand. Lee Crenshaw is a man Sylvia only met once before deciding that any more meetings were neither warranted or desired. He's an elderly, cantankerous man of bow ties and banter. At the cocktail party Crenshaw threw at the start of the semester, the man's hands glided over Sylvia as she squeezed by him on the way to the kitchen. "Excuse me," he said, all while he groped her ass in a determined, robust way.

"You remember the party, don't you?" she asks now. "I'm not posing naked and having Lee Crenshaw see it. The man of course would love nudes. Of course!"

"Liking your ass doesn't make him a pervert," Raulp says. "It makes him a man of good taste." He folds his arms then and considers his next move. She recognizes the look—it's strained, as if Raulp has popcorn caught between his teeth. "Actually," he says, finally, "I was thinking of hiring someone."

"Oh."

"That's it? Just 'oh'?"

"Oh, great?"

"It's not meant to be a slight, Sylv. It's just that I know you too well. Familiarity would cloud my vision of you, and what I see."

"What, like that I'm *round*, for instance?"

"You're beautiful," he tells her. "But there's also the fact that Crenshaw knows you, and you just said you're uncomfortable with him."

Sylvia can't help but feel rebuked by all this. Though she doesn't worry about affairs necessarily, she still feels the effects of marriage and the worry that can accompany fifteen pounds of weight gain and the effects of countless ice creams on her thighs. "Okay," she says again, nodding.

"I knew you'd say that."

"What? I didn't say anything."

"Exactly."

"I *like* the caribou idea," she says. "But, fine, if you want to paint a nude, hey, go for it. What else do you sign on for in marriage except to be supportive when your spouse needs it, right? Why else marry unless you form a mutual admiration society, or at the very least a support group?"

Raulp gets up from the table and moves to where she stands at the sink. He circles his arms around her waist. He says, "Thanks, Sylv. And just so you know, I've always *admired* you."

"Oh, and I *support* you," she says.

"Good," Raulp says. He squeezes her sides. Then he goes and gets the paper. He opens to the classifieds.

"You're advertising?"

"How else do you get someone?"

"I don't know. Pick up a tall hooker?"

"That's not very supportive."

"I *am* supportive," she counters. "I never complain about the smell of turpentine and paint drifting through the house. You know that stuff can cause brain damage." She sticks out her tongue and makes a face. He would prefer, Sylvia believes, the same steadfast encouragement he displayed throughout their marriage when she decided she wanted to study macramé, or when she decided that, come pad thai or disaster, she was going to cook some exotic cuisine, at least once. He would prefer that she smile politely and just shut up.

"You're weird, Sylv."

"Some admiration," she says.

WEIGHT GAIN and porker thighs aside, it isn't totally an out-landish thing to think she'd be the subject of Raulp's painting. First, Sylvia reasons, they *are* married, for Christ's sake. And second, he painted her once before, in graduate school, back when she was a slimmer and tighter version of the Sylvia she is today. She'd first met Raulp when he was designing the set of *A Doll's House* and Sylvia, then a wayward theater major, was learning the part of Nora—the backbreaking dialogue, the rep-etition of lines. In the end, she was only assigned the part of Helene, the Helmers' maid, and after the cast assignments she came backstage to where Raulp was painting stage windows that revealed wispy clouds, tranquil cerulean skies. She sat down on the Helmers' emperor chair, rubbed her temples, and moaned. "You know, it's because the professor is sleeping with the lead," she said.

Raulp stopped painting and stepped back to view his work. "I heard that rumor. But, hey, I've always thought the heart of the story was the person who makes the beds and orders the house."

"Right," Sylvia said. "I'm a domestic goddess."

Raulp sat down next to her. He touched the tip of Sylvia's nose with his brush, leaving a dab of blue paint. "It looks good on you."

"In clown school," she said, wiping her nose, "maybe."

He stared for a moment longer than he should have, and she felt herself blushing. Sensitive Raulp. Beautiful, brown-eyed

Raulp. Dylan-esque Raulp who, really, all the girls, and a few of the guys, had noticed. After that, he'd come in early to watch rehearsals, and, when they ran late—which they almost always did—he'd offer to walk Sylvia back to her dorm. On their way across the quad, Raulp would often request that she perform mime routines, soliloquies from Shakespeare, musical numbers. Sylvia sang songs like "They Can't Take That Away from Me" or "I Got Rhythm" despite the fact that she sounded a bit like Ethel Merman on speed. When she finished, she took long, swooping bows for Raulp, who would always offer a standing ovation.

"I'm awful," she said, moaning, but she was secretly pleased by Raulp's attention.

"So," he asked her after a performance. "Are you dating anyone? An actor? A tree? A movie star?"

"Me?" she asked, surprised. "No. Why?"

"I'm auditioning right now," he said. "To be your boyfriend."

"Oh, that!" she said, laughing. "Well, you're hired."

After they started dating, he confessed that he'd been attracted to her angular jaw, her almond-shaped eyes, her thick, almost masculine eyebrows. Sylvia was surprised; she had always considered herself homely, her eyes set too far apart, her hair too thick and unruly. "You're sweet to compliment the eyebrows, especially," she said, though it frightened her, really, to so suddenly fall in love. There wasn't anything Sylvia wouldn't have done for Raulp, really, so when, after dinner one night, he invited her back to his dorm room and asked to paint her nude, she agreed. They hadn't even slept together yet. Still, she stripped down naked and sat on the bed. She flushed with excitement as Raulp studied her. When she fidgeted, embarrassed, he sang his own, slightly off-beat version of "Why Do Fools Fall in Love?"

They were married by the end of their program. Sylvia became pregnant shortly after that. It was unexpected, and though she worried, though she'd never thought of herself as a "natural" sort of mother, Raulp took it in stride. "It'll be a change," Raulp said. "But I've always wanted to be a father."

"But what about painting?" Sylvia asked. He had just gotten a gallery showing, and he'd managed to sell a few pieces at what Sylvia had considered a good, promising price.

"I'll still paint," he told her. He also took an entry-level job at the bank. "To supplement," he said. "Until things take off." She, too, applied for work. They needed health insurance, and, even with their small house, for which Raulp's parents had generously cosigned, there were mortgage payments, water bills, trash removal, prenatal doctor visits. It was simple to trace, Sylvia knew, how one thing got in the way of another, and then something else followed, until another life—one you never dreamed of—suddenly was yours for the keeping.

They painted the spare room yellow. They rearranged furniture, picked out bedding. When she delivered, Raulp was there, helping her, urging her to push so hard she felt as though she might split open. Their daughter was born and taken right to intensive care. A respiratory complication, the doctor explained. In the days that followed, Raulp and Sylvia approached the baby's incubator with all the hopeful trepidation of parents who wanted only for their sick child to be well. They reached through tiny holes and held their little girl's hands, coaxing her to get better, to scream, to cry—anything—but after two days, the baby died.

They rarely discuss the baby now, though in the first years following her death Raulp periodically brought up the idea of having another child. When he did, Sylvia told him there was time, that they were still young, but really, she wasn't sure if she could go through it all again. She reminded him that they were still paying medical bills from their first pregnancy—Raulp's insurance didn't offer full coverage until after a year at the bank—and that for all the worry and all that time, they had nothing. But she still sometimes thinks about the baby, and how fragile things can be in the world, how there is, in everything, a desperate struggle to survive.

THE MODEL SHOWS UP the next Monday evening, a newspaper tucked under her arm. Sylvia guesses the girl is no more than twenty-two. She has a smooth, round face and a full mouth, and she's very slender. She brushes back a wisp of long brown hair. "I'm Reese," she says. "I spoke with your husband on the phone?"

"Is that a question?" Sylvia asks, thinking that there's still time to tell this girl that she's got the wrong address, the wrong husband, the wrong look. She lets out an embarrassing laugh before opening the door wider. She feels as if she has suddenly become transparent glass. "Can I get you something?" she asks. "Water, tea, bourbon?"

"No thanks," Reese says. "I'll just wait in the hall."

"Of course." Sylvia calls for Raulp. Reese slides awkwardly by, and it's then that Sylvia notices the clubbish, sullen limp in the girl's left foot. In the hallway, Reese stops at one of Raulp's paintings, a moonlit landscape done in the style of the Romantics. She inspects it with interest. "This is good," she says.

"I support my husband in his brilliance." Sylvia closes the front door. She doesn't have the faintest idea what to talk about that wouldn't involve the subject of both her husband and nudity, but she doesn't want to leave this girl alone, either. She could be a scammer, Sylvia thinks. Anyone can answer a newspaper solicitation. So much deception can lurk under a clear complexion. So she stands next to Reese and pretends to admire the painting, and she's relieved when Raulp eventually appears from his studio, shakes Reese's hand, and introduces himself in a way that is much too exuberant for Sylvia's taste. "Well, great!" he says, and shoves his hands anxiously in his pants pockets. "We can discuss payment in the kitchen."

"Perfect." Reese follows along behind him. "I'm in college, so I always need a little extra cash."

"Raulp's in night school," Sylvia says. She trails after them both, listening, hoping in vain that Raulp will say he's sorry but the gimpy leg is a deal breaker, though this, of course, does not happen. In the kitchen, instead, he pours them all iced tea while he and Reese work out schedules, payment, and sitting times. They talk about Raulp's vision for his project—a series of sketches, then a painting. "Are you okay posing nude?" he asks. "I don't want you to feel uncomfortable," he says.

Reese leans toward Raulp in a confiding way. "To tell you the truth, I *was* nervous, because I've never done this before."

"Right," Sylvia says. "A modeling virgin." She opens the kitchen cupboard and peers in, looking for something to eat. She pulls out a bag of chips and opens it.

"Like I said," Reese continues, "I was nervous, but when we were talking on the phone I started to feel really comfortable with the idea. I thought, People get naked every day, so what's the big deal, right? And I love painting. I've always wanted to paint, too, since I was a child."

"How many years would that be?" Sylvia asks, shoving a few chips in her mouth, chewing too loudly. "Two?"

"Oh, forever," Reese says, musing.

"Well, no time like the present to get started," Raulp says. "We could do some preliminary sketches tonight if you have time."

"No time like the present. I was telling your wife that the painting in the hallway is so good. Like Constable during his Barbizon days."

"Actually, it's a bit more like Rousseau," Raulp says, flushing. Sylvia almost gags, seeing her husband so obviously taken with the idea of this girl. He looks like a man who has found some precious commodity in his backyard—gold, oil, a *T. rex* skull, a rare Picasso buried under the bushes. At this moment, Raulp looks the most inspired Sylvia has seen him in years.

WHILE SYLVIA SITS AT the kitchen table, finishing her iced tea and the last of the chips, she eavesdrops as Raulp, in his studio, does preliminary sketches of Reese, clothes still on. "Until we get to know each other a little better," Raulp says, a comment that sends Sylvia's heart thumping wildly in her chest. She listens as Reese discusses her "youth" and the time she spent sketching with charcoals mostly. "Faces," she says. "I never get tired of looking at people." She even took a year off after high school and traveled, alone, to Europe, for inspiration, but when she came back home, she enrolled in a nursing program at the college. "More job opportunities," she said. "At least that's what my mother told me." Yes, she tells Raulp, she does think she's going to like posing because the whole idea of it is actually quite liberating. This, in response to Raulp's repeated inquiries. Oh, get over it already, Sylvia thinks. And it's then that Reese tells Raulp about the accident after she'd come back home from Europe, when she decided, impetuously, to take a road trip with her girlfriend to New York City. "A car just sped into oncoming traffic and crushed my compact," she explained. "My foot was shattered. Six days in the hospital."

Sylvia cannot remove her ear from the kitchen door. She waits for how Raulp will respond to all this, and what she hears in response is her husband's conciliatory tone, his saying that tragedies can only make a person stronger. Sylvia's stomach sinks. Everything within her turns brittle. She imagines Raulp taking in Reese's form, the shared moment, the thrill of new disclosures. She also imagines other, more disconcerting things, such as her husband and this young woman having wild decathlon sex in the sunroom/studio, and for the first time in their entire marriage she wonders, too, what it would be like to find herself entirely alone.

THAT NIGHT IN BED, Sylvia says, "Well, I think it's great. She seems nice, really nice." Raulp lies next to her, his eyes half closed in a dreamy way. "Tired?" she asks.

"A little. But mostly happy. It felt so good to work tonight."

Sylvia turns off the light. "Work," she says. "I'm sure the painting will be lovely. Not pornographic at all."

"It's not like that, Sylv."

"What is it like, then? Because I'm thinking work never looked so good."

"Oh, stop it," Raulp tells her. "You know I hated my job. And what about you? You can't like the bookstore much. What happened to saying you'd act again? There's still the community theater. It's not Broadway, but it's something."

Sylvia lets out an irritable laugh. "I couldn't live with success.

I love the bourgeois thing. I mean, it's not Broadway either, but, hey, it has its charm; marriage is still America."

"Sometimes I think you just don't care about anything anymore."

Sylvia says nothing. After the baby, she did take on theater roles, one of which resulted in a brief write-up in the paper. She also took up some gigs, early on, one-liners in TV ads for cough medicine, and hay-fever relief.

Thinking about this all, Sylvia breaks into an involuntary grimace. "I gave up trying, is that it? Well, let me recap for you, since your memory is so very clearly going to pot. We were young. Then I got pregnant, with your help, I might add. Then the baby died. Then we were broke and had bills. Then we grew up and I didn't think as much about art anymore. I thought about things like getting a car, and cable. I've always thought it was something of a virtue to be happy with what I have, and it turns out I like pricing books. And anyway, has it occurred to you that with all your newly found inspiration we haven't had sex in about three solid weeks?"

Raulp turns his back to her. "Fine," he says. "You're upset and I'm sorry."

"*You're* sorry."

"We won't talk about it."

"Fine," she says. "Let's not."

"Do you want to have sex?" he asks. "Because we can have sex."

"Jesus, not now. Now I don't even want to be in bed with you."

She stares out their bedroom window absently, wishes for sleep. After an hour passes, Raulp begins to snore. Sylvia gets out of bed, puts on a robe, and goes down to Ralph's studio. It is an act of desperation, she realizes, this snooping around. She rummages through the sketches of Reese that he's laid out across a worktable. She studies the softened lines of Reese's nose and chin, the tentative touch of Raulp's hand as it shaped the curve of Reese's cheeks and chest. In one sketch, Reese sits on the love seat, her gaze diverted in an embarrassed but nuanced way. In another, Reese leans forward, intently holding Raulp's gaze. There's something in this pose that reminds her of the painting Raulp had done of Sylvia so many years before. "Expectant yearning," he had joked that evening when the chill hit Sylvia's skin. "A precursor to sex," she told him, and it was.

SYLVIA WORKS at Riverdale Ink, pricing books on bird watching and art and folk remedies for things like rheumatoid arthritis. The owner, Mr. Lesser, is a shy, eighty-year-old man, and every day when Sylvia arrives to work he says, without fail, "Good morning, Sylvia. I'll be on call." Then he nods and shuffles into the back office, where he spends the rest of the day devouring romance novels. Like an old married couple, she and Mr. Lesser have fallen into a predictable routine. Her entire job, really, is pleasingly monotonous. She *likes* the old-fashioned wooden signs hanging over the aisles that read Health Care, Psychology, The Occult. She *likes* the neatly stacked books, alphabetized according to subject and author. And how else but with a job like this could she become so dangerously knowledgeable about so many things? Where could she learn about tattooing, invertebrate zoology, entropy? Theories of the universe? She'd once gone on a quantum mechanics kick, explaining to Raulp over dinner the intricacies of physics, but she had to quit when, eventually, after about three minutes, she confused herself. But that was life, there you go, the accumulation of useless and sometimes dangerous knowledge, pounds of it, in fact.

During the day's usual afternoon lull, Sylvia sits perched on a stool and reads *A Tale of Sexual Behavior*. Monogamy, in nature, it turns out, is considered *deviant*. Lions aren't monogamous. Caribou aren't monogamous, nor are cows, nor are any of Raulp's animal subjects. It all seems so evident when she reads it, and she feels that sort of desperation that comes on pre-middle age, when you realize that this is it—life is what it is and frankly, while it's not so bad it's not great either. She notes with resentment that Raulp has never painted a vulture, the one creature that is actually faithful to its mate. Of course they also spend their lives gorging on carrion, so what does that prove?

The door clangs and Sylvia catches sight of Reese, who smiles in a curt way. She sends up a little wave but then quickly averts her gaze. Reese wears a trench coat and jeans. She shakes rain off her oversized umbrella before pulling it down and leaning it against the trash can at the front entrance. Sylvia watches as Reese lumbers a few feet. She stops at a table towering with books. She picks one up absently and leafs through it.

"Can I help you?" Sylvia asks too brightly. "Coffee table read? Romance? Comics?"

Reese holds her shoulders in a rigid, determined way. She moves toward the counter. "Art," Reese says. Her eyes are sparkling. "I wanted to buy a book for Raulp."

"No kidding," Sylvia says.

"Raulp's a genius, don't you agree?"

"Let me give you some advice," she says. "Try not to act too smitten."

"Excuse me?" Reese asks.

"Let's not pretend," Sylvia says. "Art!" she adds, in her ta-da voice. "Acting!"

Reese stands up straighter. "I'm sure I can manage to find the art section on my own," she says. "Raulp is a good man. I don't think you appreciate that, or know how much he wants approval."

"Excuse me?" Sylvia asks. "You've known my husband a few hours and now you're some expert?"

Reese pushes her hair back and stares at Sylvia in a steely way. "At least I can see when someone is disappointed in me."

OH, HOW SYLVIA WANTED to throttle the girl. Absolutely throttle her. But instead she rang up Reese's sale and made change, then spent the following hour complaining to Mr. Lesser. Why, she wanted to know, are kids such know-it-alls? Why, she asked, can't men stay interested in one person? "All quite a quandary," Mr. Lesser agreed, and he lent Sylvia a romance book for good measure.

Now, at home this rainy evening, she listens to Raulp as he sits at the dinner table and talks about Reese's gift. "She brought it over this afternoon," he says. Then, when Sylvia, fuming, makes ugly comments about Reese's foot, he adds, mildly, "She's a nice kid." This, as if Reese weren't perfectly old enough to sleep with, as if an affair was so far-fetched Sylvia might as well put it from her mind.

"They could end up in bed," Sylvia tells her friend Martha over the phone later. "For Christ's sake, they could end up marrying each other. It happens. It does!"

Martha, Sylvia knows, is no putz about the ways of the world and middle-age boredom—she's been married four times. She's one of those serial marriers, which Martha often good-naturedly claims gives her the benefits of the mutual admiration society, the support group, *and* more variety in bed. "Sylv," Martha says. She exhales in a way that lets Sylvia know she's been smoking even after she promised to quit. "I don't see it in Raulp. He's just not the wandering type."

"Oh, really," Sylvia says. "Well, have you seen him lately?"

"It's a phase," Martha tells her. "So maybe he likes sketching this girl and painting—you said she was pretty."

"In a maimed sort of way," Sylvia says miserably.

"Trust me. It'll wear off and he'll get over it."

"Meanwhile there's a nude girl sitting in what used to be my living room."

"Just tell him how you're feeling." *Feeling,* because Martha herself has been seeing a shrink of late. "Tell him what you want, but do it *succinctly,* Sylvia, and nicely. That's the key—to be nice and not act like a lunatic, like you're acting like now."

"Fine, then, lunatic out," Sylvia says and hangs up on her friend.

In the days following, she begins to make excuses to come home during the afternoons. Menstrual cramps. Migraine. Flu. Stomach pain. On this fourth day: diphtheria.

"Diphtheria?" Mr. Lesser asks now. "Oh my, Sylvia. This is getting desperate." He takes off his glasses and rubs them with a handkerchief.

"What do I have to do, cough up a lung to go home? Because if you want me to, I'll cough up a lung."

"No," Mr. Lesser says. "I don't need to see that, no. I couldn't subject you to that.

"Sylvia," Mr. Lesser calls after her. "Say hello to Raulp for me, will you? I do hope everything is okay."

Sylvia's cheeks flush. She'll probably burn in hell for lying to Mr. Lesser, who is quite possibly, she decides, the nicest man in the world. "Will do," she says.

At home, she clomps into the house. "Forgot my umbrella!" she yells, too loudly. When Raulp appears in the front hallway, and when he points out that it's been sunny all week, not a cloud in the sky, Sylvia only stares blankly and says, "So what does that prove?" From the studio Reese emerges, robed. "Hey, Sylv," she says. "Home early again?"

"*Sylv?*" Sylvia asks.

Raulp pulls her into the kitchen. His voice moves to an angry, sharp whisper. "I mean it, Sylvia," he says. "I need my space."

"Nude space," she corrects.

THAT EVENING, while Raulp goes into town to order new art supplies, Sylvia stares at the finished painting of Reese. The girl sits at an angle, her right leg hanging off the love seat in an idle way, her left leg drawn up and bent slightly to her right, leaving one breast hidden, the other revealed. One arm rests on the back of the couch; the other falls to her side. Raulp's added layer upon layer of paint to the canvas, to the point where Reese's form appears thick, milky. He's given her body weight and texture. Still, there's something achingly feminine about the colors. Reese's skin appears almost iridescent, liquid. Her lips part like a split peach. Her maimed foot spears solid, whole, with no discernable deformity. She stares straight ahead in an intent, serene way, holding her gaze tightly. Sylvia runs her hand across the textured surface. She breathes deeply, letting the smells of paint and turpentine infuse themselves into her burning nostrils.

When Raulp comes home an hour later, Sylvia is sitting out on the porch steps, thinking about the two of them, and their marriage. If Reese means anything to Raulp, she decides, it cannot stand up to the years Sylvia and he have had together, to their own accidents and losses, their own efforts to hold things close over time. The smell of pine travels to her as does the faint scent of milk from the neighboring farm. It is a gorgeous early evening, really. Serene. Tranquil. The light is just starting to change, and the moon is just visible. Raulp gets out of his car and hands her a cup of coffee before sitting down next to her. "Nice night," he says.

"I saw the painting," Sylvia tells him. "It's good."

Raulp stares off, toward the open fields and wires.

Sylvia sets her coffee down, studies him. It is possible, she knows, that Raulp met Reese in town, perhaps to celebrate the successful completion of the project, or to express his gratitude. Perhaps he was even so bold as to confess that he felt the thrill of a new attraction, that Reese has helped him to realize something about himself, something important that he'd forgotten. Or perhaps Sylvia is wrong completely. Perhaps Raulp simply went into town on his own and saw no one.

"You want her," she ventures.

Raulp glances over at Sylvia but says nothing. They sit in silence, and Sylvia listens as, in the distance, the cows call out from the fields.

"You want her," she says again.

"I didn't do anything," he tells her. "And that should count for something."

They fall into another long silence, and Sylvia thinks about time, and what miraculous grace is needed to keep love intact. She stares at the yellow-blue skyline, the last bits of light. "I've been thinking," she tells him. "About trying again. I've been thinking that it's time for a baby."

She pretends not to see the hurt and confusion that spread across his face. She cannot bear to ruin the moment, her own perfect vision and clarity in it—the thought of a new life in the house, the weight and substance it will bring to their marriage. Raulp refuses to look at her. Eventually, he stands up and walks out into the front yard. From the small shed on the corner of their property, he pulls out the lawn mower and rips at the cord until the engine roars. In the near darkness, Sylvia can make out the angular lines of his body. He pushes the mower into the high grass, knocking down weeds and the blanket of Queen Anne's lace, and she waits for a sign—a wave of the hand, a smile, a nod—something that says they, despite everything, will be all right. After a few minutes, Raulp's motions become monotonous, and Sylvia, still waiting, leans back and takes a swig of coffee. She pictures them all together—her and Raulp and the baby—bound by love and time, traveling across Vandyke brown valleys, wandering under skies that open and close—pale pink, blue-yellow skies.

A FIVE-MINUTE CONVERSATION

─────────

"It's the same old thing," my father said.

This, on the phone. I usually called him on Mondays, after five, when the rates were good. He usually let the answering machine pick up first, in case I was a bill collector.

"Same old," I said.

In his later years, my father had become a philosopher, though, when I was younger, he was something of an institution. On Mondays, when I called, he spoke not of loneliness but war. In about a minute or two, he'd summarize the following: the state of the nation (*Terrible*), the government (*Liars, thieves, and murderers*), and the world in general (*Too much sorrow*).

"What do you know, Daddio?"

He told me, "I'm not afraid to die. Try living for seventy years. That's the hard part."

Before my father became a philosopher, he'd worked at a

steel mill in Bethlehem, Pennsylvania. He'd worked there since he was seventeen, which is, when all is said and done, a long time. After he retired the company went bankrupt and my father lost his pension and health care, and other things he didn't talk about.

He said: "I'm sick of people telling me I owe them. Maybe you could send me a cool million, huh, kiddo?"

"I'll bring it right over," I told him. "Be there in ten."

My father laughed—a raspy, deep laugh, a laugh full of awkward rhythms—because he knew that I lived five hundred miles away, on purpose. I made it home only once a year, if that. "Money," I said. "No time, too." But, in other ways, I was my father's perfect daughter, a philosopher-student, a want-to-be maker of meaning. And my life, like his, never did seem to work. Washers and dryers gave out at inopportune moments. The lawn mower fell to pieces. My car engine rattled furiously. A love affair ended. The laws of the universe dictated that everything, eventually, broke apart.

My father attributed all this to bad luck, the multigenerational kind.

He said, "You know, for all your education, honey, you've never amounted to much, and you sure don't have any money to brag about. You're already thirty-one and still renting. By your age I had two houses. You've got to build and fix things. You can't even change a tire. Maybe you should go into politics."

Sometimes, in the middle of saying something, my father gasped for air. A breath he couldn't complete, a failed action. "Damn asbestos," he said, and I thought, then, vaguely, that my father's gasping, like his laments, was full of sorrow. "Thank the steel mill for that, too. That stuff stays around forever, unlike institutions. And when you do amount to something," he said, not waiting for my answer, "look where it gets you. I'm probably going to lose my house, and I'm sure as hell going to die."

"What do you know, Daddio?" I interrupted. "What did you dream about last night?"

He said, "I'm sick of everything, really, dreams most of all. If you can swing it, though, I'd like a decent coffin. I don't think it's too much to ask for—"

I interrupted, in desperation. "Can I ask you a philosophical question?"

This pleased him. "Sure," he said. "Shoot."

"Do we ever connect?" I wanted to know.

"Does anyone?" he answered.

I could have said, Yes. Or, Maybe. Or, Can't we at least try? But I worried then, suddenly, about the cost of the call.

"Did you ever notice," my father mused, "that the worst things in life are said quickly?"

"Meaning?"

"Time's up," he said. "That's all."

"I have to go," I agreed, shuffling him off the phone. I planned on stepping outside and taking a brisk walk. It was a cool, gray day, the air so crisp it hurt to breathe. I knew that later—maybe a day or a month or a year later—I would regret my abruptness. I didn't really have things to do. I didn't really have to go any-where. And money is just money, after all.

"Well, then," my father said.

"Well, then," I echoed.

"Goodbye," we said, in unison. Then, as if surprised, we waited an extra moment before hanging up.

MY FATHER'S MAHOGANY LEG

⸻

My father's mahogany leg arrives via priority mail. Here is the box, lying on the coffee table, and inside the box I find the leg bandaged in bubble wrap along with a note from my father written in shaky, eager scrawl: *Dear Anna: Here is my leg. Do with my leg what you wish, My Darling.*

Of course it goes without saying that this leg is the most impractical thing I've ever received, more farfetched than the Publishers Clearing House letter lying next to it, more pointless than the Book of the Month Club and mailings that promise self-help through holistic medicine—*Lose twenty pounds with verbena supplements* and *Alter your mood with St. John's Wort.*

For starters, I have two legs already. And they are beautiful, very presentable, very *real* legs—thin and muscular, milky and always clean-shaven—legs that look good in skirts and cowboy boots, which I always wear. My legs bustle me around the city, where I flaunt them at men who wait for public transportation, pudgy men in wrinkled suits and balding men in sweatpants who have, once again, decided to walk, then finally decided to ride the bus the last few miles home. My legs hoof it ten blocks to the CD store where I work, peddling Top 20 Hits to angst-ridden, tech-savvy teens with absolutely no sense of the classics.

My legs strut and stroll, prance and pirouette. They are actually really fucking wonderful legs. Over the years I've worked hard on them—gymnastics and swimming, painful dance and hovering on pointed toes only to stare out, blankly, into a room of other children's doting fathers. In contrast, this wooden leg is idle, severed, blunted as a crutch. Like you, *My Darling,* it is simply an afterthought, an appendage, but hey, better late than never.

That the leg was sent *priority mail* annoys me.

What am I supposed to *do* with a wooden leg, a leg that my father apparently decided to will to me after his death? Should I dance with it around my living room? Cast it into a fire? Chew on it for a while, gnaw at it like a bone?

I think about calling Jimmy #3. In a rapt, seductive tone, I could say: Jimmy, you want a little extra wood tonight? Ha, ha. But Jimmy has no sense of humor, and I am never as funny as I think, so instead of calling him, I pop the bubble wrap around the leg. The cushion of air deflates between my fingertips. The popping sounds festive, like champagne bottles popping at a party. I pretend that getting this leg is like getting a rare and beautiful gift, like getting the Hope diamond without its curse, and not like getting something sorrowful, like getting someone's wooden leg, which is exactly what I've gotten.

Via priority mail.

I hate to dwell on my father, and yet here, in this moment, I have no choice. I unpack the leg from its defeated wrapper and run my hands over burnished mahogany that smells dusty with time and age. The leg has a fake foot, a shallow etching of toes. I stand the leg up on the coffee table. It wobbles but stands on its own. It is its own leg, festooned with straps meant for strapping over the nub of my father's knee. It is heavy as years, hard as my father, and more durable in the end than a body or a heart.

I have *questions*: Of all the things my father might have given, why did he leave me his leg? We were never close. He has not spoken to either me or my mother in years, and mostly only then in a few letters, letters in which he tries to explain his sense of *shame*. After my father died, who packaged the leg? A friend? A lover? Did this person think that I, too, am lumbering along, missing a vital part of myself, hence the decision to label this leg a "priority"? When this person packaged the leg, did he or she regard it, note how severe-looking it seemed, how maniacal? And did this stranger wonder who I am? This girl named Anna Lee, age twenty-seven, a girl in cowboy boots and skirts, a girl who never visited her father for well over twenty years? Could this stranger guess how many times I've wished my father dead, a wish that, now that he is actually dead, is a horrible thought to admit? If my father spoke of me, was he nostalgic? Bitter? If bitter, did his bitterness mask regret? Love?

Leg, I say. What say you?

The leg's attitude is appallingly cavalier. Only a perfectly round hole in the leg gapes at me, like a great gorging mouth. The hole is cut mid-calf and reminds me of a birdhouse opening. I peer into it and look for something, say, a canary, but inside the leg there is only more leg, there is only the hollowness of the leg, the grain of wood lapsing into uneven circles.

I didn't expect to end up with my father's leg. This is exactly what I say when I phone my mother.

She seems surprised. In over twenty years, my mother has never received anything from my father, not even his ashes. She says, Something is better than nothing. She sighs and then the moment reduces itself to a bewildered, stony silence. Tall, still slender, and always well-dressed, my mother was once the beauty queen of her hometown in Rhode Island. There is a photograph I have of my mother and father, taken on the night she received her crown. Before his accident, my father was a strikingly handsome man with chiseled cheeks and sleek hair. In the photo, my mother wears a tiara. She holds roses in her hands; her pinned hair rests in ringlet curls that hug her neck. My father stands behind her, grinning, his arms looped around her waist. On the back of the photograph my mother penned the following thought: "Together, there wasn't anything we couldn't accomplish."

Her soul, to this day, is shot with narcissism.

Growing up, I can recall many of my mother's subsequent lovers, those men who paraded in and out of our home. There were doctors and lawyers, poets and painters, businessmen who wooed her with shopping trips in the city. Over the years, my mother has received many proposals. She tells me sometimes, in a vague way, that she would have only married my father, that it was a long-ago war that separated them. They had only dated a few months before he went overseas and, by then, my mother was pregnant with me.

You always say you hate him, I remind her now. You hated him for leaving.

I say a lot of things that are entirely different from how I feel.

I hate what *happened* to him, she tells me. He was so different when he came home, and he was missing his *leg*, Anna. I never got over seeing him like that.

Does it have to be about you? I ask. There is a *leg* on my coffee table, Mother. I remind her: What we are talking about here isn't so much a man, as a *leg*.

AFTER WORK the next day, Jimmy #3 comes over to my apartment. It is a lovely apartment with large, domed windows, walls the color of burnished brass, and vaulted ceilings. When I walk, my cowboy boots clap against the wooden floor and Jimmy #3 stares at my legs. I go to the kitchen and fetch him crackers and brie, but he takes my offerings and says, Can't you give the boots a rest? Who do you think you are, John Wayne? Sit a spell, will you?

Listen, Pilgrim, I say. These boots are made for walking.

Jimmy #3 doesn't laugh, of course. He eats a cracker instead. Then he takes off his lab jacket and sits down on the couch. He works at the pharmacy on Randolph, pushing pills to the public for exorbitant fees. It's when I tell him this—that he is part of a grand system designed to screw the American people, that everyone knows insurance companies and doctors are swift bed partners and pharmacists are their dope pushers—that he finally laughs and takes me on the couch, even though, to my mind, I've said nothing funny. Despite this, I relent. My paisley skirt bunches around my waist. Off comes one cowboy boot, then the other. My legs wrap around him, my calloused feet dig into his back.

Yee-ha, I say.

Afterward, Jimmy sweeps a tuft of hair from his eyes, gets up, and goes to the bathroom—the click of the door, the subsequent quiet, a relief.

I lie on my belly, drag the leg out from under the couch, and pick off lint that has attached to it. I close one eye and look the leg right in the canary hole. When I was five, my mother first took me to the building where my father lived, and I breathed the stale air of his apartment. My father sat in a tattered chair, his hair disheveled, three-day stubble on his face. He sized up my legs and toes and frowned. Then he bent down and rolled up his pant leg, and it was then that I saw the wooden leg. When I ran from him and hid behind my mother, my father coaxed me to him, saying, Come look in my leg, Anna. Come see the canary that hides there.

I peeked in the hole but saw nothing. My father explained that the canary had flown away, that the canary was a magical bird, one that disappeared just as you tried to find it. Imagine, he said. Weird, I told him. On the second visit with my father, my mother dragged me down the narrow, corridor. Thick with scotch and painkillers, thick, as my mother said, with *shame,* my father threw a bottle at the door and yelled at us to leave. My mother's hands trembled. She walked briskly, dragging me behind her, back out into the winter day. Never again, she said. Never.

Look, I say to the leg. I'd like to think there's a reason you've suddenly appeared in my life, in however stunted a fashion.

Back from the bathroom, Jimmy #3 says, Christ, what is that, Anna?

Hello. I knock on the mahogany, and practice my mother's too-nonchalant sigh. A *leg,* silly.

I see *that,* he says, waiting for more. He stands in front of me naked, and I admire his lean stomach, the rivulets of blond hair that he continuously sweeps from his eyes. He says, finally: So you want to tell me what you're doing with a wooden leg?

It's my father's leg, I tell him, as if this explains everything.

I'll bite, he says. So where's the rest of him?

Soaring to the heights of the unknown, I guess. Then, when Jimmy appears bumfuzzled, I say, Dead. Just dead, okay?

He throws me a quizzical look, the kind of look that says, Are you from this planet? That is Jimmy #3 for you. He has that look down pat, that look that makes me feel displaced, even in my own apartment. He asks: Are you okay?

It's not exactly easy to mourn over what I don't know, I explain.

He says, That's a narrow view. It's still your father's leg.

I ignore this. I say, Some relationships are defined by what they aren't and have never been. Some histories are built upon the void of not-knowing. Would you at least agree with that?

Absolutely, Jimmy says. Mostly. Like now, for instance, with you. I'm thinking we have sex, but I hardly know you, right? I mean here you are, sitting with your dead father's leg. What am I supposed to think about that? He collects his pants from the floor and rummages through his pockets until he finds his bottle of antidepressants. He slides two green-and-white pills from the bottle, replaces the cap, and goes back to the bathroom for water. When he comes back, he says, How about next time instead of just having sex, we go out to dinner?

If you need a pretense, then sure, I say. I lean back against the stiff pillows and stretch. After all, I add, a girl has got to eat.

Seriously, Anna. I think we should at least try to get to know each other better. Then he adds: You can even bring the leg.

Ha, ha. Very funny, I tell him. I cross my arms. I am in no mood for acerbities.

A FEW WEEKS AGO, the same day, in fact, that I read my father's obituary, I met Jimmy #3 at the CD store. He was rummaging through the Beatles section, sweeping his hair back with delicate fingers. He looked up at me and winked. I am not trying to castigate him or say that Jimmy #3 cares little for Lennon or McCartney, or even the oft overlooked and always difficult to classify Ringo, nor am I saying that he uses the Beatles to garner sex from girls who work in the store, who wear silk skirts and cowboy boots every day, good-looking girls, mind you, girls who just found out their absent-anyway father had finally bought that one-way ticket to the *spirit in the sky*. But when I met him later that night for drinks, he put "Norwegian Wood" on continuous play and sang to me, "I once had a girl"—*girl,* as in a generic, nondescript, any sort of girl—which I think says a lot about Jimmy #3's initial intentions.

Of course I slept with him. I happen to be *that kind of girl,* the kind of girl who sleeps with men on the first date, that kind of *incredibly easy* girl.

I have, in fact, slept with many men. If Jimmy #3 would search my apartment he would find that aside from this leg with its gaping canary hole, I have built something of a shrine to past lovers and/or sexual exchanges: There are Jimmy #1's shirt buttons, which I scissored off one deviant night; Roger's gold cuff links with the pearl inlay lying on my bedroom dresser; Gary's lighter; Jeff's dental floss; Jimmy #2's photograph of Butcher, his golden retriever; Brad's *Dark Side of the Moon* CD; Joe's thong; Troy's Chapstick, kept in a candy bowl; Leroy's guitar strings and pick; Harold's superball; Lenny's copy of Strunk and White; Guy's metaphysical quartz, lying in the crevices of the couch cushions, *etc.*

The list depresses me.

I sometimes think: What would my father say about all this whoredom, if he knew?

To say I am *easy* is one thing, but the truth—the truth as I see it, as it might be—is that, in the absence of my father, I have thrown myself freely into the void of the Jimmys and Johns, the Williams and Guys. I have searched, in every crevice of every naked body, for that gossamer love, that pure, unfettered desire, that kind of soul-filled *wanting*. So, yes, I am *easy* . . . I am exceedingly easy. That is true. And when I have come up empty-handed, as empty as pockets or wooden legs, I have pilfered small trinkets; I have proclaimed love's trickery through dental floss and pens, cuff links and buttons, which is also to say that love has made me something of a *thief.*

THE NEXT DAY I walk twenty-five blocks to the tenement house where my father lived when he was not frequenting the veterans hospital. It is one of those community living places, the kind of place that is loosely monitored. My legs take me there without so much as a cramp or stumble, over potholes and under the moving trains hoisted up on metal girders, past the river and out into the western side of the city. Though I have never confessed this to anyone, I have often walked here, to this place where my father once lived. I have walked past the broken-down houses, the ghostly shops with spray-painted windows and iron gates shut tightly to the world. I have seen women linger by traffic lights and alleys, waiting to open themselves to strangers. I have stopped and stared at the rows of dirty windows. I have stared at the chipped, white trim of the building, the brick side choked with ferocious ivy. I have stood under my father's window—the third window from the left—and wondered about him. I have imagined in that moment I closed my eyes that my father happened to look out, that he saw my upturned face.

Once there was a plant in my father's window, but now it's gone. The curtains have been taken down. The window appears lifeless and empty. In a week or two or maybe three, someone new will come and fill the empty rooms. Someone new will come and go. And that's the way things are, I suppose. Full of comings and goings.

ON SATURDAY AFTERNOON, my mother stops by unannounced. She bends forward slightly, plants a dry kiss on my cheek, and then glides past me, her legs, her rock-hard calves, covered in silk stockings. She wears a black summer dress that shows off her back. Her perfume—deep, floral—lingers and drifts. My mother of the perfect smile, the collagen implants, her only flaw (besides her vanity) is that she self-cannibalizes constantly, biting at her nails, working her way to the flesh of her cuticles.

So at the risk of sounding barbaric, she begins, I was wondering if I might see the leg. I've been thinking so much about it—about *him,* she confesses. She enunciates perfectly, with the precision of an aging beauty queen. When I retrieve the leg from the chair, she reaches for it as she might reach for a lover if she weren't *beyond that stage.* She stares at the leg, at the gaping hole. She *beholds* it in a sad, almost sweet way. She says, If only your father didn't stay that extra year, after all but a few soldiers came home. He volunteered to stay longer; he had a nihilistic spirit of volunteerism, you know. She shakes her head. Men and their sense of duty, Anna; I honestly don't understand it.

It occurs to me that my mother holds a small, persistent grudge against my father: When he could have come home to her, he *volunteered* to stay. He lingered in the jungle and lost his leg in an explosion; he put his duty before her, ranked his order of importance.

My mother puts her finger to her lips and gives a nibble that seems so achingly private. I go to the kitchen to dry the already air-dried dishes. I put each away and watch her, noting the way she touches the leg, the way she smiles and conjures something I do not share. And then I feel *hungry,* so hungry I grab crackers from the cabinet. When I pass by her on the way to my bedroom she says, I'm not a shallow woman, Anna. I just knew when I saw him like that that nothing between us would work.

Did you ever even try to love him? I ask. After he came home, when he needed you?

My mother looks offended. Of course, she says. I frightened myself, loving him. You have no idea how love can wreck you, Anna, how love can wreck everything about you.

I leave her to the leg. In my room, I listen to Cat Stevens' "Morning Has Broken" on 45 and revel in the old-fashioned crackling of the needle as the vinyl spins. I love that airy sound, and that sound covers my mother's tears. I eat crackers and go through memorabilia, run my fingers over Roger's gold cuff links, flick Gary's lighter on and off, release the photo of Butcher, the golden retriever, from its frame, pull out Lenny's Strunk and White and read about possessives.

Then I get up from my bed, go to the window, and open it. I

break up what crackers I've left. I spread them on the sill and wait until I have a sill full of birds, pecking and scraping for crumbs. In the summer (and more so in the winter) I am visited by many small birds, ones that are sullied-looking and hungry. They fly away and then fly back. They hop nervously and twitter lightly. They carry everything away.

LATER, JIMMY #3 CALLS. He says, I know we just saw each other, but do you want to go out tonight? On a date? Then he adds: Don't forget the leg.

Ha-ha, I tell him.

After I shower and dress in a red skirt, a wrap top, and cowboy boots, I come out to find my mother still on the couch, sleeping with the leg in her arms. I clear my throat until she rouses herself, rubs her eyes, and gives me a sweet, almost starry-eyed look. I say, I have a date. And it's really time for you to get going. I add: Don't you get enough beauty rest, as it is?

She seems surprised by the passage of time, and groggy. She says, I was having the most splendid dream, Anna. Your father and I were dancing to a waltz. I never wanted to wake.

I grab my purse and check my watch. I open the door, but she doesn't move.

He's not picking you up? she asks, and smiles in that rigid way she often does. I couldn't tolerate that in a man.

Well, I say. Better than being coddled.

She frowns. I'm not entirely idle, you know, she says. I had a reason for coming. From her purse she removes a black velvet box, and from the box she removes a ring. It is a modest ring—platinum band, a small, solitaire diamond—and something my mother with all her many lovers wouldn't be caught dead wearing these days. She takes the ring and holds it up to the light, squints, then places it in the hole of my father's leg. She smoothes the wrinkles of her dress and says, I feel like I'm finally free.

I say, You told me he never asked.

She looks out the window, to the neighboring apartment buildings. She wrings her hands. I say a lot of things. He asked *after* he lost his leg, and what could I tell him then? Tell me, Anna, what would you have said?

She gets up, collects her purse, and, at the door, she stops and faces me. He did leave us behind, she says. He *changed*.

I BRING THE LEG to dinner. Why not.

Jimmy #3 arrives at Bandito's dressed in a button-down and khakis. He sits down, glances at the leg, and says, I wasn't really serious about that.

I had a change of heart, I explain. I felt sorry for the leg, being there alone in the apartment like that. Jimmy #3 gives me that look, and then, as if he gets the joke, he laughs. He laughs even though there is nothing funny.

I prop the leg on the chair between us. It sits there, looking very conspicuous, lording over the salsa.

The waiters say nothing. I come to Bandito's a lot. They parade past us, wearing black sombreros and elaborate, frilly tuxes. A man comes over, tips his hat, and recites the seviche and molé specials. We order and then sit without speaking. Around us, couples chat, raise glasses. Mariachi music plays and Jimmy sips his drink. So, he asks, finally, Are you going to tell me what's up with your father, and that leg?

I'd rather ask you a few preliminary questions first. So listen up, Jimmy. I tap my fingers against the tablecloth, smooth the wrinkled fabric. I want to know a few things before we go any further, I say. I want to know, what kind of man are you? Do you run at the slightest provocation? Are you still, after years of living, afraid of the dark? Are you waiting for your life to open? Do you feel you've failed others? Are you brave with your love? I want to know, do you believe that one event can change a lifetime? Do you hold on to the slenderest bit of hope?

Jimmy's eyes widen. He says, Whoa, horsey. That's a lot of questions. I really just wanted to take you out for tacos and get to know you better. I don't even know your favorite color, he adds. He surveys the chips and salsa and the margaritas adorned with umbrellas. He says, Anna, it's not as though you've been super easy. You're not the most open woman I've ever known. Frankly, you can be a little scary, with all your interest in sex.

Look, I say. Sometimes I really wonder if there's any person in the world who is really worth the risk. Love, I say, is a complicated thing, so maybe I should just leave right now.

He says, I'd hate to think you're leaving me for a leg, Anna.

Perhaps, I say. In a manner of speaking. I don't wait for dinner, and I don't finish my margarita. I get up from the table and leave.

BACK AT HOME that night I lie in bed with the leg, and peer into its hole. I search not for a canary but for my mother's engagement ring. I shake the leg until I hear it move then fall down into the hollow toe. It should be substantial, it should hold weight and meaning, but finally it is just what it is— something carried and discarded or put away.

I make a decision then. I ransack the apartment and return with buttons, cuff links and lighters, dental floss, photographs,

CDs, and that red thong. I take everything I have pilfered and stuff each item into the leg. The cuff links skip down to the toe. The buttons tap lightly against the wood. The Chapstick follows. I rip pages and pages from Strunk and White, stuffing each page into the leg. I fill the leg. I open the window and set the leg on the sill. It is a warm summer evening that promises, across this city, a new beginning and start.

That night, I dream of my father for the first time in years. We meet on the street, and he seems happy to see me, which is surprising. I've been trying to find you, I tell him. He says, Me, too; imagine. It's a real jungle, isn't it? Together, we walk around the city. In my dream, we talk easily. I ask him about the years I've missed, and he speaks of distant countries, my mother, the war, and all his love.

When I wake, I check on the leg. I breathe in the warm air, expecting to find that the leg has been lifted by the waiting birds that are always so hungry. But the leg is still there and there is no miracle. I bring the leg inside again and pack it away for good. When I finish, I call Jimmy at the pharmacy and tell him that I'm sorry.

Hey, he says, genuinely surprised. Why are you crying?

Please, I tell him. I want to see you now. I'll run over there to get you, Jimmy. I'll run over there just as fast as I can.

MEMPHIS

My brother Georgie has taken off again, this time armed with a leaf blower and a kidnapped dog. From my bedroom window I watch as he sneaks across the grass, his body pushing against the breezy autumn air. The purloined leaf blower is strapped to his back. The always-unsuspecting Winston trots at his heels, nosing at the pepperoni stick sticking out of Georgie's fist. It is bribery, I know, the pepperoni stick, a treat brought to coax Winston into Georgie's Jetta. The dog yaps happily, with an easy willingness that makes me curse. I decide I have the most perfidious dog in the world, the craziest brother, and a perfectly good leaf blower, which is just about the only thing that has not annoyed me tonight.

"Call Elvis," I tell my wife, Elle. "Georgie's gone off to Memphis again, and this time he has a hostage."

"Take no prisoners," she says in a pillow-muffled voice. She raises her arm in mock triumph. A mass of dark-blond hair furls the pillow's edge. It's late, too late for any of this, and I am already tired. I'd like to lie down again and drift off to sleep, undo the burden that is my brother. This is my first year married to Elle, but the honeymoon period has been anything but blissful, not with Georgie and these late-night trips, not with all of Georgie's antics. Georgie is my younger brother; he will be thirty this December. He is also schizophrenic—an ill man, a crazy man, a man who has a penchant for driving me crazy too.

Outside, Winston barks. Elle moans and says, "You'd think at least the dog would know better."

I remind her that Winston was never what you would call a savvy mutt, particularly in matters of food or trust. About a year ago—right before my mother died and we inherited Georgie, along with the doilies and the grandfather clock—we marveled at how Winston scarfed down his food at the pound, ran in indeterminate circles when we tried to make contact, and then promptly threw up. "Nervous stomach," the pound worker said, shaking her head in an apologetic way. "You'll take him?"

Elle and I looked at each other, and hesitated. "Yes," Elle told the woman finally. "We'll take him."

It will be a miracle, frankly, if Georgie or the dog even makes it to the Blue Route. We live outside Philadelphia; Tennessee is more than a thousand miles away, and all the roads to Memphis are ridden with rocks—bits of broken asphalt laid there, according to my brother, by the government, in an effort to impede his progress. This paranoia is only one manifestation of his illness, and though I often tell him that his beliefs are untrue, that all of Pennsylvania's roads are simply broken, my disagreeing with Georgie does nothing to brighten my brother's outlook or mood.

The Jetta's engine guns in a furious way, and I worry once again about noise ordinances in the neighborhood, the quiet night suddenly ruined. Georgie speeds up the road that leads away from our house and drives up past the neighboring houses with their neatly trimmed lawns and hedges. He screeches the car to a halt. After a few moments of silence, the engine guns again.

Did I mention I am tired? It does not help to worry. It does not help at all.

"Good riddance," I say.

Elle sighs and slips her head out from under the pillow. She turns on the light and squints at the alarm clock. She moans again. It is after midnight. Still, she sloughs off her covers, gets up, and pulls her long tangle of hair back into a twist. She collects our clothes from the floor and says, "You don't really feel that way, Bud. I might feel that way sometimes, but you don't."

I do feel that way, and it is the wrong way to feel, but Elle, who is generally soft-hearted, is still too nice to believe that I am mean, too nice to let me mean any of this. Instead of arguing the point, I dress. I dress even though it is sheer futility, it is absurd to keep bumbling around in search of my brother. Tomorrow if I am late for school again on account of Georgie and his antics, the principal will be angry, possibly he will take disciplinary action against me, as he has threatened to do in the past. I work at a prep school, teaching American history and English to gifted students who go on to prestigious colleges, enjoy successful careers, marry, and have expensive children and houses. The principal, a self-indulgent prig of a man who is *hardly* a pal, expects those students' needs to be met daily, without flimflam and excuses. Unlike Georgie, I do not have the luxury of work or no work.

Elle is already dressed in jeans and a sweatshirt. She throws a shirt at me. She says, "You get slower each time."

"Of course I get slower each time," I say. Does it really matter if I am slow? Does it matter if, perhaps, I grab a cup of coffee before I go out in the rain and retrieve my crazy brother? I tell Elle both coffee and slowness are options, that there are, indeed, a great many options in life.

Elle huffs at this. I ignore her and consult the calendar I keep bedside, a calendar I keep for Dr. Mulvaney to chart Georgie's "progress." To date, this is the twenty-fifth time Georgie has tried a road trip to Memphis. Each time he heads south, puts no more than thirty miles on the odometer, and, confused, agitated, he stops every time his car hits a stone on the road, one maybe the size of a pea, one just large enough to be felt under a tire. "Progress," I tell Elle. "It's all in the name of progress."

Elle stands with her hands on her hips. "It would most assuredly be progress if you finished dressing," she says. "I'll put on some coffee, but Christ, Bud, make it quick. I don't have all night, either."

"Sure," I say with a flutter of fingers. "I am on the case." But of course I am thinking what neither of us will say, what neither of us will talk about: This is just the start of things. When we bring Georgie home, we will inevitably spend the rest of the night listening to one of my brother's tirades about how Elle and I are co-conspirators against him. Georgie will storm through the house. And when I argue with him, when I attempt to inject any sort of reasoning into the discussion—Georgie will appear confused. He will shake violently. He will punch holes through the daisy-printed wallpaper that Elle loves, just as he has done before. He will kick furniture. Turn over the TV. He will break things. Small things. Things like Elle's Hummels, those perfect-looking children, so idiotically pastoral I can't say I blame him. And Elle, who only agreed to this arrangement because Georgie is my brother, will probably smile thinly and remind Georgie that the Hummels were a gift from her mother who lives in Florida. Elle will probably tell him that she always did think the statues looked too happy for their own good, and anything that happy deserves a good downing. She will say all this, and a hint of sarcasm will creep into her voice again. Can I blame her for this tone? They are her things, after all. She cares about them in a way she does not care for Georgie when he glowers and tells her simply, as if it explains everything, "Fuck you."

Somewhere in the distance, the Jetta's engine guns again. Georgie is there, still up the road, and I am here, at home, still trying to figure out our progress. I think, *progressive backpedaling,* maybe, and write this term down so that I remember to run it by Dr. Mulvaney at Tuesday's session, after Georgie huffs out in his usual way, and she and I debrief. I am very into those debriefings. I take meticulous notes, as meticulous as my brother's plans for Memphis. In his room, Georgie has a large map of the United States hanging on the wall, with red lines plotted over all the major highway markers that lead him to Memphis. He has calculated distances and miles, has marked each failed attempt with a push pin until there are a cluster of push pins surrounding the road on which we live.

Why Memphis? The truth is, I have no answer. Perhaps some queer love of Elvis blooms in Georgie's heart. Perhaps the muddy waters of the Mississippi beckon him. Perhaps he wants to learn the blues. He has never been to Memphis. He has never once expressed an interest in Elvis. I've asked, of course, and he tells me to mind my own business, so there is that. My mind unravels possibilities, none of which Georgie will confirm or deny.

I write down, *co-conspirator*? I write down, for Dr. Mulvaney, *glommed leaf blower* and *kidnapped dog*. These things I can explain, more or less. Someday I fear I will be forced to explain *Georgie*, which I cannot do. I cannot explain him at all. I cannot explain him because the truth is—the truth of it all is—I no longer know my brother. I think with mild irritation that passersby will probably see my brother out tonight on some desolate ribbon of road and wonder—Who is this man? What is he doing? And how *could* I explain? Possibly the passersby might wonder if the dog isn't in a spot of trouble, some kind of trouble that maybe a leaf blower could put an end to.

How was Winston killed, Officer? My brother blew my dog to death.

AFTER A CUP of coffee, we head outside. Elle is a good wife with a good heart and insists on coming. She pulls her jean jacket tighter when the wind blows, and she tries to make light of our nightly excursions. She tells me, "It's like having a baby, Bud, only without all the fun and sex." Then she shimmies her thin hips and sings an Elvis song. She curls her lip and bellows in a deep, exaggerated tenor: *I know my baby loves me . . .*

In the middle of singing, her foot twists and she flails her arms forward. Elle is a woman with a generally boisterous, robust nature, but she can be a real klutz, too.

"Careful," I say, catching her.

She shakes her head. "I'm losing it, Bud." Then she gives me her frequent and now tiring refrain, which is that she thought the first year of marriage was supposed to be the happy honeymoon. "The whole year," she says wistfully, her voice too loud. "Imagine."

I say nothing. It is a too-cold night, too cold, I think, for saying anything that might hurt. Rain hits the trees. The air smells sweet from dying leaves. It is dark and damp, the grass brown and soggy. We walk past the Halloween display in our yard: three drenched ghosts hang from a cedar tree, their painted mouths contorted to scare neighborhood children. Under the tree are mounds of dirt and Styrofoam gravestones that say "I.B. Dying" and "U.B. Watching." The gravestones were Georgie's idea. When we put them up, Elle said they were ridiculously morbid.

"Poor Georgie," she says, surveying them now. "All conspiracy and disaster."

"It was funny," I say. Anyway, I tell her she won't be saying poor Georgie tomorrow when she is falling asleep over toast and coffee, nursing puffy eyes. Elle—her real name is Ellen, but she's preferred Elle since being promoted to manager—starts her shift at 8 a.m., stacking thin, expensive lipsticks and hypoallergenic powder puffs at Macy's. If she's groggy in the morning and doesn't look good, it's bad for sales.

I know my baby loves me . . .

She mutilates the rest of the words. She's too young for Elvis, really, too young to know the song by heart. We take Elle's Bronco and head out the driveway, up past the neatly clipped hedges, the houses with the lights now on. Turning, I peer both ways down the road. Next to me, Elle hums Elvis tunes and draws fat men on the fogged-up window with her pinkie. "Right or left?" I ask.

"He mostly goes left here," she says.

"Left, then, it is."

Some case history: Since the onset of Georgie's illness, six years ago, he has gotten, each year, progressively worse. He has not held a job since he was fired from the car wash for threatening the manager with a good hose throttling. He has not had a girlfriend since he was twenty-four and dated a creamy-skinned girl named Rose, who dumped him when Georgie started becoming agitated and accusing her of stealing his money, and of buying too many dishes. Last I heard she'd met another man, married, and had a baby. If Georgie misses her, he seldom says.

In general—and as Dr. Mulvaney knows—my brother believes everyone lies to cover up "the truth." He thinks that his medicine is laced with mind-altering substances. He is certain our mother pricked him with a pin when he was two. He believes our father abandoned us, when in fact our father died of a complication after surgery. Georgie thinks the mafia is working with the government, and that I, in turn, am working for the government and the mafia, that prep school is an elaborate cover-up for racketeering. He has called me, several times, a flat-out traitor to a cause I had no idea I belonged to, a cause which I cannot even name.

Well, that is that.

Dr. Mulvaney likes to explain all of this to me in clearly delineated terms. She uses terms such as *cycling, word salad, onset years, paranoia.* I am so full of her lingo. We talk about neurotransmitters and serotonin, the success of new medications, the alternatives of mental institutions, the progress of shock therapy. "Shock therapy progress," I say, nodding. "Imagine that!" I chart Georgie's behavior and tell her about his appetite, his moods, how many of his pills I found stashed under his mattress this week, or how many managed to find their way into the toilet—all that scientific progress down the drain. Listening, Dr. Mulvaney sits behind a large oak desk, and she sometimes taps her pen, because she is a woman with very little patience. And behind her there's a photograph of her family—a photo of her husband and two sons, all in identical red sweaters too thick around the neck; and her sons' eyes are dark like hers, and their foreheads are round and shiny—and she leans back and says, somewhat exhaustedly, "Your brother's life is not your life." She says, "There are always other options."

I stare at those boys, those boys in their ghastly red sweaters and their pudgy arms looped around each other and their broad, smiling faces, and I think, Fuck you, Dr. Mulvaney.

Elle, bored with her Elvis drawings, turns from the fat men on the window. She is usually quiet on these trips. I can barely stand to think of all those things she might be thinking, how her thoughts and worries and dread might compound my own.

"You need new windshield wipers," I say. "I'll replace them this weekend."

"Is that it?" she asks. "Is that what you were thinking about just now?" She pulls her jean jacket tighter and rips a loose thread from her sleeve. She stares straight ahead, in an absent way.

"Safety first," I tell her. "That's what I was thinking exactly. You know me. I'm an open book."

She *tsks* this, rolls her eyes. "That'll be the day." It would be nice, she tells me, if anyone were as open as a book. She hums again, more to herself, and the entire space in the truck seems to shrink down to the size of a pebble. Finally, she says, "You know, though, we should talk more about Georgie's future, because lots of people are sick, Bud. There's help for sick people. I mean, it's just like Dr. Mulvaney says . . . there's help for Georgie."

"Thanks, Elle," I say. "But lots of people aren't my brother."

"My Aunt Zelda was mentally ill—you knew that, didn't you? When I was young, she would tell me she'd laced all the silverware with poison. Honestly, that woman could scare Jesus, *and* I think her house was haunted, but that's an entirely different story. Every time I saw a fork on the table, I thought, I'm going to die if I touch it. Mom always said, 'God, Ellen, don't touch the silverware. You never know about people.'"

"I'm glad we can still make light of things," I tell her. "Humor, after all, is a *healthy defense mechanism.*"

"Please," Elle says. "It was hardly funny. We were scared of Zelda. My poor mother tried to take care of her, but she was miserable and all of her kids, including me, were miserable in the process."

"Elle," I say. "Are you trying to nettle me?"

Elle ignores this. "Eventually, Zelda jumped from the second story of her house, broke her leg, and died of a blood clot, and my mother nearly had a breakdown of her own, she felt so guilty. At her funeral, my mother told everyone Zelda loved children. *Compensation,* yet another defense mechanism, Bud. Think about it."

"I'm thinking," I say, and I peer below the line of foggy glass. "I don't think you ever told me about Zelda."

"I'm an open book," she says. She turns the heater up to high and rubs her hands together. She scans the streets we pass, looking for signs of Georgie.

"I don't see him," I say, and I crank the window. At this hour, the streets are quiet. Cars are parked. The lights in the long line of homes are extinguished. "He might get to Memphis yet."

"A dream come true," Elle says, with a hint of bitterness. "Happy ending. Unlike Zelda."

"What the hell is your point, Elle?"

"Nothing," she says. "Just talking. Just saying my mother thought she could handle things, and really it didn't help her, or her kids, or Zelda. Everything just fell apart anyway, despite all her good intentions." She folds her arms, waits, thinking. Then she adds, more tentatively, "Did you know there were times when Georgie first came to live with us that I'd stay at work longer so I didn't have to come home?"

This surprises me. "I thought you were doing inventory."

"I think Georgie indirectly earned me a promotion," Elle continues. She leans back and pens circles with her pinkie again.

The sky is pitch black, and a heavy rain pelts the windshield. All night, it has been raining, alternating between chilly downpours and slow, damp drizzles. I search for the moon, the great gaping hole shot through the night, but it is gone.

I would like to tell Elle, if I could, that she should have seen Georgie before he started these trips to Memphis. I would like to tell her that it wasn't always like this, looking out for Georgie, bringing him home, placing two pills in each compartment of the week-long pill dispenser, only to empty and fill the container again. It wasn't always about yelling and fights and broken knickknacks and holes in the walls. There was a time—Georgie and me, my mother and father—when all of us were happy, when we sat together at dinner and talked about school and our day, when we vacationed in Florida and picnicked on the beach, our toes buried in the hot sand. There was a time we held no grudges, no hatred. But Elle would only smile, and her smile would say—as her smile most often seems to say—that she had heard enough. She should have seen my brother, though, I might insist, when he was still well enough and strong, when during the last football game of the season, he broke through the stronghold of the opposing players and bolted down the field to score the winning touchdown. He took off his helmet, his face red and moist from exertion. The crowd clamored in a raw, energetic way, "We Will Rock You" reverberating through the bleachers, and my heart swelled as Georgie, gap-toothed, grinned and raised his arms in victory. His teammates crowded around him and hoisted him in the air. They carried him from the field. Georgie ambled home that night, drunk on cheap beer, a cheerleader on his arm. My brother said, "You want some of this, Buddy?" I could only grin, wanting everything that my brother had.

I would like to tell Elle all of this. "He's my brother," I say instead.

I drive slowly. What is the rush, really? I look for Georgie. He has managed to escape our subdivision and drive out, past the local grocery store, the nail salon, and the car wash where he once worked. This is progress in clearly delineated terms, and this thought, as well as others, squeezes at me until I feel I can no longer breathe. "Truthfully, I don't know how my mother took care of him," I say.

Elle angles her head and studies me. She says, "Your mother knew what she could and couldn't do, Bud. That's the first step in caring for anyone. And, anyway, he wasn't as bad then, with your mother."

"So you're saying I make things worse?"

"I'm not saying anything," Elle tells me. "He's just worse, that's all. Who knows why."

ABOUT TEN MILES from our house, on a winding stretch of road that leads to the Blue Route, I spot Georgie's souped-up

Jetta with its one white door, an otherwise blue exterior, and bumper stickers that say *Supporter of the Fraternal Order of Police* and *Drug Free America.* The car has skidded off the embankment and hit a tree. The hood is clipped, pushed in. Black tire marks snake out from the rear wheels. George is off, at some distance from his car. Down the road, he walks under streetlights, an overhang of trees.

"Jesus," Elle says, surveying the scene. She shifts irritably, then rummages through her purse for her cell.

"Don't," I say, as she flips open the phone. I rest my hand on her thigh but she brushes it away. "It's nothing. We can handle it."

"Handle it?"

"You want the police involved?" I ask. "So we can add another two hours out here?"

She seems to consider this before closing her phone. My stomach flutters, and it's as if there is, somewhere deep inside me, a great frenzy of bats set into motion. My heart beats wildly. Down the street, my brother appears nonplussed. He's abandoned the car, abandoned Winston, who is in the backseat nervously barking and scraping at the window. The leaf blower is anchored around Georgie and he blasts it full throttle, creating a whirring noise that I am certain will wake the people in the neighboring houses. I pull the Bronco off into the gravel, shut off the engine, get out, and call to my brother. Winston whimpers, barks. "Christ," Elle says.

"He's fine," I say of the dog.

"Nothing is fine," Elle says. And it's true: Winston has thrown up his pepperoni. He whimpers more when Elle opens the door, and then makes a mad dash toward the tree to relieve himself. Elle's brow furrows. "I'll clean up this mess if you take care of the other one," she tells me. "Just go get your brother. Just go and leave me the hell alone."

With that, she is all dexterity and action. She climbs into the front seat, which is grimy and littered with candy wrappers. From the glove compartment she retrieves a box of tissues.

I walk toward Georgie. Wet leaves fall from the trees and dart around him in a restless way. The streetlight burns brightly, and in the rainy wind his jacket balloons behind him like a cape. Behind him there are houses, mostly darkened now. I call out, but if he hears me, Georgie refuses to turn around. Even in illness, my brother is all single-mindedness. He has left a discarded Coke can behind him, a slip of paper; he only cares about rocks. He moves the blower left to right, right to left. The rocks skip to the curb. What is left is the gleaming asphalt, slick with rain, broken on the edges.

I call again, louder, and this time he turns but doesn't release his grip or disengage the motor. He is dressed in a ratty wool blazer, a wrinkled shirt and jeans, old sneakers. The rain plasters his dark hair against his face. The muscles of his jaw clench. His lower lip protrudes, registers his disappointment at seeing me here, here again, ready to bring him back home.

I raise my hand, as if to stop him from yelling, which he often does. I circle wide, then come in closer. At first, it is always the same—just Georgie and me on the road, the two of us staring at each other as if we are strangers. It's true that Georgie looks like someone else, someone too fat to be my brother, too bloated from medication, puffy around the eyes. His face is dour. And, worse, what strikes me about my brother is how alone he seems. Could I tell Elle or Dr. Mulvaney that now—looking at Georgie—he intimidates me, he terrifies and saddens me, in his aloneness? "Georgie," I yell. "You've got to stop doing this thing with the rocks and Memphis. You're going to get yourself killed one of these days."

He turns the blower low, and I survey his broad face. A small cut, already clotting, juts from his eyebrow. The wind lashes against him. He says bitterly, "You're just waiting, fucker."

I ignore this and turn back to where, down the road, Elle and Winston stand next to the car, waiting for me, for us. Elle holds a hand up to her forehead to protect her face from the rain. She gestures to me, then pets Winston, and something in my heart constricts. I breathe deeply, turn back toward Georgie. For a moment, the cold feels good, intensely honest, though it's true that under my jacket I'm sweating. I hold my breath and count to five. It is a stupid thing, counting to five, a childish thing, a thing Georgie and I used to do when, as children, we passed through tunnels lined with long rows of lights that glistened like lost treasure. When I finally expire my breath, I ask, "What happened to the car?"

"Man, what the fuck do you *think* happened?" He kicks a stone, kicks it down the street, past me. Winston barks nervously. Elle yells, "For Christ's sake, do something, Bud, or I will."

My brother's face burns scarlet. He surveys his progress, glancing up and down the street. The downstairs lights in one of the nearby houses flicks on, then, in a few moments, flicks off.

I shove my hand in my jean pocket, fumble for the quarter that is buried there, the stick of gum, the balled-up lint. I speak slowly, as if I am speaking to an imbecile, which of course my brother is not. I say, "You're soaked through, Georgie."

"I am," he says. "Great observation, Buddy Boy."

I force a smile, my only goal now to get Georgie into the Bronco, to get him home.

I say, "There must be a hell of a lot of rocks between here and Memphis."

"No shit, Bud," he says. "Any idiot knows that. Every fucking time it's the rocks, then you."

"That's hardly the issue now," I tell him. "What we need to do is head back."

"Don't be coy, fucker," he says. "I'm not going anywhere anymore."

I walk a few steps toward him. I turn the quarter over in my pocket. I say, as if trying to joke and trying to console my brother at the same time, "Coy? I'm not a fish, Georgie. And I work for the school district."

A white Geo speeds by us, gunning its engine. Two teens stick their heads out and scream. I flick the Geo and the teens the finger. What do they know? They haven't ever been stuck out on a solitary road, trying to persuade someone to come home. They haven't stood where my brother and I are standing. I bend down and search for a stone, angry at the absurdity that's become my life, angry because I'm tired, and angry at Georgie, because of his illness, and because, I realize, there is not a single damn stone to throw at the Geo, all because of him. I think, Sure, go ahead and laugh, all you fuckers. Then I tell Georgie in a mean way that, in his future travels, he might at least pick a location closer to home so that we don't have to go through this every time. I tell him the supermarket is good because it is only down the street from our house, and when he's there he might pitch in and do a little shopping. I tell him if he needs something fancier, he might try the Liberty Bell and get out of my hair for good. I say, "Both of these options are better than Memphis. And why the fuck do you want to go to Memphis, anyway?"

Georgie says, "You *know.*" He aims the leaf blower at me like a weapon.

"I don't know," I say. "But I'll tell you what I do know, Georgie. I do know that this isn't progress. I do know that."

"Memphis," he says, and it is as though I am not even here, as if my brother is seeing past me to a whole different world. "Because it's sure as hell far away from this place. Memphis, because I threw a goddamn dart and that's where it landed."

I consider this. I think, What's the point in arguing? Finally, I say, "You'll never get there on your own, Georgie. Never."

"Not with that traitor wife of yours," Georgie tells me. I turn and Elle is on the cell phone. I yell to her but she ignores me. Still talking, she coaxes Winston into the back of the Bronco.

"I'm not going anywhere," Georgie says. He shivers, pulls his jacket close. And it is as if he couldn't care less that I am standing here, wet, soaked through and shivering as well, or that I am tired, or that he's even had an accident.

So we wait. We wait until a few minutes later a siren disrupts the quiet, and then another set of tires hits the gravel and crawls to a halt. Lights flash. I hear a walkie-talkie buzz to life, an officer calling in the location and license plate of Georgie's car. I don't need to turn to see Elle is most assuredly standing there beside the officer, explaining the situation and explaining my brother. Probably she is using Dr. Mulvaney–speak, as though she is in charge of the outlook and situation, and finally all is well. After all, she's probably saying, she had a sick aunt once that her mother took care of for a time.

"She's a fucking piece of work, that one," Georgie says. He's breathing hard. "Did Mom even like her?"

"You did this," I say. "This isn't what I wanted."

"Oh, fuck you, Bud!" he screams. Then he takes the blower off his back, lifts the entire unit and smashes it on the pavement.

"Hey, hey!" the officer screams. He walks hurriedly over to where my brother and I stand. He keeps his hand on his holster. "None of that, George," he says as he nears us, this twenty-something-ish kid cop, new to the force probably.

I say nothing. I survey the mess, the broken plastic throttle of the blower, the bits of wire and metal machinery scattered on the road. If I were a better man, I would clean up all the messes in the world for Georgie. I would tell Elle that if she didn't like it, she could call someone who cares. I would carry my brother home. If he needed, I would carry my brother forever. But instead I think: Everything changes. At some point which you cannot foresee, *everything* changes, and it is as though you are suddenly on the other side of your life, looking in on it as though it were a spectacle. I think, I cannot do this anymore.

The officer stands next to me. He is careful in his speech, his movement. He's probably received training in all this, I think. He probably thinks that all his training will help.

As for me, all I can think to say to Georgie is, "Brother, you exhaust me."

He says bitterly, "You don't know what it means to be exhausted, fucker."

"Your sister-in-law says you're going to Memphis," the officer says. "I think we can arrange for it, George. I think we can get you there tonight."

It is flimflam, it is mean, and I know it. I listen to the officer go on, his voice conciliatory when Georgie issues his complaints against the government, against Elle, against me. Then, when he grows quiet, I tell Georgie that we'll all go together, that we'll drive all the way to Memphis. I'd like to believe this, that we could take a road trip there, together, my brother and I. As if there were not any obstructions at all, just a breezy drive through the rainy night and clearing day, as if we could skip all the way there like a stone.

A staticky voice comes over the walkie-talkie. The officer steps back, replies, says everything is in order, that everything is okay and that the hospital has been called, and he'll be bringing Georgie in for evaluation.

"So what do you say, Georgie?" I ask. "You and me, road trip?"

My brother's look is wild and sad. He hesitates, steps toward me, then stops. He says, "Don't fuck with me, Bud, you fucker."

"I wouldn't fuck with you," I lie.

"You're finally going," Elle tells Georgie when we near the officer's car. Her shoulders straighten. Her eyes clear. Possibly she can see across the whole year. I smile at her, but it, too, is a lie.

Georgie glances up and down the street in a futile, searching way. The officer opens his car door, and Georgie's anger is reduced to that of a child. He nears me then. He lets me put my arm around him. I can feel the warmth emitting from my brother, hear the working of his lungs, his breath.

I whisper to him, "Memphis or bust."

Georgie looks at me. In the near-dark street, my brother is crying.

A GOOD WOMAN'S LOVE

It's Friday night at Leroy's Pub and, true to form, Charlie is drunk. I want to say something, but even after he's had scotch, Charlie is one hell of a nice drunk. He is nice and I am nice. Sometimes I think that's the problem, that neither of us can be mean or say what we're really thinking. When I meet him for our date, Charlie looks up from his glass, then rakes his thin brown hair back with his fingers. He shifts in his chair and takes me in—the possibilities of the night, of us—and then he smiles, as if he's still trying, after two weeks of seeing each other naked, to make a good impression.

There are other things Charlie does that make me feel sweet about him. He pulls a chair out for me in the way a gentleman or a boyfriend might. He lets out a low whistle when I slip off my jean jacket and shimmy a little, showing him the chest that the Good Lord graced me with in this life. "Daisy," he says, eyeing my sequined top and talking in that low voice I've come to love because it's both raspy and tender. "You look beautiful."

"Thank you, Charlie," I say.

"The usual?"

I nod and he gets up and goes to the bar. He orders a gin and tonic, and Leroy, a big ex-army guy, makes small talk about the start of the football season, and who will go all the way. Charlie collects the drinks and pays with tip; he's never once asked me to buy my own drink.

Charlie isn't good-looking, but neither am I. He wears a Hawaiian shirt and tan slacks that bunch at the ankles. There's a ravaged quality about his face. His lower eyelids are purple and puffy, and it looks like he's just gotten into a brawl with some-one, but I don't mind because Charlie has the most mournful, coppery eyes I've ever seen, more mournful than the patients at the old folks' home where I work as an aide, the ones who, when I help them out of their beds and into their chairs, grip my arms and lift their near-blind eyes up at me, and I know they're lonely and want to be touched. The expression on their faces and Char-lie's face is pretty much the same. Just a few nights ago, Charlie confessed to me that he wasn't sure he ever really loved a woman, and when I joked, he said, "I didn't mean I'm *queer*, Daisy." I teased him more, but I knew what he meant, really. There was a time I thought I loved Ray, my last boyfriend, because whenever he was gone my heart ached. But then Ray's knife cut into my face, and I realized that sometimes your feelings about people are wrong. Sometimes your heart just tricks you.

I don't want to get romantic about this. The truth is Charlie is drunk and needs to stop drinking if any of this is going to work. You don't always choose unhappiness. Sometimes it chooses you, but you can always change for the better if you set your mind to it.

Back at our table, Charlie sets the gin and tonic down. He says, "Daisy, you're so beautiful I'd marry you if I were a better man."

I push away peanut shells, let them drop to the sticky floor. "Is that you or the booze talking?"

"Both of us," Charlie says, and he grins. He sits down and gets quiet then, as if he's embarrassed, and because my cheeks are flushed, I do the same. You'd think with all the people who drink in town—and there are quite a lot that I know of, personally—Leroy's would pack them in. But it's also a hole-in-the-wall: dank and poorly lit, and the air smells stale from beer. The karaoke machine only plays outdated songs from the seventies and eighties, and lots of the up-and-coming drinkers have never even heard of the bands. The bar itself is long and dark, and the wall behind it is lined with mirrors. As usual it's a slow night. There are only a few locals—Ed, Joe, Jim, and Johnny sitting with their rears glued to the stools, and Charlie and me on the other side of the room, sitting at a table. I know the guys from back in high school; that's how small the town is. But I don't know the young couple leaning against the pool table, kissing each other in all manner of pre-fornication. The girl turns, and I catch her profile—her small nose and chin, her long earrings. She has strawberry-colored hair and is more than a little tipsy. She taps her foot and sways in time with "I Will Survive," but I bet she's never had to survive a bad day of anything in her life. After they kiss and sing, she and her boyfriend play pool. She squeals whenever she manages to hit one ball against another. When she does, even Charlie turns around to see what all the fuss is about. So do the guys at the bar. The girl waves at them and winks. I think there's something probably shallow about her. I try to ignore her, especially, because unlike me she really is beautiful and has her entire life ahead of her, and everything for the taking. As for me, it's true I've got firm thighs and strong arms for lifting, a good, full head of curls, and I already mentioned my chest, but I've always been homely and Ray's knife didn't make any improvements to my face. I've got bad, pockmarked skin, and a hook-shaped scar like a question mark that runs from the corner of my eye to my chin. Sometimes you don't choose all your ugliness, either.

Before these past two weeks with Charlie, I haven't been with a man in over ten years, not since Ray. Sometimes I put my hands on the old folks' faces just so I can remember what someone else's skin feels like—that warmth and heat, the wrinkles and lines that mark all a person's living and time served on this earth. I cup their faces and tell them they're beautiful. I sit with them sometimes, when I can, when there's a little lull in between cleaning bedpans and lifting them on and off gurneys. Sometimes when they're near their end, I tell them it's okay to let go and just be open to whatever is next. A lot of them hardly have family who come and visit, and if no one on staff takes the time to sit with them it's just the fluorescent lights overhead to consider, the sharp sting of them, and waiting.

I'm thirty-nine and have never been married.

Charlie hasn't ever been married, either. During the day, when he's sober, he operates a forklift at Walgreens and spends more than twelve hours holed up in the warehouse, and while it's true he hasn't ever been promoted, he hasn't been fired, either, so I'm hopeful that when he's not drinking he's pretty clearheaded. Ray couldn't hold down a job to save his life.

The pool balls crack together and the girl squeals again.

"What can you do with kids?" Charlie says, looking as the girl shimmies around, dancing, arms up in the air, body winding around her boyfriend's. The boy pats her rump. She's wearing a short jacket and jeans that are so tight they seem painted on her. "Ah," Charlie says whimsically. "Misspent youth."

"Wait until they actually have to work for a living," I tell him. "How old do you think they are, anyway, eighteen, nineteen? Underage for sure."

"It gets harder and harder to tell," Charlie says, and he takes a swig of his drink. "Anyway, Leroy doesn't care. Good for business, a little happiness like that."

"If he doesn't get caught serving them," I say.

"Who's going to catch him?" Charlie asks. "He knows everyone in town, even Billy, and Billy's the only one with a badge. Anyway, Daisy, that girl's got nothing on you."

He lifts my hand and kisses my fingers. My cheeks turn rosy, petals closing up around my scar. I say, "Are you trying to make me feel sweet about you?"

He rakes his hands through his hair. "You're already sweet as sweet can be," he says.

"Would you say that, Charlie, if you weren't drinking?"

Charlie says nothing. The girl slips one arm under her boyfriend's leather jacket and tousles his hair. She lifts her face to his and waits for a kiss. When I see them, I think about us— Charlie and me. I wish we could be like that, young and free and all our love ahead of us.

Charlie takes his last swig, then contemplates his empty glass. He says, "God, I can hardly believe it's time for another. You game?"

"I'm good," I say, holding up my glass. With that, Charlie staggers over to Leroy, who has the sense to tell Charlie that he's had enough. Leroy is a good man. He's hulking and quiet but he's firm in his pronouncements. Once when I was too young to know better and banging back shots of tequila at the bar with Ray, a rosy-faced girl like the one at the pool table came into the pub. She pulled her long blond hair back and then let it fall again against her shoulders. She angled up to the bar and asked for a piña colada. Leroy just eyed her up and down and toweled a glass. He drew a glass of beer from the tap, set it in front of her. He told her, "We don't serve none of those fancy drinks." When I laughed, the girl blinked hard at me and smiled in a calculated way. She said, "What are you laughing at, you ugly bitch?" Ray, trashed to high heaven, snorted and told her that I sure was ugly, but then again he didn't have to see my face when the lights were out. He told her she wasn't ugly. She ran her long fingers over her silver bracelets, then clanked them together and said, "In your dreams, cowboy."

The pool balls crack. Another yelp, another kiss. The girl is probably the type to drink piña coladas, too.

"What you looking at, Daisy?" Charlie asks now. "That handsome pool boy giving me a run for the money?" He smiles and I smile in that terse way I sometimes do, when I'm not entirely happy.

"Leroy denied you?"

"He's got a stone-cold heart," Charlie says, shaking his head. He sits and places his thin hand on my fishnet stockings and lets it crawl up my thigh, under my skirt. These two weeks with Charlie touching me have been heaven. And even though he's drunk, he still knows how to work his fingers in a way that makes my skin tingle. I pull his hand up, a little higher.

I say, "I wonder what it would be like if you were sober. Think of all the sweet things we could do."

"Sober is for the dead," he tells me.

I say nothing. I want to tell him that he should stop drinking altogether, that you can't really love a person until you see them clearly. Charlie and me, we don't see like that yet. We get together at night to drink and then walk to his apartment and fool around, and at first that was fine. But now it turns out that I've got other things in mind for Charlie, things that stretch beyond the night and clear into the morning. But I don't want to tell Charlie all this, or that he has to quit drinking in order for us to really love each other, not right at this moment, right when his hands are working their way up, between my legs.

Charlie whispers in my ear. His breath feels warm and thick. The girl at the pool table scratches. When her boyfriend teases her, she jumps on his back and rides him like a pony, and the entire room seems to explode and fill with a light so tangible I can feel it, feel how it threatens to pop Leroy's walls at the seams, split the place open.

Charlie's fingers stop climbing up my leg. He says, "Well, look at that pretty thing riding around like that."

"Let's skip out," I say. "I want to go someplace quieter, without so many distractions." I smile and squeeze his thigh, squeeze it tight and high on his leg, and he nods and tells me that we can get a bottle to go.

The fall night is warmer than usual, and the streets are nearly empty. I can smell the newly laid asphalt on the road, the stench of beer bottles in the Dumpster. My ears ring from the music. Above the pub, a few floors up, a couple fights, unconcerned with the open windows. Charlie *tsk*s this, and takes my hand. I look up at the stars as we walk. "Do you believe there's a God, Charlie?" I ask. "A God who looks down and actually cares?"

"Why, hell yes," Charlie tells me. "My mother didn't raise a fool."

"I'm glad," I say.

We take turns singing "I Will Survive." When Charlie sings he sounds a bit like a dog howling at the moon, and he laughs and laughs. I help him along when he forgets a line, or vice versa. "Ha!" he says, and he smacks his thigh. "Daisy we got it! We've started our own party now. Together you and me make a whole song." He does a little two-step and catches himself before he staggers. "Close call," he says.

"Oh Lord," I tell him, "every day is a close call, isn't it?"

AT HIS PLACE, Charlie slips off my jacket, sits down in his recliner, and pulls me on his lap. He rests a glass of scotch on my thigh. We kiss in the dark.

I've never stayed the whole night at Charlie's apartment, even after we've fooled around and I'm sleepy and his body feels warm under the blankets and my leg hangs over his leg. I don't want to get up and walk back to Leroy's for my car, but I slip out before the first crack of light hits the windows. Sometimes when I'm feeling really sweet about him, I like to imagine that he gets up in the morning and wonders if I was a dream. I've never been any man's dream, but I'd like to be Charlie's.

Now, in between kisses, he asks if I want a drink. I tell him that I don't want anything to drink, that I want something else instead. When I say that, he kisses my chest. "Sorry, Charlie," I say. "Not that."

"Aren't you sweet on me, Daisy Mae?"

"That's not the point," I tell him.

He stares at me hard now, as if he's thinking, only I know he's too drunk to go any place deep. I say, "You don't need to drink, Charlie." I feel foolish saying it because he's a grown man, and I don't want him to get angry. I've never seen Charlie angry, but when Ray drank the smallest thing would set him off. Then I think of Ray the night he was drunk and what he did with his knife after we left the bar and the pretty blond-haired woman told him he didn't have a chance in all his dreams and called him a cowboy.

Charlie takes a swig of scotch. He looks out the window. We both sit and don't say anything. It's the first time I notice how dark his apartment always is, with only the streetlamp outside in the alley illuminating the living room. I imagine Charlie's apartment in the morning, the tidiness of it, the simplicity of his furniture, the white walls, the clock on the mantel, the electric fireplace that he's said he uses all winter. Charlie never turns on any lights while I'm here, and even though it's never bothered me before, it bothers me plenty now.

When I ask him if he's ashamed, Charlie tells me the lights give him a headache and hurt his eyes.

"It's good to see the person you're kissing," I say.

He scratches his head and looks sleepy but says, "I guess I agree."

But then neither of us reaches over to turn on the light.

"I've been thinking," I tell him. I take the scotch from his hand and set it on the coffee table.

"Thinking never did a smart man any good."

"I'm serious," I say.

"Okay," he says. His lower lip, wet with scotch, comes down in a pout. When I smile he says, "See, Daisy, I knew I could make you laugh."

"Listen here," I say. "If we're going to try to make things

work, you need to stop drinking. I'll help you." I speak to him in a quiet but firm way, like I speak to the old folks who just lie in bed and don't want to get up and into their chairs, the ones who have given up hope. At first Charlie snickers more, but when I tell him it's not funny, he stops laughing and grows quiet instead. He nods, he's taking all this in, only I can't tell how much he's hearing on account of the booze. I tell him that this is the plain truth of the way I see it all working out. I tell him we've both had a rough time of things, but that's no excuse. "Well, what do you think?" I say. I twist the bottom of my skirt.

He kisses my cheek quickly, so that it feels like a little brush of air. He pats my leg. "You're an angel," he says.

I push his hand away, but gently because the truth is that's the nicest thing anyone has ever said to me. What Charlie says hurts to hear. "I'm not an angel," I tell him.

He cups my face. "You're Daisy, beautiful." He gets the words a little jumbled, but I don't mind. "A Daisy angel," he says. His hands on my face are warm and sweet. I can't remember the last time anyone touched me like that, not even Ray. I can't think of what to say, so I just tell him, "Charlie, don't say that. Don't make me feel sweeter about you."

Charlie says, "I'm sorry."

We sit there in the quiet because now I'm stumped about what to do next. The truth is, I'm close to crying but don't. Instead, I get up from the recliner and then turn toward him. I say, "No time like the present." I lean into Charlie and can smell the sourness on his breath, but I don't mind because I know there's tomorrow and the next day and the next, and the smell and all the bottles will be gone. He cups my breast with his hand. "Easy," I say.

"Just a silvery angel," he tells me.

I lift him with my legs and not my back. I brace my arms around his waist. As Charlie rights himself, I grab the glass. I walk him into the kitchen and turn on the light. There are a few dirty dishes in the sink, and sudsy water. I reach in and pull the plug.

"What are we doing?" Charlie asks, squinting. He pulls away, staggers back, and leans against the refrigerator. I pour the drink down the drain. Then I take the bottle from the kitchen counter and hand it to Charlie. When he sees me untwisting the cap, he says, "Oh no."

"If you think I'm your angel," I say, "then you need to get clear-sighted if we're going to be together." I hand him the bottle. He licks his lips a little and rakes his hands through his hair then over his face. He says, "I can't do it." He's almost crying, wallowing over his bottle and acting like a grown baby with his lip quivering, and even though it bothers me to see a man acting like this, I think, What else can I expect, telling him to give up what he's used to? I tell him that it has to come from him, that he has to stand up straight, pour the scotch down the drain, and promise to be clear-sighted.

I sit down at the table. I wait. Finally he says, "Christ Almighty."

"Sorry, Charlie," I say. I tell him he can't be a hound dog all his life.

He doesn't move. "Daisy," he says, "I never knew you could be a bitch."

"I thought I was an angel."

"Oh, piss off," he says.

I say nothing. My eyes well up, and Charlie, raking his hands through his hair, looks over to me and sighs and says, "Christ, all right. Don't start blubbering."

"I'm not blubbering," I tell him.

He stumbles over to the sink, promises, and pours out the half-empty bottle of scotch. "I'm the one who should be crying," he says.

"Don't," I say. "Don't start."

"Fine," he says. When I go up to him and touch his arm, he turns his face toward me and says, "You're right, and you're a good woman." He pats my shoulder.

I tell Charlie I don't want to fight. I tell him that he's sweet and brave, sweeter than anyone I've ever known. I kiss his neck.

EVEN THOUGH CHARLIE is drunk, I straddle him in bed to ride him like a pony. I'm already down to my fishnets and bra, and Charlie—well, I've managed to get him down to his boxers. He says, "You got a good body," and I say, "Thank you." His bed feels warm and lived-in.

"I want to feel the love of a good woman," he tells me.

"Thank you," I tell him again. "Thank you very much."

Amused, Charlie sings a line from "Heartbreak Hotel." When I touch him, he trembles in a quiet way, not like Ray, who was loud and rough and thrashed around. That night, after the blond girl shot Ray down, he wrestled with me on his bed as if he had something desperate to prove. He put a knife to my cheek and said, "What's one more thing wrong with your stupid face?" The knife was sharp. I didn't flinch. I barely felt anything. I thought he was playing, because he always did like rough sex. But then I saw the blade again—not silver but silver and red— and I put my hand up to my face and it was warm and moist and then there was a deep, sharp pain. Ray held the knife to my throat, pressed. Then he laughed in a bitter way and said, "Even ugly can get uglier," and I thought for a moment that my time on this earth was over. I thought, then, too, that it didn't matter if I was beautiful or ugly, any more than it mattered if I drove a Beemer to work or had a million dollars or was poor. It didn't change the fact that we all died, and no matter who was there with you in those final moments, dying was still something you did alone.

Charlie doesn't flail around, and he's still soft between my legs. He's so soft I could cry. I take his hand and place it on my rump, pat a little. "Would rough sex work, and get things started?"

"No, Daisy," he says. "I'm not going to hurt you." He kisses my bra. Then, tired, he leans back and settles onto the pillow. He makes a strange, sobbing sound, and turns his head. "I'm sorry, Daisy. I'm just so damn drunk. It's me, not you."

"All right," I tell him and roll off of him. I move to go, but he places his hand on me.

"Why are you always running off so quickly?" he asks. "Stay, and tomorrow I'll take you out for eggs."

I say, "You might wake up tomorrow and see everything differently." But when I look over at him, his eyelids quiver and I know he's asleep and already dreaming. I don't know what Charlie dreams about.

Usually I'd leave now while it's still dark, but tonight because he told me I was a good woman and held my face, and because he called me his angel and threw out his booze, I stay. I'm so close to Charlie that I can hear the sound of his heart.

Tomorrow he'll wake and his eyes won't look mournful but lustery, like the sky after a storm has cleared, and then I'll know. And it's funny, not really funny, I guess, but sad-funny. When I look at him sleeping like a stray dog under the light from the alley, I think of the old people's faces when I lift them from their beds, right before I unlatch their fingers from my arms. Sometimes their faces are looking off beyond me, and sometimes they look scared, like they're closing their eyes and mouths on death, cupping their lips over death like it's an old lover. Other times, they smile like they've quit being scared and are moving to a light that has all the love they need in the world. I think of me and Charlie in those faces. Tomorrow when the sun comes up Charlie will lift me out of bed and maybe, if he's really a gentleman, smile and take me out for breakfast.

WHAT YOU DON'T KNOW

Jess peers under his visor and squints at the sun. He's been quiet for the past hour, but now, surveying the desert, he says, "We're nowhere, Prue. Absolutely nowhere."

In the passenger's seat, Prue fans her skirt and lifts her sticky thighs from the seat, releasing them like duct tape. Somewhere back in Kansas the air conditioner went and Jess refused to pay to have it serviced. Now, as heat blasts through the open windows, Prue breathes in the desert until she feels as though she, too, is desert, part of the endless landscape, the unforgiving sky. She should feel lucky with her man beside her. But when Jess curses the absence of road signs and markers, Prue only wants to say he could have gotten a map back at the last gas station. She wants to say he is one of those men who never asks for directions, and that it is his pigheadedness that has them here—lost, the air conditioner broken, the gas gauge flirting with E, that tenuous line of demarcation. Men and directions, she wants to say, go together like coffee and Jell-O.

Instead, she says, "We're on Veteran's Memorial Highway, I think. Outside Winnemucca, like in the song 'I've Been Everywhere.' Have we been to enough everywheres yet?" she asks.

"Hardly," says Jess.

"Well, there must be a gas station somewhere."

"There's probably not anything," Jess says with a hint of bitterness that surprises her. "What you don't know is that deserts go on and on. What you don't know, *Prudence,* is that deserts eat everything up."

Prue frowns at the sound of her name on his tongue. It is a name given by her ex-hippie-turned-banker mother, a name that caused constant taunts in high school. High school is where she and Jess met, in fact, in that time when she loved his easiness, his lank, ungainly body and long hair, his sweet teasing and laughter. They are both nineteen and have been married just over a year. Jess is on leave from Fort Bragg, where he and Prue live on base, and she is pregnant, so newly pregnant in fact that she hasn't yet told Jess.

She turns up the Bob Dylan song that plays in the tape deck. *"How many roads?"* she questions, knowing Bob Dylan irritates Jess—he has often said that Dylan is for pussies—and irritating him gives her an odd sense of satisfaction. It repays him for the broken air conditioner, for being lost with practically no money left, for this unending road trip. "A tour of America," Jess had called it. At first the idea invigorated Prue, gave her a strange sense of purpose. They headed south to snap photographs of the big peach and the world's largest Coke bottle. They drove to the International Towing and Recovery Museum, then to Silo X in Missouri, with its top-secret disasters and toxic gases that turned men into monsters. In Hebron, Nebraska, they admired the world's largest porch swing. They stopped at cheap motels and out-of-the-way diners for greasy burgers and fries that coated Prue's fingers with oil. They talked about movies, alien invasions, the cost of things, and a whole lot of nothing. When they ran low on cash, they spent a few nights sleeping on the hood of Jess's Chevy, buried under blankets, her head on his chest. But now Prue only feels tired, a little too sick, and in need of home.

She releases her seat from its upright position, leans back, and props one tan leg up on the dashboard. She says, "It's been a real blast, baby, but after a while anything gets a little old. Don't you ever get tired of going everywhere and nowhere, all at once?"

Jess glances over. "You don't even care that you've never seen anything, do you? If we turn around, we'll miss the *Hornet* in Alameda. It's only a national treasure, you know. A living monument to our history. One of the guys went to California *six* times to see it, it was that good." Then he adds: "There's a lot that's good on the West Coast."

"Home is good," Prue says, pointing. "That direction."

Jess snorts in disgust. "The *Hornet*'s better than home. Bet you didn't know it's haunted. Real live ghosts in *that* baby."

Prue rolls her eyes. "Only kids believe in ghosts, Jess."

"Bull-*shit*," he says. "Two hundred sightings of soldiers lost in battle. *Doc-u-mented*. That ship's seen more action than *you'll* ever see, that's for damn sure. Everything holds on to its ghosts. There's not anything that's been through war that gets off scot-free."

"Gas," Prue reminds him.

"*Pru-dence*," Jess retorts. For a moment, his stare is unyielding, but then, suddenly, he snickers. He glances at the gauge, snorts again, then leans back and steers with his wrist. As is a recent habit, he runs his free hand over his crew cut, back and forth. It is an act that somehow hurts Prue to witness, just as it hurts her when, late at night, Jess turns and tells her they can never go home again, that he's seen too much to ever go back.

Prue feels a strange tiredness, an unaccustomed ache. She knows she should feel grateful that Jess wasn't sent home to her in a coffin, like so many other husbands and wives. She has often tried to imagine what it was like for him to be in the desert, to be caught in its swirling storms. Did killing, she wondered, ever become as easy as pulling in a breath of air? One, two, three, breathe, and it's over—no real discomfort, no real shock, but only a sweet relief that you are the one left standing? And what—if anything—dies, in the process of all that? Prue wants to ask Jess now but she can't. He would only say she is talking stupid. He would only give her that hard look she's seen so many times since he's been home—jaw clenched, eyes deep, concealing—and Prue would feel unsettled, cast-off, as if longing for the boy she knew in high school weren't enough, as if she'd met a stranger coming home instead. And that is the truth, she realizes. The boy she knew is gone.

"I bet you didn't know they give you at least twenty extra miles after empty," Jess says. "I bet you've never been out of gas in your life, *Pru*-dence."

"I've been out of gas plenty," Prue says.

"Bullshit. I bet you don't even know what real empty feels like."

"Oh, I know empty," Prue says. She glides her tongue over her teeth and tastes the bare, gritty sand. "I know *real* empty, too." For a moment, she thinks of Fort Bragg and North Carolina's lush forests, that weedy heaviness that hangs over everything. She says, "I don't give a rat's ass about the *Hornet*. I bet you didn't know *that*. I don't give a rat's ass anymore about a whole lot of things."

"Oh, I know," Jess says, nodding. "And I agree with you on that last part."

Prue cranks up Dylan and turns over possibilities. She will leave him, she knows. She won't keep the baby. One, two, three, breathe, and she will walk away. She says, "I know no desert can go on and on and eat up everything, you're wrong about that. Not if you don't want it to, it doesn't."

"You don't know shit," Jess laughs. He cranes his head out the window and lets out a fierce, sad howl. He speeds, kicking up dust behind them. "And I know *that* just like I know it's only pussies who cry for home, just like I know that we've got at least twenty miles before real empty, and that the *Hornet* is sure as hell loaded with ghosts *you'll* never see. It's what you don't know that kills you, that's what I know. Bang, bang, bang, dear Prudence. Knocks you real dead."

CONVERSIONS ON THE ROAD
TO DAMASCUS

───────────

I think, though I am unsure, that my flatmate Cass knows what I have done. She has been stalking me around our apartment for days, laying word traps, hoping I might confess. I want to remain inconspicuous about the whole affair. We are not friends, she and I. We have only lived together six months, since the start of the school year, and we are bound by the necessity of shared rent that is due to our landlord, Mr. Tannen, on the second of each month. Beyond this, I have no commitment and refuse to suffer through the cumbersome condition of affection.

She has said I am godless.

Cass tells me her first mistake was rooming with an ethics student, that this fact alone should have alerted her to the potential for what she calls "certain problems of spiritual affinity." She's very dramatic when she speaks. Cass is an actor and a second-year graduate student in the Drama Department, both of which facts, I tell her, are something less than a miracle of nature.

Presently, we are in the bathroom, I am peeing, and once again Cass has breached the boundaries of social etiquette by barging in. Her rear end plants itself on the tub. She sits with her arms folded. Cass wears faded carpenter jeans with frayed holes in the knees and a white V-neck sweater. She has coarse black hair that falls below her waist, and she's wearing a pissed-off Polish look that I find intimidating. She asks if I think her boyfriend, Evan (also an actor), has another girl. She has only been seeing Evan for a month. They are not committed, but she is obsessed. Cass has a certain weakness for imposters, actor-men. She says she adores anyone who looks like a young Robert Redford, even though she also admits Evan is an oversexed dog.

I find that when enclosed in a small room it's best to say nothing incriminating. Now would not be the time to tell her, for example, about being tied to Evan's bedposts, or about his deft use of electronic devices. Cass's intuition can take her only so far. I have been very careful. After our lovemaking, I've washed Evan's smell off of me, soaped every orifice, and arrived home from his apartment smelling of Irish Spring.

You're awfully quiet, Moira, she says. Her look reeks of suspicion. At the beginning of the school year, I once saw Cass run down an undergraduate (the girl on foot, Cass in her Jeep). Yes, she said the gas pedal stuck; yes, she was cleared of wrongdoing. Still, I can only imagine what she might do to me.

She asks if I'm nervous. I tell her no, I'm not nervous, not especially, no more than usual, et cetera. I tell her her obsession is bound to breed psychiatric bills.

Actors are full of fictions and lies, she says. She smacks her hand against the tub. I wish I didn't always find myself in bed with thespians. Betrayal, she says, pervades all thespian interactions.

Whine, whine, whine. For any proposition to be meaningful, love or affairs alike, circumstances must be verified, I say. Empirical evidence, hard facts. Show me the proof of betrayal, I tell her. Then I sniff the air, somewhat tauntingly, and say: Do you smell Irish Spring?

As is customary habit, Cass slides a small medallion, a picture of Saint Stephen, back and forth across her necklace. She narrows her eyes in a most predictable way.

It's true I am not without some feelings of guilt. But once you have committed the crime, there is always the business of cover-up. Self-preservation in circumstances of betrayal is essential, and I am all for that.

EVAN WILL SOON PLAY Jason opposite Cass's role of the Colchian princess in the college's production of Euripides' *Medea*. He practices his lines while naked, standing over me in bed, and sometimes when he is reading, he jumps up and down, causing all manner of extremities to whirl and fly about. Like many men, Evan aligns himself with the classicist school. He believes his penis is an embodiment of nobility and that he can discern truths such as love or beauty which he then approximates with sex and nipple rings. All this should make me leery of him. The truth is, I have always imagined that I would end up in bed with a man who looked like Nietzsche, a little on the morose and philological side, possibly someone who listened (as Nietzsche did) to Wagner's music. But it seems that, like my flatmate, I have a terrible weakness for gray eyes, good looks, and clean, classical features. (I suppose Evan *does* look like a young Redford.)

Once, before we first kissed, Evan said, simply, Risk it, Moira. Before that moment, I had never risked anything. Normally I suffer from a terrible interiority of the soul that causes me to dwell in the corners of familiar, often crowded institutions— campus libraries, coffeehouses, et cetera—and pass judgments. But here, in Evan's bed, I feel other things: sheer whimsy over our naked bodies, an unexpected affection.

Evan plops down and nibbles my belly. He quotes Jason's lines in a zealous way: *I will listen to what new thing you want, woman, to get from me!*

I am normally not a jealous person, but today, since he has asked, I give Evan a good-natured ribbing about having two women. Is it necessary to have us both? I ask. I do not mention that I have on occasion indulged horrible images of Cass and Evan naked, a thought that makes me feel slightly ill. I tell him I want to know which one of us—Cass or me—he prefers. I say, It must be difficult to have relations with two flatmates. I ask him if he has ever indulged a certain fantasy that he might, on some occasion, end up in bed with both of us, if only out of sheer confusion, carelessness, or the simple act of forgetting. And then where would you be? I say. Think about it.

I am thinking about it, he says. And wow. I'd be a guy in bed with two women.

Not funny, I tell him.

I thought you said no attachment and no jealously. I believe you said, "I'm much too smart to get attached to you."

I said more that smart people know better than to get too attached, and then they go ahead and do it anyway.

I can't help myself, Moira, he tells me. I always fall for my leads. And this, he explains, combined with a certain dogged appreciation for the female form, repeatedly gets him in trouble. Condemn not, but pity me instead, he says.

Boo-hoo, I say. Poor Evan.

After more lovemaking, which today consists mainly of discourse (a carryover from my love affair with Nietzsche), Cass texts Evan. There are tears involved, drunkenness, incoherent phrases. Apparently there has been an abundance of tears and drinking and texting lately.

She's obsessed, he says. He scratches his head. He asks, Who would have thought?

She *knows,* I tell him. Evan-Jason has taken a second lover (you know who) and Cass-Medea is planning her revenge. It's all so very textbook, I say. Suddenly I think Cass is probably on her way to Evan's apartment as I speak. I remember the running down of the freshman; it was no laughing matter. I get out of bed and search through the tangled pile of clothes scattered on the floor. I tell Evan every interaction is eventually terrifying.

He yawns. Like most people after sex, Evan has a very low attention span. He busies himself by draping a Kleenex over his penis like a toga. The whole draping ceremony pleases him, confirms his own spectacular wishes about the splendor of his body, its classicism, its containment. I go to the bathroom and wash. I slip into my jeans, button my shirt, and pull on a sweater. Head still wet, I rush out into the frosty air and into the descending dark.

A PERSON DECIDES that she is going to have an affair with her flatmate's boyfriend, and, while in theory this should be easy, the situation is soon mired with complications. First, there is a small pang of guilt I feel constantly, along with my unexpected interest in classical theater. Also, over the last two weeks things with Cass have gotten uglier. After each rendezvous with Evan, I arrive back to the flat and Cass sniffs the air with canine cunning to see if Evan's warm and spicy scent clings to my coat. *Irish Spring, Irish Spring,* thank goodness for the thin scent that masks our deception.

Constant supervision! When Cass is not attending classes, she stalks me to the point where I am almost never alone. Cass has sworn that if I'm guilty, I will pay. She's asked if I think I am beyond reproach. She's said: Who do you think you are, some superwoman? I believe she is searching for proof of my amoral nature, secretly reading my books on Nietzsche while I am attending classes.

Now, while buying a cup of coffee, I catch her peering through the window, her eyes and hair wild, snow falling all around her. She places a gloved hand to the glass, taps, and gives me a most cunning smile. Then she comes in and stands next to me. I inhale, hold my breath. Cass studies me. She slides the medallion back and forth across her necklace, tucks it down into her sweater, and eyes me suspiciously. She says God sees everything, Moira. And in case God fails, she tells me, she is also gathering evidence.

I've done nothing wrong, I say, but she escorts me to the library, because she says she is *going that way,* even though Cass has never set foot near the library and cannot use the UCLID catalog to save her life. She watches, preys on my nervousness, and when she sees I am shaken, she smiles. It's insanity. Cass is falling off the rocking horse, cracking up.

On campus it snows and snows and the tree limbs are coated with ice.

Peril lies at every corner.

THESE ARE the hard facts of my guilt: When Cass and Evan first began dating, Evan stopped by the flat one morning while Cass was attending Professor Klodhaven's History of Drama seminar. Wagner was playing on the stereo. On the coffee table lay *Beyond Good and Evil,* which I might have been reading had I not decided to paint my nails and take a quiz I found in Cass's *Cosmo* concerning my disposition for true romance.

When I opened the door, Evan brushed snow out of his hair, greeted me in an informal, lazy way, and invited himself in. He sat down on the couch and propped his feet up on the table, stretched, and scratched his head. Where's Cass? he asked. Gone, I told him. I hobbled back to the couch, wads of tissues jammed between each newly painted toe. Water trailed from his boots and onto the table. When I pushed his feet down and said *Excuse me,* he smiled in an amused way (straight, white teeth, very Redford), and patted the empty space next to him. Sit, he said. I'm not a *dog,* I told him. I don't take orders, you know. Had I been dressed more appropriately, I might have told him I was on my way out to a class or the library. But as it happened, I wore only a T-shirt and cut-off jeans.

He watched as I leafed through the magazine in an annoyed, distracted way. He picked up my philosophy book and studied it. Finally, Evan said: I don't *believe* in either *Cosmo* quizzes or the master-slave morality of Nietzsche; both kinds of indulgences in thinking can lead to trouble. He cited various historical instances where both Nietzsche and *Cosmo* have been misapplied to horrible ends. He said if I wanted to know where the real evil lay, I should look to women. Really, Evan has such an awkward way of flirting.

I said: That sort of thing, oppressing women and their sexuality, feels a little old. Men have been using that kind of evil-woman nonsense since the Fall, I explained. I told him I personally was sick to death of always being mistaken for the devil.

Hmmm, he said, watching as I removed the tissues. Pleased, I admired my toes.

Nice, he said. His voice was surprisingly soft, and doting.

Thank you, I said.

Has anyone ever told you you look like Jodie Foster, very studious and intense and cute?

As a matter of fact, yes, I said.

Can I tell you something?

What?

It's flirty, he said.

I don't fall for flirtation, I told him, even though I was already blushing.

It's deviant, he told me. I can't say it.

Oh, please, I said, glad for such a disclosure so early in the day. Now you have to say it.

Red toenails make me horny, he said. Now I can't look at you without imagining you naked.

Discourse, intercourse. They are not so totally unrelated. And in my defense, it does sometimes happen that strangers come together in a fevered, frenzied way. In such instances, the less clothes, the better.

However, of the times Evan and I have slept together since that day, and how I've blatantly lied to avoid detection, I cannot speak without further recrimination.

I DO NOT THINK she has showered in days. Cass has let her hair grow ratty-looking. She skulks around the flat with a butcher knife in one hand and a script in the other. I am fairly certain Medea used poison, but I do not belabor the point or break her already fragile mood. Perhaps, I think, this is only Method acting and not some act of bewildered aggression or a veiled threat against my life.

Cass throws the knife down onto the floor. I can't stand it, she says, disgustedly.

I am taken aback by her current state of being, which is something vacillating between severe depression, anxiety, and unleashed rage. She looks at me and sighs. We are in a mostly depressive episode currently, I see.

Evan hasn't called, she says. Not once in two days. She laments his loss and curses what she now calls his "paramour."

I say: Why is it women always get the curses? What is Evan, I say? An innocent?

That's not the *point*, she tells me. I'm Medea, she says. He can't just do this to me.

Uh-huh, I say, because her nerves are clearly frayed. What I think, however, is that acting = schizophrenia = illogical progression of discourse = psychiatric bills.

Take the running-down of the undergraduate, for example, an event that landed the girl in the hospital with a sprained ankle (she fell) and landed Cass on probation (the dean was present, just arriving to his office). That whole fiasco happened because before getting into her sedan, Cass had a fight with her boyfriend Gil (predecessor to Evan, also an actor), and Cass had accused Gil of flirting with the girl, an understudy. The fight put her, in Cass's exact words, as recorded in official college documents, "on edge," and when she pressed the gas pedal, the pedal stuck, the car flew forward, and the poor girl had to jump into a ditch to avoid being hit.

Let's not get crazy, I tell her now. Let's not do anything rash.

Cass sits next to me on the futon. Evan smells of another woman, she confesses. She stares at her script absently. Her hands tremble.

How many women can he have? I say. I have not slept with Evan in almost a week and have never before considered the possibility of another woman (besides Cass) in his bed, car, on his sofa, et cetera. I am not a jealous person, but I feel miffed just the same.

Evan has gotten the upper hand, clearly. Cass and I look at each other. She shrugs. We sit in silence. It is this moment, as *Medea* suggests, when a woman takes a man for her master, that she is exiled from her home and dispossessed.

LATE THAT SAME NIGHT, Cass haunts our apartment. She sobs, speaks to herself, quotes lines from the play. Until they are on stage, actors live in a kind of darkness, a limbo. For all actors, I decide, life is only a performance, and events on the stage are the truth. There is no way to argue it otherwise.

Other news: I found two of my Wagner CDs mysteriously cut in half. My Nietzsche book is missing. Cass is working up to something. There is evidence of this all around.

AT EIGHT O'CLOCK the next night Evan arrives, script in hand. He drags in the cold, along with a trail of slushy snow. He says, Hello, Moira, and shakes my hand with great formality, as if there weren't other things besides his extended arm that I have seen protracted and stiff.

I am finding you a little unbearable of late, I say.

He says, I have absolutely no idea what you mean by that.

Cass says nothing. She watches us from the futon, where she's been firmly planted all day. She twirls her hair and stares in a morbid way.

Jesus, Evan says, addressing her next. What's gotten into you?

Cass ignores this inquiry. The awkwardness between Evan and me seems to please her, and she smiles in a vindicated way. Evidence, evidence. Cass slides the small medallion back and forth. There are signs of deterioration. I go to the kitchen and down another cup of coffee. I watch as Evan sits down next to Cass and places his hand on her knee, but she brushes it away. Cheater, she accuses.

Evan is an ennobled Jason, an actor to the end. He says, *Even if you hate me, I cannot think badly of you*. He kisses her hand.

She says, I could kill you right now, if I wanted. She nods knowingly, makes a slicing motion across her throat, and then kisses him full on the lips.

Thespians!

I down the last of my coffee and decide I will have no part in the evening. I collect miscellaneous books from the table (along with a few *Cosmo*s) and gather my coat. I tell them I will be at the library, but Evan, not wanting to be alone with Cass, says: Moira, you can watch. He tells me, We need an audience, don't we?

As if this is a good option. Look, the whole thing is getting sticky, I say. I am no fan of acting, I tell him. Or the classics.

He says: Have you seen *Medea*? There's no telling what she might do. He laughs nervously. I sit, and even though I feign disinterest with a copy of *Cosmo*, I am forced to see Jason and his Medea embracing, her body limp, her wild eyes gazing at me. Evan, I decide, gets some kind of sick pleasure from all this. Having two women (possibly more) has made him bold. Cass begins to cry.

It's true, I am beginning to feel amoral.

Later that night I wake to hear Evan through the walls, his groans in synchronicity with the rhythmic banging of the futon against the wall. They have made up. He has taken advantage of Cass's affections, possibly gotten her to shower. I get up from bed and peer around the corner of my doorway. Cass is sprawled out under Evan. She pulls him closer, strokes his hair. It is a sad and fearful sight, to see them, the contours of their bodies, the pliability and frailty of their flesh, the frenzied way in which they come together again and again, and how, when finished, they disconnect, spent, exhausted, still only themselves.

Medea opens in two days and will run for one week only. After the play ends, I can only hope that things around the flat will return to normal.

MR. TANNEN CALLS the next day and says he has received complaints of lewd activity, sexual trysts, loud noises. I tell him he's got the wrong flat, even though the air smells thick with sex and there are two used rubbers in the bathroom trash. I am on a bit of a caffeine kick. I am missing my Nietzsche book, and my music has been destroyed, not to mention other things—pride, morality, the start of any affection that might have moved me to love Evan. Mr. Tannen cares little about any of this, of course. He's a short man with thinning hair and it's widely rumored that he sleeps with students in exchange for rental discounts. I say: Look, Mr. Tannen, I am in no mood for harassing phone calls, but he tells me he's heard rumors about both Cass and me, that he's on to us and has our number. He says, The walls are thin, miss. He clears his throat after every sentence. After he clears his throat for the fourth time, I say: Are you touching yourself, Mr. Tannen? Are you?

He tells me I'm insane.

I CAN NO LONGER hold any eye contact with Cass. She wears the same clothes from yesterday—an old flannel shirt, yoga pants, and sneakers. She stands at the kitchen counter and butters a slice of burnt, crunchy toast. In the middle of breakfast, and for what reason I don't know—love, abandonment, fear—Cass sobs uncontrollably. After she eats, she lies on the futon, watching *The Price Is Right,* and when I tell her it's almost time for classes, she yawns in a sedate way, shifts, and turns under her blanket. I sort through mail: coupons (there is one for *Irish Spring,* which I discard); a credit card offer; a letter to Cass from her old high school sweetheart, who still, after all this time, writes; and a letter from Mr. Tannen to all his tenants saying that unpaid rent is subject to prosecution.

Tannen is out to get us, I say. I toss his letter on the coffee table.

Tannen is a pervert, Cass moans. And Evan is no better. She rouses herself, drapes the blanket over her shoulders, and goes to the window. She stares down to the park below us.

By nine at night, there is other evidence of problems: Two empty wine bottles are in the trash. I find Cass's research paper there, too, which Klodhaven has given a D. Later, I wake to find Cass standing over me. She leans in close, a knife in hand, and I can smell the acrid stench of wine on her breath. She speaks of betrayal, in both friendship and love. She says: Some friend you are, Moira, then she quotes *Medea,* saying, *I wish I might die*. She slides the small medallion back and forth. She stumbles back, falls to the floor, and then stretches out, turns, and sleeps.

I could press charges—I would be within my rights—but instead I decide it's enough that I stop seeing Evan altogether, that I put my torrid little affair behind me, and journey anew into the future. I cover Cass with blankets and return the knife to the safety of the kitchen drawer.

SOME MISCELLANEOUS FACTS: First, when considering the ethics of power, right and wrong, good and evil, there is no place for attachment, as attachment corrupts. Nietzsche, before he became so lonely and morose, sitting around listening to Wagner, all philological and suicidal, knew this fact, subscribing to what he called a pathos of distance that grows from differences between certain classes of people (actors, ethics students, a perfect case in point). Now, as I am faced with Cass's weeping, with my own feelings of guilt, I wonder if distance is really a possibility bewteen flatmates. There are, as Nietzsche also knew, occasionally attempts at reconciliation, times when certain types of actors/thespians and nonthespian sorts come together despite their differences. It is becoming clear to me that despite Evan's rather classical detachment and Greek obsession with his penis, and despite my own cynicism and judgments and concern with literary discourse, Cass has *suffered*. That we are *alike* in our suffering. Tragedy, absurdity, and meaninglessness all abound because of one plain and simple fact: I have been an inconsiderate friend.

ON THE MORNING that *Medea* is scheduled to open, the park's groundskeeper finds Cass lying in the snow, dressed in a pink housecoat and clogs, laughing wildly and trying (unsuccessfully; she is drunk) to make angels. The ruckus drives me downstairs and out into the cold. I huddle with other students and watch, shivering, as the groundskeeper tries to help Cass up. She bites him, draws blood. The police are called. The dean is called. There is a suggestion, as she lies there, shaking, that she might need help, that she is rambling incoherently and possibly an indigent, but the dean disconfirms this, tells everyone about the incident with the freshman. Icy blood lines Cass's mouth (from the biting episode), and her whole body turns blue from overexposure. Someone (I don't know who) covers her with a blanket. The police escort her to a hospital (mental institution).

LATER, IN MY DESPERATION, I go to the dank, ill-smelling hospital. I ask the desk nurse how they are certain Cass is not simply Method acting, how they know she is not playing out a derivation on the act of revenge, abandoning the knife and poison for a form of self-destruction instead. The nurse, who looks a bit like a female version of Nietzsche, seems alarmed by my appearance (cut-off shorts, a T-shirt, no coat, hair a mess). She assures me that Cass is clinically depressed and a danger to herself, that she has probably been like this for years. She says: Are you a sister?

An unlikely proposition, you she-man, I say, but thank you. I want to see Cass.

The nurse tells me that Cass is in an "extreme state" at the moment and that I can come back in a day or two. I am going to be up the creek with rent problems, but I tell her, this philosopher-nurse, that I am a millionaire.

She asks me if I need some sort of assistance.

No, I say, of course not. You've done enough, I tell her/him.

THE COFFEE SHOP is already abuzz with news of the "nervous breakdown," and the people in my department, a serious and sober bunch of nose-pushing bibliophiles, say they are concerned that all actors possess, at some profound level, feeble minds. When I come to the table, they say, Christ, what's wrong with *you*? They produce judgments as I leave. I am certain I am already the butt of their ridicule.

An understudy, an up-and-coming freshman, has taken over Cass's part as Medea.

Evan calls to ask about Cass, but beyond that, we have little to say. I tell him we betrayed Cass, that our cynicism and detachment collectively have done her in. He sounds apologetic and tells me in a glib way that he understands. He says that even though he feels exhausted and sad, he will continue to play the role of Jason, as this is what Cass would have wanted. He tells me that when *Medea* closes, he will sleep for years.

I am filled with some indescribable sensation, some need for Cass, and a feeling of duty toward her. I drive to the hospital, but when I arrive, Cass is being escorted out by an older couple, possibly parents or grandparents. Cass appears to be a wholly fragile thing. When she spots me getting out of my car, running toward her, tripping in slushy snow, she turns her head away, denying me atonement.

I SPEND MOST of the days and weeks afterward sitting in Cass's room, filled with regret. I tell myself, I ought to have been nicer, that a little kindness and consideration goes a long way, especially with regard to flatmates, if not the world at large. All action, I realize, is bound by space and time, and each moment, significant and insignificant alike, is unrecoverable. This premise, I am certain, is at the root of all falls, from grace and sanity alike: We cannot get back our lost time.

I am thinking seriously about quitting school.

I am definitely, at the very least, quitting German philosophy.

At night I no longer sleep. I imagine I hear Cass roaming the flat and am burdened by both dreams and nightmares, all of them involving her and, oddly enough, a school of thought Nietzsche abandoned. My dreams mimic the conversion on the road to Damascus. In them, Wagner is playing in the distance, and as I ride on a horse, the strains of music grow weaker. Cass waits on the side of the road, and when I pass, she asks me why I have persecuted her. I fall, weeping. In my dreams, I lose my identity, change my name. These dreams, at the end, are filled with a certain quality of hope. In my nightmares, Cass's ghost haunts my room with a knife, a possessed, tragic, lonely figure, and she tells me only that I will pay, that our sins follow us into eternity.

I have begun to sit in on Cass's History of Drama class. Professor Klodhaven has noticed and eyed me suspiciously, but he has said nothing. Yesterday, when I tried to hand in a paper I'd written for Cass, one which I am certain would have earned her an A, Professor Klodhaven refused to accept the work. He looked at me as if I were deranged.

On the fifth of the month, Mr. Tannen stops by the flat to remind me of my commitments. When he sees me, he seems to take pity. He does not look like Redford except that he has, I am sorry to say, blue-gray eyes. He tells me that he will deduct fifty dollars from my rent if I am having problems, and I am so grateful for this kind gesture, I sleep with him. Afterward, when he tells me we can sleep together every month, I come after him with the knife I now keep under my bed.

I LIVE IN EXILE. The desk librarian finds me asleep in the book stacks, my head resting upon a shelf. Around me, there are pages and pages torn from Nietzsche's books and scattered about. The librarian demands to know who I think I am, but I cannot tell him. He turns me in to the dean, who places me on probation and orders me to see the school counselor. The counselor is a *humanist,* and so I have found my little corner of hell. In his waiting room, there are endless copies of *Cosmo,* reading material that paves the New World. I weep inconsolably and tell him I cannot go back to the flat, that I have suffered through long, lonely nights there and fear for my sanity. He suggests only that I learn forgiveness and love.

I nod desperately.

Mr. Tannen, however, is out to deter me. This morning, I receive a certified letter in the mail demanding overdue rent and money for damage to the floors. With it, there is a crude, handwritten note, telling me I was the worst piece of ass he's ever had. He tells me I have cost him money, he repeats that I have ruined his floors, and if I do not remit payment, he says, he will have his day in court.

PLEASE, IF YOU LOVE ME,
YOU SHOULD KNOW WHAT TO DO

═══════════

My wife wants a cow. If I don't get her a cow, she says, she's going to take little Alice and move to the country and I can fend for myself with microwave dinners and scraps. She's quite serious about getting a cow. She tells me it must be a Holstein with dewy eyes and thick lashes and a long tail to swat flies. She'd like me to also purchase a bucket and a sitting stool because she says that of course she will milk the cow once she gets it.

The cow is to be named Claraluna. My wife believes this to be a pretty name.

I don't know what to do with my wife when she gets hysterical. Everyone knows you need to have some kind of special permit to own a cow in the city, or you need to be someone famous. I tell her that the air is unsafe for cattle and that the skyline threatens to fall. I tell her this, but she says it doesn't change anything. She says, Please, if you love me, you should know what to do.

When my wife says this, I don't know what to do. When I want something that is outrageous and will never happen in a million years, such as a leaner stomach, a fuller head of hair, a magical pill to keep fear or sadness at bay, or just a wife who doesn't make such extravagant demands, I get up and take out the trash.

My wife never takes out the trash; she simply sits on the edge of our bed, sniffling, holding little Alice in her arms.

We live on the fifteenth floor of a tall building. When I take out the trash, I walk down a lot of stairs, but it doesn't make my stomach leaner, and if I perspire I lose more hair. Sometimes, when I take the trash out, I see rats behind the Dumpsters in the alley. They twitch their whiskers, then scurry and hide. Thinking of this, I say to my wife, Would you settle, honey, for a rat?

She weeps when I say this. When she weeps her shoulders jerk up and down and baby Alice bounces on her lap. The baby laughs when my wife weeps.

LATER, MY WIFE PACKS a suitcase while little Alice rolls over and over again on our bed. When my wife closes the lid of her suitcase, it makes a *click-click* noise, which is like the sound of a great heart closing. I'm leaving you, she says.

There's nowhere to go, I say. There's no one for us but each other.

The baby bangs her chubby fists on the bed. She kicks her legs in the air and laughs in three short bursts.

My wife grew up on a farm with cows and other livestock. She lived on this farm until we met and married and moved to the city. My wife's father was never around for her, and last September when my wife was pregnant and big as a house, my wife's mother died, and the bank sold the farm, along with the horses, the cows, the chickens, and all the eggs.

My wife was very tight-lipped about the whole thing. She didn't even get along with her mother and thought the country was a real drag. After her mother died, my wife said, I don't want to talk about it. Then she had the baby and said things like, The baby is crying and needs to be fed. She made meals in Crock-Pots and added lots of butter. She even tried to add butter to the baby's bottle of milk.

I called my wife crazy when she did this. I told her they lock women up and take away their babies if butter goes into the milk, or if the milk turns sour. My wife said she was sorry. She said she was sorry over and over again. I told her even so, she should try to be more careful. I told her butter and babies don't grow on trees.

IT'S POSSIBLE THAT a cow is just a cow. It's possible my wife wants an exotic pet, like she wanted the baby. Maybe my wife is one of those demanding wives you hear so much about, the kind who up and leave for no apparent reason and without sufficient warning and you can only sit on the bed for years afterward wondering what in the world went wrong. It's possible my wife is just flat-out crazy. She *has* been known to put butter in the baby's milk.

But now my wife is stroking the blond curls of little Alice's head. She is balled up on the bed and cradles the baby against her breast. Her closed suitcase with the locks that go *click-click* lies next to her.

I'll say this much: When my wife talks about the cow, there is no way to reach her. She is here on our bed with baby Alice and not here. She has traveled backward in time to a place where the light shines softly and there is a sweet buttery smell that lingers in the air and all her love is ahead of her. When she goes to this place, she has a double vision, a way of looking both forward and back. My wife says *cow* to Alice as though the word were the start of a story she is whispering but can't fully remember. In the story, it doesn't even matter if my wife really loved her mother, or if things were better here in the city or there on the farm. Grief has its own peculiar language, and its manifestations are endless.

Sometimes I imagine that behind this story of the cow there is another story, that my wife, like so many others, is lost, locked in a great dungeon where rats crawl around in Dumpsters and the air smells sour and she is alone. For some reason, the only thing she can think to tell me is, Please, if you love me, you'd know what to do.

I want to touch her when she is like this and tell her that it's true that in our grief we only have each other. But then my wife looks up, as though I could never possibly understand, and, as if that look has its own peculiar language, I suddenly don't. I don't understand anything about my wife at all. I think, Maybe my wife just wants to leave. *Click-click,* end of story. When that happens, I don't know what to do except leave her curled up on the bed with the baby. When that happens, I don't know what to do except go to the kitchen and take out the trash.

THE THIN BORDER BETWEEN HERE
AND DISASTER

━━━━━━━━━━━

Dobbin had bought the mask on eBay because the price was good and he was a history buff and liked that sort of thing: vintage, canister, the kind used in the First World War, the kind of mask that protected men from chemical attacks and toxic compounds such as chlorine gas and white crosses. At the time, the entire country was recovering from disaster, and he'd felt the sway of sorrow, the sharp pull of grief. But then, gradually, slowly, in the months that followed, he felt a counterpull toward meaning, one that brought with it an almost unexpected hopefulness. He reasoned he *should* be hopeful. He and Julia were newly married, he'd landed a job teaching in the South, and he was determined that, for all the world's chaos, he could at least make his own life good, his love more lasting.

Now, ten years later, in the midst of their separation, Julia stands in their bedroom and holds up this very mask. Dobbin sees a faint flicker of recognition—the shape of Julia's mouth changes—before she places the mask on his side of things: snorkel gear from a vacation in the Caribbean, a leather bomber jacket, and binoculars she has fished out from the closet. She is rummaging through old things these days, deciding what is hers and what is rightfully his, splitting up what is both of theirs, in the interest of fairness. Julia is the kind of woman who is most always fair, if not a bit severe in her pronouncements; Dobbin sometimes feels she levels them like her own brand of atomic weaponry. Sorting through their things (*their* things; Dobbin still thinks this way), she seems so oddly purposeful that it frightens him. He feels a small, persistent sorrow in the knowledge that she blames him for everything—being in this state, her long years of unhappiness, his mistake with Annie. If he blames her for anything, it is that she somehow seems too finely honed to this ritual of breaking away. If he blames her for anything, it is that she has not managed to learn the art of forgiveness.

Orange, a hint of spice envelops him when Julia walks to the bed, clothing in hand. Dobbin sits, watching her, and runs his hand over her sweaters, which she has laid out and folded, all to be boxed up. He wants to plead, loudly, bang his fists, but there is something in Julia's demeanor that preemptively forbids this, and so he picks up the mask and inspects the thin fractures in the yellowed glass, the molded rubber face covering, the breathing apparatus that Julia always thought looked like a miniature elephant's trunk. "Ugly," she said when she first saw it, but wasn't everything ugly that was connected to combat? They were in graduate school then, living in a cramped apartment with small windows that barely filtered light. Studying for his dissertation, punch-drunk from a continual lack of sleep and a profound nervousness, Dobbin believed—actually believed—it was a good idea to own a mask, that everyone in the country should own one, just as a matter of day-to-day survival. He saw himself in a jaded yet oddly optimistic way, as a revolutionary on the brink of a new world. "Do you remember?" he asks now. "What things were like when I bought this? Do you remember when you came home that night, and I had this mask on?"

Julia wears a neutral, perhaps cautious, expression. She folds a summer dress and places it in a box. "You were tired and delirious," she says. "Craziness abounded in all directions, as I recall—dissertation and anthrax scares in the news, suspicious powder in envelopes."

"Everything was so chaotic," he says. "So frightening."

"It was."

"Julia," he says. "If we could talk."

She's near him, so close he could reach from where he sits on the bed and touch her hand.

She tilts her head out of habit but no longer pays him any real attention. Instead she folds shirts and pants that are of course hers. She packs a CD by a folk singer they discovered when in the Southwest. The CD is in question—it might be his—but Dobbin says nothing. As she moves briskly between the closet and the bed, Julia has the distinct air of a bird of prey. She's a tall brunette, slim, though imposing, with her hair pulled back in a twist that makes her face appear sharper. She's forty, never bothers with makeup, and still always manages to look dignified. Still, despite this, she's not the type who will forget any wrong done to her or turn away from any grievances, and this trait has always made her a solitary woman—no one can live up to her standards, not even him. Thirty years from now, when she is old, she will probably live alone, behind closed doors, like Dickinson. Or she will own fifty cats and set about the arduous task of feeding them each day. This is what Dobbin thinks, begrudgingly, as he traces the slender line of her neck, the birthmark at the base of her chin that looks like a miniature country. He wants her to stay here in their house with its many bookshelves and oriental rugs and antique furniture, and not move into the subterranean apartment of another man's house. He tells himself he will win back Julia's love. Things work themselves out, he knows. Even sorrow ends.

Because, after all, they are civil. It seems to him, that even if Julia ignores him, such as she's doing this very moment, they don't hate each other. They have had years together that were, all in all, solid, their home established, defended, held dear. And Julia isn't so unkind as to hate, or to be malicious. She's perhaps too serious, too honest—she frightens most people, really—but mostly she is a smart, astute woman with a sometimes plaintive sense of humor. And under her harsh honesty there is a sensitivity that Dobbin easily loves. When they lived together they rarely fought. They shared chores, held dinner parties, decided—mutually, agreeably—not to have children. There is nothing terrible he can think to say of her, no catastrophic flaw in her demeanor to pinpoint as the origin of fracture. And he has made only one mistake.

She emerges from the closet with sandals, boots, a pair of high heels. "Leave it to separation to make you clean out the closets," she says.

"You don't have to do this," he says. "You don't have to go."

"Leaving is the one thing I do have to do," she says.

"You'd rather live in Poe's basement?"

She places the sandals and boots and heels in a cardboard box. "William. Not Poe."

"We used to call him Poe back when we made fun of him. All that angst and fussiness in one man, it's criminal, Julia."

"William is fine," she says. "He's hardly the problem." Her jaw twitches, and her anger passes over him with a nauseating effect. Even though it's a warm, pleasant day, he can practically feel the chill in the air between them. She packs more persistently, with less attention to folding and arrangement. "Anyway, he had the room, and it was affordable. It's not like I'm making a ton of money, I'd like to remind you."

Dobbin says nothing. He knows it's unfair to hold three degrees, to be well-read and to have two chapbooks in press, only to have that translate to a job teaching composition and rhetoric on a limited-term basis, expendable at a moment's notice. He knows Julia could have done better in terms of a career, had they not had to negotiate the two-body problem so common in academia. And he knows that in this small, conservative town of only a few thousand people, there is so little for her here, only one or two in the department who dabble in poetry, Poe being one of them. To reach people who share even a remote sense of her interests, she must commute more than an hour and a half to the nearest city. Over the past year, she's become uncommunicative with many, and Dobbin most of all. She's buried her head in books, hidden herself away. Though he can't blame Poe for any of this, he also can't help but feel that Poe has probably been saving up for this moment for years.

Dobbin places the gas mask on the bed and picks up a sweater that has fallen to the floor. He says: "I'm sorry."

She pauses, shakes her head, adjusts. She wears an overly

formal expression that she reserves for moments of hurt. He watches as she sorts through a stack of photographs, some old letters—the exquisite line of her hands, the ring she still wears—shaking.

Dobbin gets up, reaches out to comfort her, but she jerks away. It is an act so jarring, so unfamiliar that it makes him cry. "Julia," he says.

"Don't," she warns. "Just don't." She carries a box out of their bedroom. Downstairs, in the kitchen, she pauses and looks around as if she has forgotten something. Dobbin wonders if, after she leaves, she misses these still-familiar rooms. But perhaps she doesn't allow herself to dwell on their home, or their years together, or him. Perhaps she's already relegated them to the annals of history, closed chapters, done deals. Perhaps she'll simply return to Poe's and decide that this entire separation can be the source of inspiration, a reason to write more: sestinas, ghazals, sonnets. Regardless, he knows that soon he will be alone. He will chastise himself for not reaching to touch her again, now, if only he knew what to say.

After Julia leaves, Dobbin mulls over history papers on WWI and anti-German propaganda. One of his criminally smart students writes that the war started over a domestic disturbance. He writes down, in response, yes.

OF COURSE by Friday everyone on campus has heard that Julia's moved out. It is a small college in a small town of southerners who still view outsiders with suspicion, a polite distance, and interest. Both Dobbin and Julia are known, even by strangers. This fact alone has singularly unnerved Julia, who can't even go so far as the grocery store without bumping into a colleague, or a parent of a student, or, worse, the students themselves. It is uncomfortable for her when a student takes that moment to ask about his grade on the final paper. "It hardly matters," Julia once said. She already knew by the end of classes who would pass and who would fail and so instead spent finals week at the kitchen table, not grading but folding research papers into origami shapes of birds and frogs and other woodland animals. If later at the grocery store the well-meaning student would mention that he never received a graded final, Julia, slightly mortified, might nod vaguely and say, "Right, the turtle. Good job."

Now, of course, there is a new wave of speculation, about Dobbin, about Annie. Almost everyone in Dobbin's department seems bent on disclosure, though so few publicly acknowledge him or what has happened in any real way. The departmental secretaries exchange knowing looks, their suspicions about Dobbin's affair finally confirmed. To compensate, Dobbin has avoided prolonged conversations with both the secretaries and his colleagues. He has walked around this week in a strange, comforting haze of denial. He generally operates at a hurried pace, often exchanging quick pleasantries before slipping into class or retreating to his office. Today, though, Clint Barron, the department chair, takes Dobbin aside to ask if his "situation" is going to be a problem. He hints that, if so, Julia is on a limited-term contract and he might be able to speak to the English chair. "Pull some strings," Clint tells him, nodding affably, though Dobbin knows Clint is concerned and doesn't want any pro-longed scenes. Dobbin stops him before he can go any further. "It's not a problem," he assures Clint. "We'll work it out."

In the safety of his office, Dobbin unloads his shoulder bag, his laptop and papers, and then walks to the window. His gaze travels across the wave of still-tanned students that descend from the steps of the Humanities Building and out across the once verdant but now blanched quad. A few students talk idly on cell phones; a group of boys gather for a game of Frisbee. Eventually he catches sight of Poe's skinny, restless form. Though Dobbin is tall and paunchy, though he has thinning brown hair, he still feels more stately and attractive than Poe. Dobbin feels Poe dresses like an indigent—a wrinkled shirt only half-tucked into shabby-looking pants, no belt, an old leather satchel strapped across his chest, long hair despite the advancement of middle age. Poe stops and extinguishes his cigarette before entering the Humanities Building. There, on the third floor, he and Julia have the benefit of proximity, his office just down the hall from hers. Julia once confessed that she and Poe often mull over scansions at lunch, or discuss Simic's latest collection, share new work. It seems to him no more right or wrong than things he's done with Annie.

A wave of bitter jealousy comes over him, and Dobbin calls the adjunct office for what feels like the hundredth time this week. Once again he's greeted by the palsied voice of one of the female instructors, who tells him Julia is unavailable. She urges him not to come over like he did earlier that week. No one really wants another scene—Dobbin calling down the hall after Julia, her ditching into the bathroom, his shouts to her increasingly urgent. Disgusted, he hangs up the phone. He feels hotly embarrassed at how public his life has suddenly become.

Dobbin knows—he believes—he should be able to place the matter of his marriage into perspective. Given all of history, the fallout of love could only be seen as a small tear in the fabric of American life. Compared to problems experienced by countless others—war, famine, genocide, poverty—his problems are insignificant. Still they are *his*, and as such they are amplified in his mind and heart to catastrophic proportions. He tells himself that if the world at large can recover from war and terror, if the earth can replenish itself after nuclear fallouts and mass extinction, then surely he, with his personal disasters, can recover, too. But who knows how to decode the covert gestures of love? He feels certain Julia remembered their own complicated history—the accumulation of it, the sheer mass of days and years—in that moment she held up the mask. Her face contorted when she saw it. He wonders: Isn't contortion practically synonymous with love?

IT IS CLOSE to noon when Annie arrives at Dobbin's office, holding takeout from the sandwich place downtown. She knocks, peers in, and gives Dobbin a friendly, slightly tactical look, as if she's trying to gauge his mood in the wake of Julia's leaving, measuring it against her own feelings regarding this development, the new possibilities inherent in it for them. A more recent hire, Annie is twenty-eight and pear-shaped. Her broad, attractive face is framed by a mass of blond curls. Her dark eyes are always alert, probative. Dobbin serves as her faculty mentor, and that is how their friendship, and then affair, began—going out to lunch to discuss teaching and research expectations, questions about student advising, that sort of thing.

She sets the takeout bag on his desk and sits in the chair across from him. Her tone is gentle, teasing, when she says, "I've been sent on a reconnaissance mission."

"Barron?"

"Now what *did* that man say, exactly? Something about a line of demarcation being crossed among the tenured and untenured. He was very concerned about boundaries, so I guess my three-year review is sunk. Did you ever notice that Barron looks like George C. Scott?"

"Everyone says that." Dobbin leans back, regards her. "Anyway, I doubt you're sunk," he says. He knows that this type of fraternizing with colleagues is generally frowned upon, but it's also understood that among like-minded people, things frequently can and do, often, happen. It's only an issue when students are involved—that's when you have to worry. That's when your job is really put on the line. He says, "Barron is probably jealous he didn't think to do it first."

"A compliment," she says, and unfolds her napkin. Her silk blouse brushes against the desk. "Well, thanks."

Dobbin knows she wants to talk about them, but the truth is, he doesn't quite know what to do with Annie. She's been his undoing, yes, but he doesn't, after six months of their affair, actually see them together in any long-term sort of way, either.

He eats in silence, while Annie talks about changes to the curriculum that the provost proposed, the addition of new classes for history majors. She's spirited, her hands gesturing as she speaks, yet however much she motions, however much her facial expressions change from willful to earnest to amused, her dark eyes never veer from him, as if she were locked and loaded, ready for whatever he might say.

And though he wants to play along now, he finds the situation a bit contrived, too—Annie's visit, the casual way she talks to him, as if nothing has happened this week at all. It irritates him, really, how she believes she has the upper hand in all this. And she does, in a way: She has nothing to lose.

"You okay?" she asks finally, after she exhausts her small talk. "About Julia?"

"I'm fine."

"Rumor has it she hasn't taught her Tuesday or Thursday class. *That's* not going over well. Maybe she's been busy with the move?" Annie bites her sandwich and waits for his response. She watches him with an effortless concentration that he finds alarming.

He feels suddenly defensive, angry. Annie has no right, he reasons, to ask about Julia's state of mind, or emotions. He reclines in his chair. He says, "What is it about southerners and gossip?"

"*Southerners?*" she asks, amused. "Everyone talks, Dobbin. Southerners hardly have the corner on the market. Everyone's entitled to their opinions."

"Talk, then," he says. He tosses the remains of his barbeque sandwich in the trash, wipes his hands with a napkin. "What do I care? You should know we're working on things. Talking things out."

Her voice becomes falsely appeasing. She smiles in an indecipherable way. "Good," she says. "That's all anyone wants."

He wants to tell Annie not to obfuscate things, not to confuse sex—or the sometimes false sense of intimacy that being naked and next to someone can create—with love. When they started sleeping together they both defined the terms, as well as the situation. They were attracted to each other, plain and simple. They met in parks and at Annie's apartment, stripped each other bare, took pleasure in those few, stolen moments. Perhaps for a few weeks or a month maybe, Dobbin fancied himself in love, but there was never a time he indulged being without his wife, never a time he thought he wouldn't in the end stay with Julia. Julia, after all, was substantial in his life, solid. She was there every night when he went to sleep, there in the mornings when he woke up, there at the table eating breakfast or dinner with him. Though Annie could be spirited, fun, eager in bed, it was still Julia who remained a permanent fixture in his life. He could imagine a time before Annie. He couldn't imagine a time without Julia. Finally, he says, "What happened between us was a mistake."

Annie holds his gaze. Her eyes are penetrating. "I know," she says. "But it did happen, so there's no point in acting like it didn't. There's certainly no point in ignoring me. And anyway, let's not forget. It *was* fun."

TELLING ANNIE IT might be fun was an error in judgment; Dobbin realizes this now. But they had spent so much time together and seen each other so regularly that he started to indulge the possibility of an affair. When they first began having lunch a year ago, Annie was so freshly idealistic, so opinionated and comfortable with herself. She was easy to talk to in a way that Julia hadn't been, and he sensed that Annie found his experience and age refreshing, perhaps even attractive. He'd give her advice on how she might win more departmental favor for tenure, what high-profile committees she might join that would garner notice. If she found his discussion of pedagogy or departmental politics to be too pedantic, she never let on. She'd tilt her head, listening intently as Dobbin discussed what amounted to petty departmental gossip, old stories and rivalries, and she'd give him her undivided attention. They'd talk about the antebellum period—Annie's area of specialty—and localized regional conflicts, Confederate grave sites that were still, after nearly 150 years, being unearthed in the region. She'd ask him questions about the Great War and Germany. Sometimes when she'd talk she'd absentmindedly touch his hand in a tantalizing, pleasant way, and she'd let her hand rest there a moment longer than she should.

After a time, their lunch conversations turned into a little window shopping or a walk in the park afterward. He savored those walks, the smell of new leaves, the clouds that stretched thin above them. Annie would speak pleasantly and keep a brisk pace. She confessed that she was trying to shed twenty pounds in time for her old college friend's summer wedding. Julia knew about the outings, of course, but Dobbin perhaps made light of how often such things occurred. Then, on a drizzly afternoon walk when Annie needed to pick up a textbook she'd forgotten, Dobbin walked her to her apartment near campus. If he was flirting, he wasn't doing it strenuously. He simply joked that he hadn't stepped foot in another woman's place in years, and Annie casually replied that it might be fun to have an affair with a married man. "For the experience of it, only, of course," she said. How that one statement and his teasing response that *Yes, for the experience of it, it might be fun* turned into a tryst Dobbin scarcely wishes to remember. But she came close to him then, chin upturned, and everything in the moment seemed to reduce itself to her intense look of desire. He's ashamed when he thinks of how he delighted in Annie's body—her rounded stomach and breasts, her full bottom dimpled in the dim afternoon light. There was nothing else—not Julia, not his marriage—to consider. Afterward, he considered everything, of course.

"I can't leave my wife," he told Annie.

"I didn't ask you to," she said, and dressed.

He had crossed a line, but once it was crossed there was no going back. He asked to see Annie again. He needed to see her. And that was how the affair began, and continued.

Dobbin admits that in his insignificantly small life the absolute worst memory he holds was the ruined expression on Julia's face when she finally confronted him. There was a frantic tone in her voice that was so uncharacteristic of her when he came home that night, only a few weeks ago—came home, actually, from Annie's.

"Why are you doing this?" she screamed. "Why are you lying?" He denied it, of course, denied Annie, denied everything. What else could he do? They were rumors, he told Julia, but tears ran down Julia's face, and she only shook her head. Then she proceeded to smash dish after dish on the kitchen floor, until there was a mosaic of porcelain around him. "I know you," she said. "Don't you think I can tell when you're lying?"

THAT AFTERNOON IN CLASS, Dobbin shows black-and-white slides of aerial attacks, airplanes dropping large cylinders down to the ground, soldiers in the trenches, wind gusts carrying gas in the enemies' direction. He discusses, how, in those early years before artillery shells were marked with red, green, and yellow crosses, the wind would often shift and send toxic gases back to the very camps from which they came—an act of subterfuge by nature, men choked by the miscalculation of their own actions. He talks about the dangers of excessive force, the isolationism that ensued after the First World War, the implication of that national sentiment when it came to entering into World War II, Nazi Germany. Dobbin teaches because he believes that it gives him the opportunity to transform students into freethinking individuals. But what he sees today is a room half-full of students who are overwhelmingly disinterested. These are young men and women who care little for history and who anxiously await the end of class, or simply slink out from the lecture hall early and pass—hopefully unnoticed, unscathed—into the world of fast food and tanning salons again. He surveys the future generation. "You all depress me," he says unexpectedly. "You know, someday your networking grid will collapse, and then where will you be? You might have to actually read a book."

After the lecture, he drives out past the orange-and-white banners that designate campus grounds, then out to the main road, past the IHOP and the park where lovers meet on weekends. He passes under bridges encrusted with kudzu, drives out five miles from campus. He's careful to park at some distance from Poe's house, because he still believes Julia knows him so well she will sense his approach, hear the familiar rattle of his car engine. He gets out. He glances over his shoulder. Then he skulks down the hill, past the still-full trees and the row of bungalows with white, scalloped lattices.

At the bottom of the dead-end street, he sees Julia's sedan parked next to a compact that Dobbin suspects must be Poe's. He looks right and left, but sees no one short of an old woman carrying a grocery bag into her house. A black Labrador stalks around a fenced yard, and, as Dobbin passes, the dog barks. He feels foolish, immensely so, but he crouches against Julia's car and takes cover. His heart races. He waits but hears nothing—no doors opening, no one asking the dog, "What is it, boy?" If he could see himself, he guesses he'd be filled with dread and disgust—his heavy breaths and sagging stomach, his beard grown to compensate for his thinning hair. Not only is his life an abbreviated spectacle, but now he's a bona fide Peeping Tom. Still, he feels desperate to speak with Julia. He's certain that being in the same room with her is the only thing that will afford him any solace, and so he continues.

He walks across the cobblestoned garden, ducks behind shrubbery, moves around the side of the house. He peers down through the smudged basement windows. The space below is fully furnished, equipped with a small kitchen.

He doesn't recognize any of the furniture: a square kitchen table and chairs, a sofa and love seat with broken rattan, a simple glass table with boxes and stacks of books and papers piled on top of it. On the facing wall there is a mirror, positioned to catch light, though now, with the sun going down, the room looks small and darkly comfortable. Dobbin's eyes adjust. Is Poe here? he wonders, imagining Poe's scrawny, naked form emerging from the bedroom. Sickened, slightly titillated, he waits, anticipating. He senses disaster, as if he's released the pin on a grenade and somehow absentmindedly forgotten to throw it.

After a while, when his knees ache from bending and the warmth from his pressed hand has fogged the window, Julia walks out from the bedroom. She is dressed in jeans and a bulky sweater. He pauses momentarily and holds his breath until he's certain she's alone. Relieved, he taps on the window, and when she looks up he gestures. "Julia," he says through the pane of glass. "Hello."

Julia nears the window. She does not seem alarmed, not really. Didn't she know he'd come after her? How foolish, how possibly romantic it might seem to her, her husband squatting outside, waiting in a hopeful way just for a moment to see and speak with her. He knocks on the glass again.

"What do you want?" she asks.

He reads her lips. "I already said: To T-A-L-K. Can we please just talk and put this behind us?"

She shakes her head, and, gradually, her look registers a feeling that Dobbin can't quite decipher. There's a sudden angularity, a stiffness that comes over her face and lips. She walks rigidly back to the bedroom, slams the door. Dobbin pulls his jacket tighter. He bangs on the window, yelling at her to open up, to just open up for Christ's sake.

After a few minutes Poe calls out to him, and Dobbin turns to see Poe rushing toward him, his look serious, his face slack, his ridiculous hair pulled back in a ponytail. "What do you think you're doing here?" Poe demands.

Dobbin stands up. He's flushed, he's breathless. "This isn't any of your business," he says. "So just go and let me speak with my wife."

"It *is* my business," Poe says. He comes closer to Dobbin, so close that Dobbin can smell Poe's spicy aftershave. "Your *wife* just called me. Your *wife* asked me to tell you to leave."

"You fucking presumptuous twit," Dobbin says. He's faintly aware of his clenched fist, the rush of adrenaline. He lunges at Poe. He wrestles Poe to the ground. His fist connects with Poe's jaw, hard, cutting. They writhe around. Dobbin punches Poe again, then hits him once more, in the stomach, before he hears Julia's screams and feels the grip of her hand on his shoulder. He turns toward her and then feels a sharp blow from Poe, right above his eye. "Stop it, both of you!" Julia yells. "Just leave, Dobbin! Just leave."

AT HOME THAT NIGHT, Dobbin takes two shots of whiskey, to dull the pain from the cut above his eye and to dull the headache that is already forming. He watches television in the living room, commercials that warn against the dangers of soapsuds. The fight ended badly and relatively quickly, with Poe threatening to call the police, a threat issued with such sincerity and outrage that Dobbin tucked his loosened shirt back into his pants, wiped the dirt from his knees, and left. His marriage and Julia aside, there was his career to consider. An affair might not leave a permanent mark on his record, but an arrest surely would. Now the room spins. He pours another shot of whiskey, then greedily downs it. He sits in the dark room, the glare of the television the only light. He listens to nothing in particular—the voice emanating from the TV, the clock striking the hour, the occasional car that drives by his house—and he feels as though his entire life has been reduced to a state of madness, as if everything he's spent years building is collapsing, slowly, around him.

The phone rings, and the sound travels through his throbbing head. He picks it up and hears Julia's unnerved, oddly distant voice. "Why did you do that?" she asks. "Poe almost called the department chair and the provost after you left. It was all I could do to get him not to."

Dobbin adjusts the phone against the crook of his neck. A new pain cuts through him. He can feel the burn of the whiskey in his throat and a heaviness in his limbs and voice. "Julia," he says. "I was just thinking about you."

"Oh, Jesus," she says. "Are you blitzed?"

"Blitzed, bombed, would it matter? Because, yes, all of the above."

His words are met with silence and he strains to hear Julia breathe. "Look," she begins finally, her voice shaking. "I'm not saying it's all because of Annie. Do you understand?" She pauses, and then, in a vague way, she tells him that she knows what it's like, that new attraction, that wanting someone different, that needing to start over again. "Really, it's impossible to speak of staying together when so much has changed," she says. "For both of us." From her conciliatory tone, from her hesitations, he understands, implicitly, that Julia has slept with Poe. Dobbin also understands that she's stopped loving him, that she probably has not loved him for quite some time, though when pressed, she cannot or will not pinpoint when exactly her feelings changed. Nor will she admit that she's had any part in their undoing. If there is in Julia any sense of failure, any thought that there might be something she's done to concede or retract, it never seems to occur to her to confess this now, in the moment.

"There was a distance," he says finally. "Which I regret."

With that, Julia takes in a sharp pull of air, and Dobbin hears a distant kind of muffle, a click, and the abrupt flatline of the phone. He stares at his large hands, aware that they seem strangely disembodied. He goes to the kitchen for another shot of whiskey. Then he calls Annie and invites her over to the house.

"Finally," she says. "I was wondering about you."

"Just come over," he says.

An hour later, love, his life has gone diffuse again. He thinks of Julia, how he once stood in a room full of people and promised, yes, of course he would treat her right—always. He thinks then on random things: weekends holed up in the house, painting walls; nights lying next to her, that familiar warmth. He thinks of this all, sees it in black and white, as if in a movie. He sees, too, bombs and plumes of smoke and skylines that suddenly collapse. He wants to hide, he wants it all to be over, and he wants—he simply wants—to be new and blameless again.

They—he and Annie—are in the bedroom, the bed rumpled from the night before, from Dobbin's own restless sleep. He feels tired, heavy. His head throbs under the weight of Annie's flowery perfume. She's near him, warm, her look beguiling. She caresses his arms and shoulders. She's already unbuttoned her blouse, stepped out of her skirt. He kisses her, feels a subtle thrill, those sensations that aren't yet diminished, those feelings that are still new.

"Yes," she says, and she begins to murmur in his ear. He holds up his finger to his lips. "Shhh," he says. He sways a little as if he is dancing with her now. The room pulsates with white light. Dobbin can almost hear the bombs being set off, one by one, feel the trench he—they—are digging, deeper, deeper, between him and the life he's known. He hears Annie whisper something about protection, so he staggers to the closet and steadies himself against the doorway. From the shelf he takes down the gas mask and fits it over his face. He breathes and turns to see Annie, half naked, through the collusion of time and yellowed glass. He likes her like this—hazy, distant. "Okay," he says. "Protection."

Annie wears a bemused, slightly cryptic expression. "Oh my," she says. She unhooks her bra, watches him. "You are just a little drunk."

"Pretend I'm someone else," he says. "An infantryman." He salutes her.

Annie moves toward him. "A history fetish," she says. "Well, then, let's get those clothes off right quick, soldier, before the next battle begins."

WITH ANNIE, in the coming months, Dobbin feels a certain measure of emotion, though nothing as strenuously labored as love. It's more as though he feels the mechanisms of love, the machinery of it, and the slow chug of time. Some nights he still dreams of Julia and he wakes, weeping.

In conversations that happen with greater infrequency, Julia never mentions reconciliation, and that, too, gradually begins to seem like a dream. She never discusses their past or goes into details about her life apart from him, her time with Poe. She tells him only that she's writing, and eventually will find a new place to live. On those occasions when he sees Julia and Poe across the quad, she sometimes glances in the direction of his building and office, but never for long. After a while any talk between them peters out, and Julia changes her number at Poe's, does the usual things. Dobbin sometimes drives by Poe's house, but he dares not stop. Rumors persist on campus, of course. Julia, he's told, shows up less and less for classes; she leaves her students waiting on her for inordinate amounts of time. Dobbin listens with interest, though he seldom says anything. Gradually whatever pain he feels turns into a dull ache, not exactly a forgetfulness but something that keeps life moving along at a functional pace.

In June, Julia relocates back east and Dobbin receives paperwork in the mail. He feels almost relieved, as if there is something accomplished in the simple signing and fragile markings of the pen—a forgiveness, an absolution, even a certain amount of generosity. Any regrets he has are eventually tempered with a feeling that everything turned out for the best. He finds comfort in this thought and does not indulge other possibilities, because he's certain that if he did, he'd be forced to admit that everything, our lives, our love and happiness, only straddles the thin border between here and disaster.

WHITE TREES IN SUMMER

———————————

E ven with his bedroom window open, Viktor had heard no noise during the night, not the tree branches that scraped against the exterior of the house or the neighborhood teenagers' laughter as they gathered outside with rolls of toilet paper in hand. He was not ordinarily the type of person who, at eighty-two, found that a restful sleep came easily, but that night Viktor had barely tossed or turned, so close was he to a hopeful dream in which he heard Bella's voice calling to him. It was a simple dream, really, but he woke crying and, chastising himself, he wiped his eyes, got up, showered, and dressed. It was not until morning coffee that he looked outside and found that everything had turned a furious white—the tree, the rosebushes, and the hedgerow of privets that separated his small yard from the house next to his. The paper hung in long, flowing loops that billowed unpredictably in the June breezes, just when the sky above Viktor had seemed almost bright, the trees green in their hopefulness. From his window on this Saturday morning, he surveyed the yard and was reminded of winter, just when he had resolved himself to life pushing forward again.

Though he was confident many were involved, he suspected a certain Ryan, a troubled boy with dark hair and a nose ring that Viktor found repulsive. Ryan was living with a foster family down the street. And if Ryan was involved then surely Ruth Powell's daughter, Trish, was involved too. Ryan and Trish were dating, pooling their individual resources of friends into a collective free-for-all. Since March there had been gatherings on Trish's front porch, twenty or so seniors who smoked herb-scented cigarettes, who laughed noisily through the dark hours of night. Viktor would raise the blinds and gaze down to the street, to the solitary porch light, the silhouettes leaning against the banister. It bothered him, the noise, but it bothered him less than it would have bothered Bella. Still, he huffed irritably about his bedroom each time the teens woke him, even though Bella was not there to hear his inarticulate complaints.

He considered retrieving a ladder from the garage and disentangling the paper from the leaves, but reaching and grabbing all of it seemed only a remote possibility, a difficult venture at best. His eyesight was poor. His legs might have managed well enough, but surely his knee would knot up and his fingers would, with one grasp, curl and tighten.

He called the police instead. A retired security guard for the high school, Viktor knew most of the officers at the station. By eight in the morning Officer Bryant showed up, just as he did six months prior—when he worked the night shift, when the snow fell furiously and Bella had to be taken from the house. Bryant was in his midthirties and had a responsible, serious-looking face, and glasses that pinched him at the nose and temples. Still, when he got out of his car and inspected the yard, he smirked. "So," he inquired. He draped his arm around Viktor, even though Viktor was a slight, frail man who didn't liked to be touched. "Who the hell did you go and piss off this time?"

Viktor ignored Bryant's profanity. He gestured down the road, toward Ruth Powell's house. "The Powell girl, Trish is her name. I would like you to go over to her house and talk to her." He held up his hands beseechingly. "She will respect you, your authority." He pronounced his words carefully, with the faintest hint of a Russian accent; it was a stiff formality that lingered in him, one left over from years ago when his parents, now dead, first arrived in this country.

Bryant looked up at the tree branches, and squinted. Above them, the sky had accumulated moisture. Swirls of gray clouds mounted atop one another. "Well, first we better get this all down before it rains," he said.

"You don't think it's in my right, to have you go over there and talk to those children? My right as a citizen?"

"It is. But there's nothing like wet paper, and you could use a hand, I bet." He went to the back, where Viktor told him the ladder was stored. He came back around, leaned it against the trunk, and climbed.

"Last week," Viktor said, calling up to him, "after nightfall, I was watching the CBS news and I heard a flat-sounding thud. I thought perhaps there was an intruder, so I took my gun down from the closet. This is no longer a safe town."

"Can't be too careful," Bryant agreed. "We get a lot of calls worse than this."

"Yes," Viktor said. "I read the paper, and that is why I have a gun."

The officer glanced down. "Alarm system would work, too."

"Alarms," Viktor said, waving the officer off. "A waste."

Bryant ripped down more paper. "So what was it, the sound?"

Viktor leaned closer to make sure he'd heard him. "Nothing. Only eggs, smeared down the window. A waste. These children do not understand hunger. They do not understand need."

"I don't know what to say about that," Bryant told him. "And I'm not going to be washing windows today, either."

"I washed the windows," Viktor said irritably. "Wire brush, soap, water."

Bryant came down the ladder and picked up the piles of paper from the ground. "Hey, look," he said, "you can report this, but things like this aren't what I'd call a priority around here, just kids being kids."

PERHAPS THE PAPERING had meant nothing. Perhaps it was simply an act of boredom, one brought on by the end of school and the easing of curfews. Didn't Viktor, when he was young, sometimes play silly pranks on others, with his friends? Perhaps in this town one might expect—should expect—small, random acts that bordered on the criminal. But still, he felt certain it was more, an outright retaliation. Who couldn't tell, as they passed by the street littered with cigarette wrappers and dime bags and used condoms, that Viktor's garden was a prized possession? Bella's garden. He still tended to it after her death, breaking up roots with a small shovel, pruning back thorny stalks with his bare hands. It was Bella who planted the roses years ago, the peonies and laurel and lady's mantle. It was Bella who cut clusters of lilacs before they drooped and rotted, who brought them inside and arranged them in vases. She was a big woman, thick around the waist, and she had capable, strong hands. Around her, the garden bloomed, the sweet smells felt as deep as promises.

When they'd first married, over fifty years ago, gardens filled the entire neighborhood. Neighbors shared tomatoes that split apart on the bottoms. They gave gifts of jellies, jams made from grapes they grew in their backyards. Now the town was considered old and historic, both of which translated to run-down and forgotten. Plywood covered up buildings that once housed small boutiques and bookstores. The only people who came through town were those on their way to someplace else, those who traveled with the windows up and the car doors locked. Even the high school where Viktor had worked most of his life had become a haven for problems—mold in the heating systems, funding that over the years had dwindled, halls where fights erupted that involved knives or guns. The people who lingered on the streets so often haunted Viktor. Their faces reflected a pinch-eyed anger, one raw and exposed, the kind that comes from being forsaken.

Things changed. That seemed simple enough. The town. The people in it. Bella was dead, had been dead since winter. Viktor now lived alone. He felt frightened by the people around him. He even felt frightened by the teenagers, by their raw defiance when they walked down the street late at night, smoking. And watching them, Trish and Ryan in particular, he also felt a pang of jealousy, not because Trish was a particularly pretty girl—she was tall and thin and often seemed angry—but because both she and the boy had everything ahead of them still, possibilities they seemed content to squander, and all the time in the world, it seemed to him, for living.

THE TERRIBLE HEAT gave way to showers, and by noon rain pounded the pavement. A few remaining strips of paper first stuck to the uppermost branches and leaves then fell and dappled the grass and ground. Viktor left his house and walked the length of Irving Street. He had given up umbrellas years ago, and now, as he walked, the rain fell on his scrawny tanned arms, his silver hair. He crossed the street and headed a few doors down, to where Trish and her mother, Ruth Powell, lived. He climbed the rickety porch steps, and, at the front door, he ran his hand across his forehead. He had not been to the Powells' in many years, since they'd first moved in and Trish was a round-faced, plump-looking girl who hid behind her mother. Bella had ushered Viktor over with a homemade pie, a welcoming present.

"You should take it over," he'd told her in a firm way.

"Oh, no," Bella had blushed. "They will think I am vain, holding my own pie."

He thought, with an extreme sense of longing, that if Bella were with him now, she would have brought something to offer in advance of conversation. Without anything to hold, he rang the doorbell, then stuffed his hands into his trouser pockets.

Trish held the door open and Viktor squinted to see her better, her bony shoulder blades. Recently, she had dyed her hair jet black, a change that made her skin seem stark, ghostly, her large eyes more deeply set in their sockets.

He cleared his throat. He peered inside. "May I please speak with your mother?"

Trish turned, looked up the stairs, then looked back at Viktor, unsure.

"Do you remember me?" Viktor asked.

She stood up straighter, anchoring herself against the door

frame. "I know who you are," she said after a moment. "You're that man who lives down the street, the one whose wife died."

"Yes," Viktor said, and he stepped forward a little. He felt compelled to jog her memory beyond the most recent fact of Bella's death and all that had happened afterward, to remind Trish that they had ties—they were neighbors—and ties, however small, were things best left unbroken. "But do you remember me? Years ago my wife and I visited you, your mother."

Trish said nothing. She turned her head again, briefly. Then she looked at him in a blank way, refusing to acknowledge anything.

"I have something to discuss with your mother," Viktor continued. "There is the matter of my tree. Please. Get her."

"She's not home."

It was a lie—Viktor could see it in the girl's face, how her eyes darted away from his, toward the ground in an ashamed, adolescent way. And it was only a moment later, anyway, that Mrs. Powell called downstairs, asking who was at the door. When she appeared, Trish rolled her eyes and slunk away, leaving her mother and Viktor in the foyer. The air smelled musty, damp, though she kept the house neatly. The living room, off to the left, appeared dark, the large window draped with thick curtains. The room was sparsely decorated—a few photographs, a clock—but it was comfortable enough.

"It's Viktor, isn't it?" Mrs. Powell asked. She was now a woman probably in her late forties, Viktor guessed, a woman with a sloped and wary look, though her voice was plain, direct, and more than a little tired. She worked nights, he knew. She'd pull her car out close to eleven in the evening and didn't return until the morning. She probably hadn't even been to bed yet.

He smiled slightly. "Yes. Yes, Viktor."

"You live down the street, the house with the garden."

"Yes," he said again, leaning forward, pleased that she noticed, pleased that she remembered. He thought of asking if she remembered Bella's long-ago gift, but he refrained.

"I was at work the night they brought your wife in," she said now. "I'm sorry."

He said, "You work at the hospital, yes? A nurse?"

"Yes."

"Ah," Viktor said, nodding, thinking now of that night, the horrible pace of it all, the ambulance, the questions later posed to him by officers. "I do not often go there, myself, these days. I decided quite a while ago that I'm done with doctors, that when the Lord sees fit, then I will go." He thumps his chest lightly in a smug, determined way.

She glanced at her watch. "I haven't slept yet," she said. "And Trish has to eat lunch before heading to work."

"She works?"

"During the summer, yes. If you call being in charge of the barista bar work."

"Ah," Viktor said again. "Any work keeps a person out of trouble, my wife always said. I know you have things to do, so I will just ask: Did you happen to see my yard?"

Mrs. Powell studied him. "Yes," she said finally.

"The children," Viktor continued. He looked down at his hands, trying to find words that would sound less like an accusation, more like a polite inquiry. But this, of course, escaped him. He surveyed the living room, the curtained window, the moss-colored rug worn thin from use, the floral sofa that sagged in the middle. "Trish, has she been well? Sometimes children do things—stupid things—when they are upset."

Mrs. Powell's expression turned chilly. "What makes you

think my daughter would do anything like that? What makes you so certain she's upset?"

"No, of course not. I did not mean—"

He heard the creaking floorboards upstairs and knew that Trish was probably listening, and a silence followed, during which time Mrs. Powell's expression grew sharper.

"She is a good girl, you are right. My wife, Bella, always watched her play outside when she was small. She was fond of your daughter. We were never able to have children, you know, but Bella wanted them. She wanted many children. It was my fault we could not have children, the doctors said."

"I'll remind you, since you're accusing my daughter, that there were a lot of accusations, too, surrounding you and your wife's death."

His mouth went dry. He felt as if he were chewing on grit. "I did nothing," he said.

"What you did," Mrs. Powell said, "is your own business. I know what people go through when someone is sick. But Trish. She's my daughter, and you have no right to accuse."

The statement was an affront. He believed she was kind, but now he felt rebuked, and his own anger rose in him like a sudden storm. "Of course," he said, looking down at his hands. "I am sorry to have bothered you. I'm sure you are teaching your child well, particularly since she no longer has a father."

"My husband died in an accident," Mrs. Powell said flatly.

"I know," he said. "I'm so sorry. But my wife was very ill at the end. I do not know if you knew that. She did not remember anything, even her own life. She could not swallow on her own."

"You should go," Mrs. Powell said. "There's really nothing more to discuss."

LATER, AFTER TRISH CAME HOME from work, Ryan's old sky-blue Civic pulled up in front of her house, and Trish ran outside, down the steps. She signaled to him, barely gave him a chance to step out and close the car door before she hugged him tightly.

"Hop in," he said, pinching her sides. "We'll drive. Where do you want to go?"

"How about L.A.?"

Ryan grinned in the fierce, reckless way that Trish liked. He was a short, muscular boy, good-looking, rugged. He had been through everything, it seemed, and had continued to push on. He rapped on the hood of his car. "We probably only have fifty miles before this piece of shit gives out. How about Jersey? We could sneak in and gamble, win a little money."

Trish kissed him. When she pulled back, she studied his rugged face. "Wrong direction," she said.

"Get in."

She looked back at her house. "Can't. Jersey, L.A., or otherwise," she said. "Grounded."

He looked down the road. Then he took out a cigarette from his pack and lit it. "You're too old to be grounded. What does your mom think, you're a baby?"

"Don't turn eighteen for another month. Her show until then." She didn't tell Ryan that it was the old man's visit that led to her mother's refusal to let Trish go out that evening, nor did she mention that was only an excuse. It was Ryan her mother disapproved of, really.

Ryan glanced over his shoulder, toward the old man's house and yard. He flicked his cigarette anxiously.

"You didn't help that old man take the shit down?"

"Why would I?"

"Because you're you," Ryan said, eyeing her up and down. "Miss Nicey-Nice."

"Hardly," Trish told him. "I think a cop helped him." ·

"Doesn't matter. He'll pay more by the time we're through."

"I don't know why you hate him so much," Trish said, though she knew this could lead to an argument, or worse, Ryan getting angry and just taking off, as he sometimes did. Still, regret had crept up on her; Ryan was right. She had seen the old man through the living room window, saw how he stood outside for a long time, staring helplessly up at the tree. It was a stupid prank. The old man was hardly worth the energy that Ryan so mercilessly directed toward him. "He's just an old man," she said now. "He's not worth it."

"He's a fucking murderer," Ryan said. "The bastard should be in jail."

"You weren't even here when that all happened."

"You told me," Ryan said. "Everyone did."

"So what does that make you?" she asked. "Some administer of social justice?"

He gave her a stony stare. His nostrils flared. "No. Makes me the damn hanging court."

"Come on," Trish said. She tugged at his T-shirt and went to kiss him again but he turned away. Silence passed between them—she hated when he refused to speak to her, when he gave her the silent treatment for hours. She huffed and leaned against his car while Ryan got in and sat there. The truth was she wasn't sure about the old man—he was cranky, he was practically a cripple, and he often gave her a look that said he didn't approve of something about her, the way she wore her hair or dressed or talked—who knew? But she didn't think he was a murderer.

That seemed beyond the old man's capability. And, anyway, Trish thought, after living so long with someone? It didn't make sense. Still, she remembered that night, how the snow came down heavily, and the siren in the distance, coming closer, its shrill sound still cushioned by all the snow that blanketed the ground. When the ambulance finally skidded to a stop, the flashing lights burned through the whiteness, and workers carried the gurney up the steps and into the house. Within the hour, the woman was being taken out on a stretcher, her face already covered. The old man tumbled out behind her, still in his pajamas, weeping.

Ryan had heard the stories, of course. The old man had murdered his wife. He'd gotten away with what many thought to be unthinkable, given her pills, overloaded her system until she stopped breathing altogether. There was a note the old woman left, one that exonerated her husband of any wrongdoing, written, it seemed, years before, when she first realized she was ill. And there was a liberal judge, new to town, whose mother had suffered from Alzheimer's as well. Still, every time Ryan saw the house or the old man out in his garden, he'd grow intense, brooding, angry. The previous night, when they were all on the porch, drinking beer and talking about plans for summer, Ryan had gotten out of his chair suddenly, swaggering a little as he did. He said, "It's not right." Then he knocked the chair over and cursed it. "He can't expect to do that and not pay."

She didn't remember who rallied behind Ryan first, or even who decided upon toilet-papering. What she did remember was how Ryan commanded the attention of her friends, and how that impressed her. "He'll be fucking clearing this shit for hours," Ryan said, tossing the roll up into the branches, waiting until the roll caught and tumbled back down to him, or to Trish, who waited on the other side. The others tossed more rolls, and soon the entire tree was white, billowing with paper.

"Please don't be angry at me," she said now. She did not turn to look at him.

He gunned the engine. "Why should I? I'm out of here."

She shimmied her rump a little against the door. "I could use some company."

"We doing it?"

"Mom's sleeping," she said. "Later, after she goes."

"I'll come back then," he said, still irritated with her. "Later."

"Stay." She hated when he did this, and she hated herself more for pleading with him. Ryan cocked his head, and finally he shut off the engine.

They sat out on the porch steps. Ryan leaned back, drew in the smoke from his cigarette and tipped the ashes. He flexed his biceps. He could bench-press two hundred. When Trish was in his arms, she felt overwhelmed by two contradictory feelings: First, she'd feel as though she couldn't breathe, that he could crush her, that the intensity of him was too much, and then she'd feel as if the entire world were shut away from her, and that feeling wasn't altogether unpleasant.

"We could break in, tie the old man up, really have a go at his house, or him," Ryan said. His jaw tensed.

This was the kind of talk that frightened her. She was sure Ryan wouldn't actually go that far with things. At least she hoped he wouldn't. She shifted her weight and ran her hands over her shorts. She stretched her long legs.

"Did you hear me?" he asked, nudging her with his huge arm. "I got a baseball bat."

"Oh, *give it up*," Trish said. "The guy will have a heart attack, he'll fall over dead, and then you'll be the murderer."

She shifted again and felt the tension pour through her limbs. She twisted the silver ring he'd given her, worked it around her thin finger. She looked up to the gray sky. She slipped her hand around his arm, moved closer to him, but he pushed her away.

"You don't just go fucking with someone and not pay."

"The old man?" she asked.

"You knew his wife, didn't you?"

"Only a little."

"What was she like?"

"I don't know," Trish said, and made a face. "She was, I don't know, *motherly* or something. What you'd expect."

"Right." He nodded. He exhaled a thin line of smoke and his jaw clenched again. He smothered his cigarette on the step, leaving a circle of ash against the gray paint. "We'll do it tonight. We'll get everyone together."

"I'm grounded, remember?"

"Don't act like a kid, Trish," he said. He got up and looked down at her. "I don't like hanging around with kids."

Her face flushed hotly, but she knew there was no arguing with him when he was like this. She lowered her eyes and stared at the ground.

"Don't do that," Ryan said.

"What?"

"Remember," he said, lifting her face so that she had no choice but to look at him now. "We've got a pact."

SINCE HER FATHER'S ACCIDENT early last fall—during a night when temperatures slid suddenly and rain turned to black ice—Trish often felt that the promise she'd made with

Ryan was the only thing that really mattered anymore. It comforted her in a way that nothing else could. She didn't find solace in the guidance counselor's assurances that everything happened for a reason, nor did she find comfort in the stories she'd heard in whispers after her father's funeral was over. That night, her father had driven home from New Jersey and had been drinking; there was a young woman with him in the car, a girl from work. "Poor Ruth, what she put up with," a once favorite aunt had said. The rumors stabbed at her, made her sick. She began to blame her mother. She slipped out that night to be with friends, girls who were both cheerleaders and stoners, girls who she'd hung around with since the beginning of high school despite the fact that many of them, she knew, wanted Ryan as much as she did—that attractive boy who showed up in the hallways, looking like he was ready for anything.

It was perhaps because of her father's death that she and Ryan got together at all. He'd heard about it and came up to her after classes. He leaned against her locker, arm up, and asked how she was doing with everything. They started hooking up, and when she lay there next to him, she felt as though he was the only one who understood her. Ryan understood, Trish soon realized, precisely because he didn't try to act as though he knew all the answers. He didn't know if her father was cheating, if he was drunk, if there was more to her parents' life than Trish knew about. "Wouldn't want to venture a guess," he said, staring up at the ceiling, pitching his cigarette into the air. This was on a night when they lay outside in the park, on blankets, when the night was cool and the sky so black it seemed to swallow everything.

Trish shivered and pulled Ryan close. He was always more comfortable at night, in the dark, and she could feel his warmth, hear him breathe. She placed her hand on his chest, and he covered her with a blanket while she slipped into her jeans again.

"You know there's nothing that'll make it hurt less," Ryan said.

"I guess." She buried her face into Ryan's stomach, wanting all the warmth that lingered in his body, all the strength. She hated herself for feeling so weak. Ryan ran his fingers through her hair, pulled back the long strands from her face. "You should dye your hair black," he said offhandedly. "As a sign to the world, you know, that you're through taking all its shit, that you're strong, a survivor."

She nodded, wiped the tears from her face.

He lifted her chin and kissed her. Then he stared at her, in a hard way. "You know, my dad was hardly around, and when he was he was hitting my mother. She died from that fucker's fists."

"That's terrible." Trish held on to him harder.

"Hell," he said. "Nothing to be sorry for. You didn't do it. Besides, he's paying for that now. Thirty fucking years for that."

She shivered, then closed her eyes. "Let's run away together," she said. "After graduation, let's just go. There's nothing here I want to remember, anyway."

Ryan seemed to consider this option. "Maybe," he said. "Okay."

"Swear."

"Swear what?"

"That we'll always be together."

"Okay," he said finally.

"And if we break the pact?"

Ryan grinned and made a slicing motion against his throat. "Kidding," he said. He took off his ring, a simple silver band with a skull engraved on it. In the dark, he slid it on her third finger, and it hung there, too loosely.

"I'll wrap the ring in red thread," she told him. "I'll dye my hair black."

Ryan leaned back and laced his fingers through hers, turning the ring over. "Till death do us part. You renege and I'll kick your ass."

"You wouldn't," Trish said.

Ryan thought for a moment. "No," he said. "I'm not like my old man. I'm better than that."

VIKTOR SAT on the porch with his gun positioned on his thigh. His skin felt clammy. The front lights were off. It was just past eleven in the evening and the air threatened more rain. He felt alert, filled with a sense of purpose, and he watched out over the street, toward the neighboring houses, waiting for any teenagers who might gather again, thinking to do something to his house, his property. It was *his* house, he told himself again; he *owned* it. It was *his* yard. Anyone who came onto his property was an intruder, a trespasser. He was within his legal right to hold the gun up, in the trespassers' direction, to threaten force if necessary, to shoot. They'd run off with their tails between their legs, he told himself. Let them tell people he was crazy. Let them call the police. What did it matter now?

He looked out across the garden and listened to the sound of distant sirens—always sirens in this part of the city, always someone in trouble, always someone in need. Every once in a while, he'd cock his head, catching sight of a shadow moving across the road, and he'd wait, the adrenaline pouring into his arms. But then there was nothing more, and he'd decide it was only his eyes and imagination that had toyed with him. Still, the light down at Trish's house was on, and though the front porch was empty and silent, he knew they'd come. He ran his hand over the metal barrel. It felt strange, just as it had felt strange the night Bella died. She would not have the gun, of course, though in the end it would have been quicker, less painful. He said, "Bella, pills will hurt." He smoothed her hair. "I do not want for you to hurt any more," he said.

That night when the snow grew deep and everything around him seemed perfect, he removed the letter from her jewelry box and placed it next to the bed. He washed her bedspread and tucked it neatly around her. He placed flowers on the night-stand. Then he smoothed each round pill in his trembling fingers and gave her one after another, massaging her throat and working her mouth in his hands until she swallowed. She never opened her eyes that night—he might have told that to someone if he thought he could explain the night at all, to anyone. Who would understand all the years, the pain? She convulsed once then twice and a third time—much of the bottle was gone. He told her: "Tonight, I go where you go."

But not with pills, he decided. He feared he'd awaken in a hospital room with Bella gone and life ahead of him. He rummaged around on the top shelf in their bedroom closet until he felt the metal box tucked in the back. He unlocked it and removed the gun and box of bullets. He went to the kitchen and sat at the table. He loaded each bullet, one by one, finally bringing the cold metal to his mouth, his hands shaking so violently that it would have been possible for the trigger to be pulled without his consciously willing it. He didn't know what finally stopped him. Sometimes he told himself it was Bella he felt coursing through his veins. Perhaps, though, it was only life, the quickness of his heart, the air drawn into his nasal passages, his lungs, which expanded, then contracted again. He put the gun down on the table in front of him. He knew even then that he would fail to do what he'd promised Bella. He once considered himself a fearless man. He once believed he could do anything if necessity called for it. But he was only a coward. He poured himself a drink to settle his nerves—another promise to Bella broken, after so many years of not drinking at all. He chastised himself. But what he knew was simple: He didn't want his own life to end sooner than it might have. He was grateful, if not happy, for what life there was.

Now he heard laughter down the street, saw the slinking shapes of teenagers gathering outside on the road in front of the Powell house, the tall shapes of boys, the smaller movement of the girls as they talked anxiously among themselves. They moved closer. They walked slowly. Surely they saw him there after a time, even in the dark. There were five of them—Trish, her arms wrapped tightly around herself, as if she were cold; the boy Ryan, who held a bat; two other boys with sweatshirts on, hoods drawn tight around their faces so that he couldn't see who they were at all, or if he knew them; and another girl with braids throughout her hair, someone he'd never seen before, talking now, louder, saying, "That fucker's up waiting for us."

Ryan slapped the baseball bat into his open palm and stood at the gate.

"What do you want?" Viktor called out. He stood up, peered out nervously. He kept the gun to his side.

"You know what we want, old man," Ryan said. He slapped the baseball bat again.

"Ryan, *don't*," Trish urged him.

"I told you to stay home if you couldn't handle it," he said sharply.

"You don't speak to her like that," Viktor yelled. "You don't speak to *me* like that, either."

The group moved toward him, and Viktor could barely catch his breath enough to remember to hold up the gun, to point it. They stopped. "I'm within my right," he said, waving it. "This is my house, and you are not welcome."

VIKTOR AWOKE in the morning. He was out on the porch and didn't know how many hours had passed. A dampness clung to his skin, and the sun was just rising. It had rained during the night, but nothing else had happened—he'd waved the gun, which was empty of bullets, and the girl, Trish, started pleading and crying and the boy came closer before the others said, "Let's go," and they all separated then, running off in different directions, calling Viktor a lunatic, all while Ryan and Trish stood there a moment longer, Trish tugging on the boy's jacket. The boy shot him such a look of hatred—such hatred—before he threw down the bat, hard, on the ground, and he spit and wiped his mouth and told Viktor—told him—that the old man wasn't worth his time. They walked off, and Viktor, shaking so urgently, sank back down to his chair, his heart beating so fast he thought he might die himself that night, finally make good on a promise.

In the ensuing weeks, a few incidents persisted. Another egging. A smashed mailbox. It was more than a month later that, while tending to the garden and weeding the overgrown flower beds, Viktor noticed the faint trace of lettering across his walkway, white paint on the cement. He looked more closely—

MURDERER. He wondered how long it had been there. He made out each letter, then finally the word itself, before he went into the house and returned with a bucket of soapy water. He bent with difficulty and washed what he could with a wire brush. He hosed his walkway down with water, then took to scrubbing again. He would not call the police. Let them call him a murderer. They were children. They were scared, they were as scared as he was of this life. They were children, he told himself. What did they know? And he could defend himself.

He heard Trish's voice before he actually noticed she was there, listening to him complain under his breath. He looked up from his work, wiped his brow, squinted. Trish was at the gate. She had a dog with her, a mangy-looking mutt much like the ones Viktor and his friends used to kick when they were younger, when the mutts came too close to trash cans, sniffing for food. This dog, too, sniffed nervously around before lifting its leg on the fence.

"No manners," he said, nodding. Then he went back to his work. She didn't seem to be waiting for him to say anything. She simply watched as he struggled to remove the paint from the sidewalk. "What do you want?" he asked sharply.

She debated, pulled the dog closer. She was about to say she was sorry when she realized there was nothing she could say to make anything better. The old man could barely hold the brush without it slipping from his hands. She tied the dog's leash to the fencepost and opened the gate. She said, finally, "I'll help clean it up."

She came over then and bent down, her bare knees scraping against the pavement. She pushed her hair behind her ears and took the brush from his shaking hand. Viktor said nothing. He sat back, exhausted, on the dry grass. One more moment, Trish thought, and he might have wept, right in front of her. His hands came up to his face, then fell suddenly back down into his lap.

"I know you didn't do anything wrong," she told him. "I mean, we're all sort of assholes sometimes."

Viktor wiped the sweat from his forehead. The dog sniffed at the flowers and grasses that poked through the fence and into the sidewalk. "I had a dog once," he said. Then to Trish he said, "Where's your friend?"

She glanced up. "Ryan? Gone."

"Ah," Viktor said. "That's good. Whether you know it or not, he wasn't the right boy for you."

"That's what my mother said," she told him, but when he looked at her, he could tell she was upset by his statement. He didn't understand youths—he could admit that—why a girl with so many possibilities would want to be with a boy whose life would never go anywhere.

Trish continued her work. She scrubbed hard, intent on making the letters fade. She could have told the old man it wasn't Ryan who did this—if Ryan had decided that the old man wasn't worth his time, then he meant it. He wouldn't go to that place that would, finally, make him like his father. She still believed that. No. It wasn't Ryan but the remaining gang. They egged the house, smashed the mailbox. They stepped back after spray-painting the letters, satisfied with their own actions. They were the ones who came over to her house after leaving Viktor's; they were the ones who called her out on the porch, wanting her to come see. But she felt years and years older. She was finished with all that business, too. They laughed, and she couldn't help but think they were mocking her, too, in a small way. *He is gone,* their smiles seemed to say. *We all knew that would happen.* After he had thrown the baseball bat down onto the sidewalk, Ryan stopped talking to any of them. Within the week he'd run off from the foster home, and no one, not even Trish, had heard from him since.

She scrubbed harder. Viktor sat next to her, watching. Perhaps he was thinking she deserved this, that she deserved everything bad that had happened in her life. She glanced up at him. He ran his hand through his damp hair and then pulled a small towel from his pocket to wipe away the sweat.

She said, "I'm sorry about this."

"Ah," he said again. He frowned, and she couldn't tell if he was resolved or angry. He stared off to the roses and hedgerow. Finally, he told her, "My wife was very ill. I promised her I would help her die when the time came, and I did. That does not make me a murderer. I still have a promise to keep. It is like a great burden in my heart."

Trish inched down the sidewalk on her knees. "I don't believe in promises."

"It is probably just as well," Viktor said. "They are difficult things."

She got up and dropped the brush in the bucket. She thought of telling him about the promise she and Ryan had made, but it hardly seemed to matter anymore, and she didn't want the old man to dispense fatherly advice. At least she didn't think she wanted it. "I don't care what people say anymore. It doesn't matter much. It's not totally gone, but it's better. In a few months, it'll be covered with snow anyway. That's the thing about this place, there's so much snow."

"Winter is a cruel season," he said. "But sometimes summer is worse. I do not want another summer. I wait, eagerly, for the first snow, and then I will keep my promise to Bella."

"You'd be the first." Trish brushed off her knees. Overhead the sun beamed brightly. The breezes blew but didn't stop her from sweating. She undid the leash from the fencepost and yanked the dog toward her, but the dog pulled away, not wanting to come to her. "Stupid dog," she said, twisting the leash. "My mom thought he'd be good for me, to learn responsibility."

"Ah," Viktor said, nodding. He lifted himself up slowly, ignoring the sharp pain in his back and legs. His face twisted. He picked up the bucket. "Responsibility is also a difficult thing, but your mother is a smart woman," he told her. "And you're a good child. My wife always said that about you."

Trish wasn't sure if she was good or bad or anything but herself. Anyway, she didn't owe him anything else. She'd apologized, and she helped him, and that was it. "I don't think you'll have any more problems," she said now, nonchalantly. Viktor nodded as she closed the gate and pulled the dog down the street, not urgently, toward home.

RILKE

⸻

Although I am preoccupied with words, I cannot say what I want. Once when traveling in a foreign country I negotiated my desire while lying naked on a bed, legs up in the air, toes gripping the flesh of a stranger's shoulders. And when this man asked me, in between wet, jaunty kisses, what I *wanted*, all I could say was *Je ne veux rien* and not *Prenez votre temps, s'il vous plaît*, which is what I actually thought.

I do not remember this man's name. (I am not certain I ever knew his name.) But his small, dingy apartment smelled of smoke, and his body felt sinewy, racehorse lean, moist with sweat. His hair fell across my shoulders as he moved. He spoke of things I dare not say, and some of which, truthfully, I did not understand. When we finished, I grabbed my purse and buttoned up my blouse, slipped on my jeans, and stole a pack of cigarettes from his shirt pocket. I quoted Rilke, not in French but in German, and said, *We are never at home in our inter-preted worlds.* And the man, this stranger, lay back in bed, blew me a kiss from his cupped hand, and whispered in a smooth, soft voice, *Va-t'en!*

I do not believe that French is the language of desire.

I am unsure about German, though I confess that, like Rilke, I believe that if I cried out no one would hear, that I would be reminded of my own divisions.

ENGLISH IS NO BETTER. Always I must approximate. Back home in the States, I once dated a man who was forty-three, twenty-two years older than I was then. This man never said I love you, though it's true he did have a cat and a mother, so he may have been lying. Perhaps he simply did not say everything there was to say.

I gave him pet names, Peanut Butter and Honey Pie and Bear, because everything about him was thick. But most of the time I just called him Bash, a shortening of his Lebanese name, Bashir.

I called his cat Kitty because that was the cat's name.

I never met his mother, and so did not know her name.

Bash usually called late at night, not because he wanted to talk dirty but because he wanted to discuss philosophy. After midnight he became extremely lucid and could speak in the most straightforward manner about Husserl and Hegel. He could breathe the body politic, phenomenology. He quoted Buber's *Ich und Du,* which he struggled to read in poor, broken German until finally he gave up to read in English instead. When he read, his voice put me to sleep because he spoke in whispers.

I do not think Buber has been translated to Arabic.

Bash called me Cutie and took me out for ice cream and walks late at night, under the moon. When he and I kissed, our glasses knocked together, and I shook beneath his hands as if everything within me were imploding. I nibbled him and he sucked in his belly. The black hairs on his body felt full, furry under my fingertips.

Take the advice of the Marquis de Sade, he once said while we lay in bed, arms folded around each other, sheets twisted between our legs. Don't ever have children. He told me that at twenty-one I was already very frightening. He asked me if, like Sade's female philosopher-monsters, I preferred an alternative kind of sex.

What a pickup line, I told him.

Afterward, he said it would probably be better if I remained single.

I never quoted from Rilke because Bash thought all poets possessed feeble minds. I told him that of all the poets, Rilke was the hardest to pin down, born in Prague, raised in a German-speaking neighborhood, offended to be called a German and an Austrian, both in equal parts. I spoke of his soldier-father, the destruction of his homeland in war, his time in Paris with Rodin. Rilke, I said, never felt himself a native anywhere; he was his own country—body, mind, and heart. In his *Duino Elegies*, I said, Rilke spoke intimately with his readers, as if in a whispery confession, and tried to overcome distance.

Bash asked me why anyone would ever do that.

I wrote him a poem but never sent it.

Once after we'd taken a shower Bash wrapped his arms around my waist and asked what I wanted from life, but there was too much, then, to say. We stood in front of a foggy mirror, his chest hairs wet against my back, steam everywhere. He bit my neck. With my pinkie, I penned on the mirror what I wanted (not sex but love), and when he pulled away from me, I told him I was only joking. I tried to laugh but felt unearthly and foolish.

Sometimes when I see the moon and it's low and full of itself in quiet ways, I still think of him.

SPEAKING OF THE MOON, a word here about our alien natures. It is a widely regarded belief that mathematics, and not words, is the universal language. Do you know what desire translates to, in math? Would Rilke know?

When I married my husband, he plotted our spending habits on charts, month by month, line by line, until a grid became full. He said he wanted to see what we were worth. When I laughed, he didn't understand what I thought was funny.

I'm not exactly telling you the truth about him because my husband was not technically a mathematician. Actually, he counted time lines on five-hundred-million-year-old fossils—*Olenellus*—in Cambrian rock. He entered all these numbers in a database and performed statistical calculations about extinction rates.

When I first met him in a library and he told me all this, it made me horny. I said I didn't believe anything could last that long and asked him to bed. We had sex among fossils because he worked in the Collections and had a key.

My husband wore boxers with symbols of πr^2 on them that glowed in the dark. He bought the boxers from The Gap. The Gap has a sense of humor about things.

He was so sweet when he smiled I knew I would devour him like chocolate, bite by bite.

My husband's naked body did not look like rock and did not look old. His cheekbones stood in high relief, his flesh contoured like a cherub's. Most of his skin was smooth and white, though he had fine brown hair all over his chest that I would not have expected. I called him My Angel. I wanted to carry his skin on mine as a soldier carries a flag, announcing himself to others.

Once during a rainy night he said he would give me anything I wanted, but at that time I couldn't think of a thing I could actually keep.

He said, Let's stay together until we die.

I quoted to him and said, *Every angel is terrifying.* I read him all of Rilke's *Elegies* in bed, before we slept at night. I said, *Beauty is nothing but the beginning of terror.*

He said, Poetry sounds beautiful, but I just don't understand it.

I told him I didn't understand how to calculate time and the earth's history on a one-dimensional line, from beginning to end.

We washed dishes together, cooked meals. With him I became so full I gained weight. He read articles while I graded papers on Baudelaire's *Les Fleurs du mal.* We turned off the lights at the same time each and every night.

After ten years things became so quiet I developed a predilection for the future. When we gazed at rocks and mountains, I could hear the smallest cracking and knew that neither the mountain nor I could do anything about this fact.

I didn't know how to describe the sound of erosion in a way that my husband believed, but I still marveled over fossils. For a long time, that was all we could talk about. Finally, I said, Are we any less subject to time than rock?

He said he didn't understand the question. People aren't mountains, he said.

When I left, my husband said that he was better at loving, though when he said this, it didn't sound childish; it only sounded like a statement of fact.

Last I heard, he had married an actuary. She computes insurance risks and premiums. I can only hope they are happy. Sometimes I wonder what she thinks when she sees his boxers from The Gap. I am sure he hasn't gotten rid of them. He never gets rids of anything, even things that are old.

THIS IS GETTING OLD, you say now. We are in bed together, and I can't tell if you are angry or joking, though I have seen you naked and felt you pressing between my legs, so I feel as though I should know. If you're going to talk like this every time I ask you what you want, you say, I may have to reconsider sleeping with you again. Then you add, I was really just asking you what you wanted to eat. I always get hungry after sex.

You are a good lover with strong, nimble fingers, and it's true, I suppose, that you are still hungry. You rub your belly, lie back, adjust the pillow. You stare at the ceiling fan, which swirls above us. Rain hits the window. I have seen the sky tonight, a shattered, pearl gray.

I want to say you are a sweet man even though you are hard, emotionally balled-up like a fist. I want to say you have the most lovely milky-brown eyes, and your skin is warm and heavy.

I sit up, lean over and kiss your stomach instead. It's true, I tell you. I said too much. Should we fix a snack?

Not now, you say. Now you've ruined it. Now I'm only tired.

It is tiring, I agree, all this history and desire.

I could die while listening to you, you say. I've aged twenty years since you've started. I'm really glad you didn't start from the beginning, or go on about all the men you've slept with.

That's true, I say. There's a lot I left out.

I want to tell you that, as with the foreign man, we are still strangers, and, as with my Lebanese man, I have no way to know if I reach you, and unlike my ex-husband's charts, there is no good way to measure the distance between us. Instead I ask, Why did you let me talk for so long?

I dozed off, you confess. I remember the French guy, and war, and also something about the Marquis de Sade.

Oh, good, I say, leaning back on my pillow. Those were all the best parts.

Maybe I can listen when you can say what you want in one sentence or less, you tell me. Really, you need to make things simpler.

I pull up the blanket and turn to face you. I cover your leg with my leg. Truthfully, my wants are so large that I can't fit the words around them. I want to tell you I feel lonely. I want to ask if, on rainy nights, you are ever moved to speak the language of the poets. But mostly, I want to feel proximity of body, mind, and heart. I want, like Rilke, to cover the terrible nakedness in you and in me, to cast the emptiness out of us and into the open spaces.

Perhaps Rilke was wrong. I cannot ask you this. You teach history and speak frequently of soldiers, countries, and war.

Do soldiers, away from their homeland, carry flags? I ask instead.

You scoff at this and shift under the covers. Only if they're insane, you say. Only if they want to get shot.

It's frustrating, to be without a home and country.

Not really, you say, as you strip off the covers and get up to make a snack. There are always borders and opposition. Sometimes, you tell me, it's easier to remain quiet and say nothing.

HUNK

1.

Hunk, he calls as he pulls my sister close and loops his thick arm around her—flesh and bone, his mottled elbow, her pale neck and shoulders. She's a pretty girl—too pretty, I think—tall and lean; dark eyes; a Gypsy forehead that, when it furrows, makes her seem older than almost-sixteen.

Hunk, Hunk, Hunk. Hunkie, the people of Eastern Europe. Or Hunk, a slab of meat. He musses her hair, then pretends to bite into her until she screeches and laughs, leaning into him, leaning in and not away. Raspberry gloss coats her lips; her smile tightens. I love my sister's laughter. It's as deep as a secret she hides inside, and, as it runs through her, her entire body shakes. Her head bobs forward, a mass of long chocolate curls. Her head bobs back, gently, like a buoy.

Here in the kitchen, the light shines brightly through the worn curtains, exposing fine particles of dust in the air; here the day is beaming and beaming more, the hot, sticky August sun promising never to go down. The air pushes so insistently through the screen doors. My sister laughs when he whispers something in her ear. Beyond her, the house remains almost quiet; a fan hums, pulsing on and on and on. There are fans all around the house, in hallways, in bedrooms, set up in strategic places to circulate and cool the air.

Who's my favorite? What does the favorite get?

2.

I am the baby of my family. Eleven years younger than my sister, I am an accident, the grand failure of a breaking condom. Life pushes forward, I joke to people, years later. I am happy to be alive, I say, and I mean it.

Here in the corner of the kitchen, I sit at a rickety table with legs that always wobble, my own legs never touching the ground. I lop up too-sweet cereal with a spoon, lick what runs down my chin. At five I am all yellow curls, all sweet chunky cheeks. Jealous little thing, I want to be the favorite. She is mine, I want to say. I watch the intricate weave of bodies, the play of skin on skin, like wrestlers, or like dancers twisting in both graceful and violent maneuvers.

She is mine and mine and all mine. I have woven my hands into that mass of hair, nuzzled against each curl, threaded my fingers through her fingers, pressed my lips to her lips, a good-night kiss, a good-morning kiss, a glad-to-see-you, to-be-alive kiss. She is my sister. I have breathed her and felt her and been her, and she is all mine, right down to the bones and blood.

My sister, still in a stranglehold, looks over at me, winks in assurance, and says, Hey, Goldilocks, what does Goldilocks do? And I know then I am to hunt for bears—my sister has made me fierce, telling me exactly how I must be: I am to be the hunter and not the hunted, which is what she tells me when she doesn't want me to be afraid. It also means I am to go to my room and stay there and be quiet and wait for the sound of closing and opening doors again. It means I am to look under the bed, search through the closets, poke around the dusty corners for things that might devour me.

Okay, my sister says, to something my father whispers. She looks down to the floor, at the forget-me-nots springing from woven baskets, and she laughs. She looks out the back door, to the yard and trees, to my brothers, who are outside in the sun, enjoying the day, and she laughs.

I do not know what her laughter means.

3.

Yes, there are boys. They are tough-and-tumbling brothers who wrestle at night, who give each other bloody noses over yard work. Outside, on this particular day, they rake crunchy leaves that have fallen down early—a drought in August—and then throw the leaves up in the air, out of their arms. The boys spend all day outside. The boys *are* the outside, wild, unkempt down to the last hair. They smell of warm breezes and sunshine. They wear the wind on their backs, have tree limbs for arms.

Later, after they finish their work, they will dangle themselves from branches, falling backwards without concern for the smallest injury. They will burn insects—ants and katydids and cicadas in this summer when the cicadas awaken. They will burn them all with magnifying glasses, just to see.

The brothers aren't exactly hunks, though they are lean and muscular—almost, but not quite, fleshy. They do often hunker around, though, practicing Travolta moves in the driveway— a little hip, a little lip—a routine from *Grease*. Their smiles widen when girls in the neighborhood ride by the backyard on bikes, all curvy, shiny knees and floppy sandals.

4.

Years have passed since I've seen my sister. I am thirty-two now, and, mostly, I am alone. There are several reasons for this. I like to be alone; I am used to it. And I am difficult to know. Impervious, deliberately so, I push most people away.

There is a woman I know who wants to be my friend. She is a beautiful woman; she has thick hair like my sister's. She keeps her hair cut squarely, bluntly, just as everything about her is blunt—her forehead, her smile, her manner of speaking. My friend loves the truth. She's as relentless with it as a sewing needle, threading and threading bits of truth into something substantial. She tells me not to hunt for bears, but to chase down the words instead.

We exchange stories, hers always truth, mine always lies. Because I prefer the idealism inherent in lies. I tell her I don't see the point in truth, and I mean it. It's never served me well. I bring her stories about unending road trips and warring roommates and people who want rather absurd, funny things— things they have no hope of getting—like pet cows and love that will never leave them. I write all this so I don't have to write about my sister. My friend reads my stories, finds in them the one or two slivers of something that sounds like me. She finds something else, and suddenly there is a pattern. She is stitching me together, putting me on the mend, which I suppose is an act of friendship.

5.

Many times I've thought of writing about my sister, because I often miss her. But I don't know what I would write about, or how I could keep her from becoming just another fiction, just another character I invent to pass lonely days, to have someone to talk to who understands without all that saying. It's been twenty-six years since I've seen her. The amount of time that I've known her has been eclipsed by the amount of time I have not.

Once, with the very first man I dated seriously, I tried to speak about her. I said: This truly awful thing happened, and she left, just like that, up and disappeared. I was far less circuitous in those days, much more haphazard with both my love and my intentions. I would tell anyone anything, if only they seemed as though they might listen. If only they asked.

When this happened with my boyfriend, we were at dinner, a fancy place with white linen—he worked for the government and had a lot of money. As I spoke, he cleared his throat and glanced around to see if anyone else might be listening. He leaned forward and said: No one wants to hear *that* kind of story. He said: Tell me one about a man who battles the enemy and wins the foxy lady. You know: action and blood, secrets and death. Maybe a rhetorical flourish or two. Now *that's* a story.

6.

My sister is so insistent, though, so small in what she offers me. The secret to beautiful hair, she says, is to lather and repeat. You've got to coax the shine into it.

She has just come from the shower, and I have heard the doors closing and opening again, heard her secret knock at my door—five quick knocks, a *bumpity-bump-bump* rhythm, a language she and I share through the walls at night. I have smelled aftershave and lotion and sensed my sister's salty tears. I have searched the corners of my room but come up empty-handed.

She sits on my bed and adjusts the pillows. She sits bundled in a robe, even though it isn't even dinnertime. No bears, Goldilocks? she inquires. When I say no, she growls and tackles me, tickling my sides until I laugh. She lets me roll her over—she is so easy, my sister, so gentle in her rolling—she lets me go bang-bang-bang into her heart with a pretend gun.

Oh, she says, covering her forehead with her arm. I'm dying. As she leans back, her hair falls, the soft skin of her neck exposed, the faint impression, raspberry marks under her ear.

Don't die, I say, suddenly regretful. Come back to life, I tell her. I plant a kiss on her cheek. I coax her with another kiss, but her eyes are closed and she does not answer. She lies perfectly still. I push at her shoulder. I nudge her a bit, check her heartbeat and pulse like doctors do on television.

7.

September pushes life on and on. I feel it pulse through me, like wind scattering the dead leaves. September is also the month of Aunt Judy's pumpkin bread, sticky on the mouth's concave roof, sweet on the tongue, melting like butter. She stops by to check on my father, to see if there have been callbacks on jobs. Laid off from the textile factory, my father has been home all year, and people are starting to worry, notice small things, changes in demeanor, a certain quietness that has settled over the house. Is he depressed? she wants to know. Are things okay? Does he seem all right to you girls?

My sister and I rally around him. We are his girls—we are such good girls. We stay inside, neglect friendships, help out around the house. My sister does not ask to drive, though I know she wants to. She has a secret love, a kiss-me love, a boy from school named Alex. Sometimes Alex prowls by the house late at night, waiting to catch a glimpse of her. He coaxes her with promises of weed, tiny pills, and beer. He throws small stones at her window. Come out, he whispers. Can you come out?

8.

We prepare for Halloween a full month early. We are secretive in our preparations; my sister holds clandestine meetings in the basement, telling me exactly how the skeletons must look. When we finish our cuttings of cardboard and charcoal, we hang the skeletons on the front door, a warning to those who enter—Beware! We plant gravestones in the front yard, speak of death and goblins, ask Aunt Judy if she knows what it's like not to sleep. It's not Judy but my sister who seems most tired, those half-moons under her eyes, her hair barely combed. She cracks lame jokes anyway, parades around the living room, dancing like a zombie.

Girls, Aunt Judy says. You girls, always living in a fantasy world. Can't you ever come down from your clouds? She tells my sister she's surprised at her—almost sixteen now and still talking nonsense. Silly, she says. Your mother needs your help. She's been working so much, trying to keep up. There are important, adult things going on, you know.

Aunt Judy is silly. She wears entirely too much makeup: blue eye shadow and peach lipstick, and her red hair always shellacked. Her clothes are too tight for her round body. She believes she can be twenty again. What is sillier?

9.

There must be a mother. I open the white shutters of her closet, step into the mothballed air and inhale until my lungs hurt. There are pretty shoes lined up against the floorboard, long dresses hanging on metal wires. I go a-hunting through the house, down the long corridor that leads to the kitchen, where soup has been left on the stove too long. I run my hand across curtains left on the ironing board. I find dictation in the living room, take-home work from the office, her almond-shaped reading glasses lying atop a mass of papers. In my room, I find clothes laid with exacting detail in the places body parts should be: a yellow Lynyrd Skynyrd shirt lying just under the pillow on my bed, a pair of brown slacks under it, a braided belt in between, socks under the cuffs of the slacks, clogs on the floor. And then I sleep.

It is not my mother but my sister who kisses me goodnight, who tucks blankets all around me. It is my sister who tells bedtime stories. Before she pulls up the covers, she lets me drape the sheets over both of us. This is how we tell stories: under the sheets, hiding in ourselves. If someone were to look in through an open door or window, if ever there were open doors and windows in this house, they'd see us bunched up, flashlight barely seeping through the fabric. We are like ghosts, my sister and I, already disappearing.

10.

My sister ignores the knock at the door. We are busy, go away. She intones: It was a cold night, just like tonight. She pretends to shiver. She has just taken a pill, one that will dull her senses, one that Alex gave to her the night before. I listen more to the sound of her voice than to her actual words. Her voice is light, like a song waiting to be lifted, full of its predictable, often sorrowful, rhythms. I try to braid my sister's hair—she has left it looking wild—but it tangles so easily. She pulls me from her, in no mood for my wandering fingers.

It was going to snow, my sister continues. It was just about to snow, actually; the sky was black and the air so cold it hurt. The mother pulled her entire family out of bed—two boys and two girls—and she scooted them outside in their housecoats and slippers, their jackets still open. The children thought perhaps there was a fire, but there was no smoke. The children wondered where the father was, but he stayed inside, sleeping. The mother piled them all into the car. She had packed a suitcase for each child, my sister says. There were icicles hanging from the door. A brother broke one off, just for something to do; he carried the icicle in his bare hands, licked it. The mother started the engine running to warm everyone up, but then she just sat there, crying, not knowing where to go or what to do. The baby slept through all this, my sister says. The baby was only three, going on four, and she had curly blond hair, just like yours. She looked like an angel, sleeping like that. I bet the baby doesn't even remember.

11.

My friend frequently speaks about lies and how bad they are, though mostly it is with regard to the government and politics and the vitrolic flow of information. My friend's brother died in Vietnam, and she is still very angry with the government. Truth, she says, is the only thing that can save us, restore our voices, our common humanity.

Sometimes I think she speaks the truth so much in an effort to remember her brother. Maybe, in speaking the truth, she soothes some hurt, calms some grave injustice. I do not know for certain. I rely on speculation, innuendo. In that regard, I believe I am like my sister. We are not easy girls, my sister and I. We leave out the most important things, rely on pauses and hesitations, which we also look for in other people. But, even then, intuiting, what can we say we really know? I will never be like my friend, who searches for truth and seems disappointed when she can't find it. Even the smallest pieces of my knowledge are fraught with complicated interpretations, large, gaping holes, lies.

My friend and I sit at the kitchen table. We drink wine and smoke cigarettes. We read tarot cards and palms and laugh hysterically when we say that we'll never lose our beauty and luster, or that we'll be rich and famous.

What was your family like? my friend asks later. She is still trying to get to know me, still piecing me together. She is so intent on uncovering anything I hide.

Mostly, I say, we were a normal family. This is not a lie. I love my parents. They are my parents, after all. And my father and mother took care of us. We had warm clothes every year, breakfast, lunch, and dinner. We went on picnics in the park. We took vacations to Florida. My parents had friends, people who visited. In the winter months, my father would take us all sledding. He waxed our sleds with candles. He made sure we bundled up. He warmed the car before we got into it—he always did that for us—and he drove us to the highest hill in the neighborhood, where he'd wait as we got out, one after the other, and flew away on our sleds, screaming. Then he drove down to retrieve us and drove us back up again for another go. He did that for hours, which was very nice.

That *is* nice, my friend agrees. But it seems to me that this is not enough for her, that she is still waiting.

Most of us, these days, don't have much of a relationship, I tell her. We hardly speak, if you want to know the truth.

She looks at me sympathetically. Of course you all have a relationship, she says. Even if you don't speak at all.

I would like to believe this. I would like to believe that's how all love is—that love is carried with us, on our shoulders and inside our bellies. I would like to believe this about my sister, especially, even if it is rather foolish.

12.

Hunk, Hunk, Hunk, my father calls. He wants her to come and clip his toenails. My father is a slack man, with skin that is like leather treated too long. My father is also extremely superstitious. Did I mention this? He believes he once saw a ghost. He speaks of his own mother casting spells that could bring the dead back to life.

Hunkie, he calls my sister. He praises her Gypsy good looks. Hunks can call one another Hunks in affection or recognition, in the way that another friend, years later, would talk about calling her sister Dirty Irish, or in the way that my friend Greg would call his lover Queen, or Queenie, or Louis, you fag.

13.

In January, we pour a new basement. My sister has been living these days in her room with the door locked, and my *bumpity-bump-bump* coaxing doesn't bring her out. Even Alex doesn't draw her interest, coming to her window, offering up weed and small tokens of his affection. What is wrong with her? Aunt Judy wants to know. Come down, she calls. Come down now.

My brothers, Aunt Judy, and I help my father mix cement that will turn hard and crumble. My brothers call each other *goofball* and *moron* and *dumb ass*. They throw cement into each other's hair, claiming peanut butter gets anything out. They laugh when Aunt Judy chides them.

My sister finally comes down to help. She is dressed in sweat-pants and a T-shirt that exposes her thin arms, the paleness of her skin, the fine dark hairs that travel over her and stand on end. My brothers tease her, tease her tiredness, her aloneness. They smear wet cement on her back, to try to egg her on.

We mix and pour and level things off until everything about the room seems gray and cool, thick and wet. We move back-wards, edging our way to steps that lead upstairs to the kitchen. We leave no footprints. Right before we finish, my sister bends down, and, at the landing, she writes in big, chunky letters: THE HUNK. Years later, after my sister has left, my mother will cover this up with ugly fragments of carpets that do not fit any-thing. And my sister, what is left of her, will disappear all over again.

Who's the favorite? What does the favorite get?

14.

Time passes and life thaws outside the window. Things push on and on. A full summer later, after the summer of closing and opening doors, the summer of bears and more bears and rasp-berry kisses and briny tears, I walk into my sister's bedroom and find her packing a small duffel bag, with only the basics: shirts, jeans, underwear, a bra and panties. She is so willing to leave everything behind. She is so willing to go. She tells me: I'm sorry, baby, but I can't take it anymore.

I do not understand what my sister's packing means, just as

I do not understand her laughter or tears. There was a mother, I know, who packed things and only made it to the end of the driveway, so I am not too worried. I watch as my sister packs, as she takes a family photo and cuts our two faces from it—same pale skin and hooked nose, same deeply set eyes. She holds us up and says: I'm going to keep you with me forever.

Years later, in her one and only letter, she will send this photograph back to me, worn and blanched and wrinkled. She will send it to let me know she hasn't forgotten, to remind me of her promise and to break her promise all at once, to both lie and tell the truth, simultaneously.

15.

For a long time—years, in fact—nothing happens, which makes me sometimes wonder about my sister. Before I leave home for college, she sends a letter to me, along with the photograph of us taken years before. In the letter she says horrible things. She speaks of doors opening in the middle of the night, marks left all over her body. She says so much that I have to skim over large portions of her words, skip entire passages, block out pieces of information.

These days I never read the letter, but I know exactly where it is, in the third drawer of my lingerie chest, buried under fishnets and garter belts, lacy bras and other things I don't often wear. That is where I keep my sister, and that is where I keep her words.

I have learned so much from my sister about the importance of walling myself off from the world, of keeping things inside. And I have been clever, in my own right. At twelve, I took up voodoo. I turned Goldilocks into a crone, magically. I practiced the evil eye. I could tell my sister: One inconsiderate look and I was at the needle, stitching away, making dolls from old scraps of clothing, spitting on the face. I was never labeled the favorite. No one ever called me Hunk, though my father, to this day, calls me a witch.

My parents are now very old, and they live alone without many friends. They never speak of my sister. Her name, like the clothes of the seventies, has fallen out of fashion. Each year, their house becomes darker and quieter, their reasons for celebration less.

If ever I mention my sister, on days when I am feeling brave or those days when I just need to remember or piece things together, my mother is always the one to say: There are two sides to every story. Your sister was smoking so much pot in those days; she was taking pills. She would run off in the middle of the night. You really don't even know the half of it, my mother says. You were too young to understand anything, so I don't appreciate your tone.

I do not tell my friend any of this, just as she rarely speaks about her brother, except in fragments.

16.

It is so unlikely that my sister will ever read this. It is so unlikely that if we ever passed on a crowded street she would turn her head in the smallest recognition.

Still, I hold entire conversations with her in my head. I could tell my friend this, but frankly, why should I? Like my mother, she would only arrive at too-quick answers. I am practically a lunatic with all my chatter. I am like Goldilocks on speed, held up in some abandoned building with a gun, trying to formulate a plan that will let me get to her. Because I sense that my sister needs me, that she is lost somewhere and hurt and in need of resuscitation. Only, to find her, I have to murder many people, and say things no one likes to hear, particularly in stories. What order could possibly come from such chaos, what happy ending? Already I hear the blazing sirens down the road, anticipate the disaster that is us, that wreck of my sister and me.

Sometimes I like to imagine that I bump into her somewhere, on a street or train, or in a coffee shop. She recognizes me immediately, even with my hair dyed jet black, even with all the angularity my body has taken on in recent years—hard edges around the chin and cheeks, arms that frequently cross when I am speaking. She recognizes that certain pout of my lips, that quality of sameness in us. I know you! she exclaims. I'd know you anywhere, you, oh you.

We sit down, at a table or in a nearby restaurant. Even though I have aged, my sister, miraculously, has not. She appears tall and her hair is still long and full of shine. I say: What have you been up to all these years? Start slowly, take your time. I've got all day. I've got forever for you, actually. You, I say, are forever in the present tense.

But my sister does not answer, as if she herself doesn't know what happened to all the time. I thought about calling, she says vaguely. I wrote you that letter, but you never responded. Alex said maybe you were frightened, but I told him you were so small—you were really just a baby—you probably blamed me for everything. It's good to see you don't.

No, I say. I never blamed you.

It seems as though she wants to touch me, perhaps my knee

or my shoulder, but she keeps her hands planted firmly on her lap. Only her body leans slightly forward. You held up pretty well, she says. I bet you're a real fighter; I can see it in your face.

Maybe, I say. But I'm not as brave as you. I do not know whether my sister has been brave or not, but it seems to me this is something you tell people you love who have been through a great ordeal and continue to live. I had it pretty easy, I say. The bears never got me. I moved far, far away. I also mastered the evil eye; it does wonders in a pinch.

Funny, she says.

I confess: Sometimes I try to write about you, but I can never make the words fit. I leave out entire passages and all the big moments. I keep abbreviating everything.

Then you lie, she says. About the bears.

I don't know, I say. It's true I have had to forget things. I do not tell my sister that part of this means forgetting about her at times, that part of this means having to let her go. It's amazing what you can live with, I tell her, if you just commit to it.

Oh, I know, my sister says. Then she says something a little stupid and hokey, something like: I understand you, really. You never have to explain to me. She leans forward and plants a tiny kiss on my cheek, one that is terribly light and breezy.

Thanks, I say. I needed that.

My sister leans back, smiles. You girls, she says, imitating Aunt Judy. Always making up stories, always living in a fantasy world.

Yeah, I say, imitating Aunt Judy back. Can't you ever come down from your clouds?

Then, suddenly, we laugh. Can I tell my sister how much I love her laughter, how much I've missed it? Or how much I've longed for her? In a few seconds, my sister will get up from the table and leave—magically, just like that, she will disappear—because that is also how my sister is: full of comings and goings. But for now we are both alive and well and laughing. We laugh to cover the silences, to cover the tears and all the years between us. If I strain, I can hear under our laughter the smallest fractures and sense the greatest losses, those spaces in us where nothing fits anymore.

ANTS

She wakes to an infestation. From beneath her bedroom window, ants have crawled in from the garden and formed a haphazard line along the lattice. For a while now, she's been watching them. She's been admiring their bodies, their threadbare legs, their groping antennas. Against the glass, the ants seem to form phrases: *Adsum. Ecce signum.*

Not so surprising, actually. Nothing surprises her anymore.

Look, she says when her husband, Paul, comes in from his office, pencil in hand. She says, Darley, the ants have learned Latin.

Paul frowns, ruining the superb line of his face. He asks if she's been playing with the morphine drip again. Once, after she'd first begun morphine, she believed she saw cockroaches scurrying down the walls. She screamed until her voice grew hoarse and her cheeks burned with tears. Afterward, she tried to joke to cover the terrible silence, to stop Paul from looking away. She said, No more Kafka, Darley. That's a promise.

But the ants—if not the roaches, if not the words—are real. That, she reasons, must be so, because Paul says, I'll get the spray.

She waves her free hand. What for, Darley? It's spring. It happens.

It's spring, she thinks, that makes everything worse, the aching inside her, the pain so sharp it feels as if a barracuda is nipping at her insides. And the infestations, the ants, they have happened in previous years, in previous springs. Last year, she pinched the ants between her thumb and index finger, one at a time, and felt like a god. But that was a different time. Things bothered her then: an unmade bed; dust on the table; a fine, graying hair out of place. Ants storming the house? What would the Mulhaneys, the Forbeses, the Walkers have thought when they arrived for Friday cocktails, all of them with their manicured fingers and pressed suits, their leather soles clicking against the floors? And what would Paul have thought? After being married for thirty-five years—good years, in which they raised their daughter, Rebecca, and taught her to enunciate when speaking in foreign countries—she still worried what Paul thought of her.

Back from the kitchen, Paul tucks the pencil behind his ear and sprays until the ants begin to fall from the window, disappearing below her line of vision. His silver-rimmed glasses gleam in the light like minnows flashing underwater. A fumy cloud drifts toward her.

It's dastardly, she says, or thinks she says. Just exactly the last thing this house needs.

Shhh, Paul says, raising a smooth finger. *Don't breathe.*

SHE DOES NOT FEAR the last breath, that slow draw of air, that raspy rattle. She does not want more sunsets, the dying ball of flame sinking below the horizon, nor has she wanted the pale-blue, too-expansive sky. She does not want Paul to confess his late nights, his extracurricular business meetings. She refuses to ponder the unfathomable world, the even more cruelly unfathomable God. Her mother once questioned too earnestly, and where, in the end, did that get her, lying on the floor, frothing at the mouth?

Paul goes out to the kitchen again, comes back carrying paper towels and Windex. He sprays a fine, vinegary mist over the glass and rubs until it squeaks. Everything about him—his high forehead, his thin, gray hair and sea-blue eyes—seems to shine in the bright morning light. When he finishes, he kisses her forehead, then leaves, and, within moments, he settles down at his drawing board next door. He is all business, all pencils, all protractors and blueprints. He is gone.

Left alone, she is willing to consider small details. A globe that rests on her nightstand, for example, the couple suspended in glass, their openmouthed laughter, their circular spin through iridescent snow that swirls when the globe is shaken. It's a gaudy thing, really, but still a gift from her sweet Rebecca, Rebecca at eight, all dark pigtails and ruddy, fat cheeks. She is willing to consider this room that Paul built for her. This space around her. The domed ceiling like a church, exposed oak rafters, large windows that filter too much light. The walls of the room are yellow. Flowers surround her. Daffodils border the white linen sheets. Orange-yellow trumpet flowers, morning glories twist and turn just outside the window. Wilting dandelions fill a gold-colored vase, a gift from the nurse who tended to her until Paul finally sent the nurse away. What was there to do? Thank God the nurse left the small dispenser. Thank God for her kind pity.

FOR A WHILE, he has been laughing. She has forgotten the sound, and it startles her. It begins low, in Paul's stomach. It rises and falls, then ascends again, finally choking out the stillness. Robert Mulhaney, Paul's partner at the firm, says, *What?* then he laughs, too. Since Paul has taken to working from home, Robert sometimes stops by during the week. Perhaps today is Tuesday. She often loses track. Time seems to slow, then stop altogether. It bends backward and forward. It speeds up, and she tries to catch it.

There, on the other side of the wall, Paul and Robert discuss blueprints for the new municipal building in the city. Robert will stop by her room before he leaves and she will pretend—as she always pretends when he stops by her room—that she is sleeping. He will turn, quietly, but for now there is laughter.

When was the last time she and Paul laughed like that? It had to have been on her fifty-eighth birthday, last year, when Paul surprised her with a cake. That morning he snuck into their room, nudged her awake. He wore a mischievous look. A dusting of flour powdered his forehead and cheeks. She said of the cake, Darley, *Pisa leans less.*

Such compliments, he said. Quiet, and make a wish.

Disastrous, she said. Wishes.

Money?

She swatted him with the morning paper.

World peace?

She pressed her index finger to the chocolate frosting, and Paul shooed her finger away.

Rebecca's success?

She has a job in D.C., she said. Soon she'll be president.

Fine, he told her, sighing. You're always so difficult. How about happiness, then?

We are happy, aren't we? She touched his arm, smiled playfully. Have you neglected to tell me something during all these years, Darley?

He set the cake on her bedside table. There was that affair with my ego, he said. I got successful and suddenly fell in love with myself.

Such vanity, she said. You're terribly vain. I don't know why I ever married a man better-looking than I am. He laughed, as did she.

If he knew, though, how unhappy she often was. If he knew those times she felt as though they were strangers, as though *she* were a stranger in her own life. If only Paul knew how much she'd grown to despise her teaching, to cringe when collgiate mouths massacred the language she loved: *mirabile dictu, meum et tuum.* And Rebecca. She couldn't count the times she spent resenting her daughter, resenting that Paul catered to Rebecca's every desire. If he knew, then perhaps he'd hate her. He'd hate that he'd married a woman who wanted to break the fine bone china, sabotage the parties with too much pepper, stand up from the dining room table and, in front of everyone, scream.

She screams now.

Paul rushes into the room. The silvery flash of minnows moves closer. She feels as though she could almost touch that light. The morphine drips slowly. One, two, three crystal drops, like melted snow. Behind Paul, in the doorway, Robert Mulhaney stares down at his shoes. What they must all talk about in private. What things they must say. Paul wears a look of exasperation she's often seen lately, a look that already eulogizes.

Stop that, she whispers.

What?

That look, Darley, she says. I hate it.

THE NEXT DAY the ants reach with their delicate legs and attach themselves to her covers. They crawl across the white blankets, climb the hills of her bony knees and stop at her chest. She lets the morphine drip from the dispenser.

Paul comes in from his office to check on her, just as he claims he comes in every hour to check on her. He surveys the window and says something under his breath, which she must strain to hear. He says, I'll get the spray.

Please, she says. No assault today.

He stares out the window. It's a fine day, really. There have been so many in a row. The purple lilacs are in bloom, the daylilies are open. All right, he says, bitterly. He adjusts his glasses. Rebecca called, he says. She sends her love, of course. She met a man in the city, a lawyer who she likes. I think it's good she has someone to talk to about everything.

How terribly useless to talk, she says, or seems to say. She looks for the ants, but they have disappeared from her blanket. They are so much quicker than she once thought, in those springs when she pinched them between her fingers. She wonders, vaguely, if this is how Kafka felt, destitute and alone with only the company of bugs.

Rebecca asked if you ever read the book she sent awhile back, Paul says.

Yes, she lies. She did try to read, of course, until the words blurred and seemed to move about on the page. Once, she read many kinds of books, books on Buddhism, Jainism, animism. Many -isms. But Rebecca had sent a book about cerebral functioning, with one page dog-eared that talked about firing synapses, those terrible spaces within the brain that create a final need for God. A parlor trick of the brain! And her daughter's inscription, that there was no need for a Bible when the science told us all we need to know of God. It occurred to her, then, that Rebecca hated her, that possibly she blamed her for being slightly overweight, for subjecting her to unnatural cruel hurts as a child—an impossible quest for perfection, Latin tutorials, a weaning from the nipple too soon. Who knows how many complaints the heart holds, quietly and forever?

Paul turns to face her now. *Every spring,* he says. He grabs a tissue and wipes the ants from the window. He throws the tissue away and sits down beside her. He says, You were talking to yourself again.

Was I? I thought I was praying. Her mother often prayed, though this is something she does not tell Paul. There is so much, in fact, that she won't say.

Have you forgotten you're an atheist? he asks. He lies down next to her. He lifts her hand, kisses each of her fingers. He says, Whether you realize it or not, I *do* love you, despite . . .

She breathes deeply, smells the coffee on his breath, notices a small mole just at the base of his neck, chafed from his shirt collar. In all their years of marriage, how did she never notice this mole? She is in love with it, with the small, humble shape of it, its dark color that seems to pull her toward it. I love you, too, she says.

Probably, she tells herself, she still does love Paul. He *is* a good man. He has taken care of her since the nurses went away.

He has simplified her as he would a building, removed her onyx ring, her gold necklace and watch. He has cleaned her hands, palm up, twisting her wedding ring around in his careful fingers. He has tended to her closings and openings. Cleaned her messes. He has laid her back on pressed sheets, stiff with starch, and tucked the covers around her. But when she is gone, Paul will remarry. Perhaps Laura Mulhaney, that tall imposing blonde, such a serious, studious woman, so right for him if she weren't already married. Paul needs the stability of marriage, she knows, just as he needs the frenzy of affairs.

You're tired, he says now.

No, she tells him.

The thing about sleep, he says, is that you have to let it in.

But I'm not tired, she says, or thinks she says. You're the one who's tired. Darley, you're the one who needs a rest.

HER MOTHER, lying on the bathroom floor like that. She was only ten then, and at first she thought her mother had slipped on the floor, hit her head. But the tub and floor were dry, the air cool, and her mother, she noticed, was frothing at the mouth like an animal. The slow, choking gurgle of fluid. Black and white tiles. Her mother's pale, uncovered arms. Then that terrible gagging. If only she'd thought to move toward her mother instead of stepping back. If only she'd placed her own hands inside her mother's mouth, cleared the obstruction. But of course there was no obstruction, only pills. Those white pills, their perfect round shape.

She ran outside instead and waited for her father to come home from work. She wore a pale-green dress that day, one which her mother had picked out for her, and as she sat on the concrete steps she counted the goose bumps that formed on her exposed legs. After a while, she got up and walked to the window box that was filled with pansies. From the box, she retrieved a nest. *A secret,* her mother had told her when they'd first found the nest in the weeks prior. *Such a secret under the flowers.* She sat Indian-style on the macadam, letting the ruffles of her dress fold between her thighs, and with a mason jar, she cracked open the blue eggs, crushed the featherless bodies, touched the closed eyes, the thin mucus that covered the birds' beaks. Then, ashamed, she buried the birds under the window box, dug the dirt up with her hands, ruined the border of hostas. When the sky grew dark, her father's car pulled into the driveway and she said nothing.

Perhaps, in the end, her mother was too light for everything. Perhaps she, too, floated through the parties, a slender-faced woman with pale eyes. Her mother's smile, her airy laughter, her high heels and flared dresses, what did all those things matter when she stood in the kitchen at night, choking back tears as she prepared dinner, as she pounded a slab of meat until it became paper thin? When her mother would call her to dinner, she would pause at the door, wait just a moment before speaking. What was under those pauses, those brief hesitations?

She never told Paul the truth about her mother, of course. She never would dare tell him about the birds, her own murderous ways. As she got older, she stopped thinking of what to say about any of it. She set out the candles on the dining room table instead, arranged the trays of fruit, and laughed when the Mulhaneys, the Forbeses, the Walkers stopped by to visit on Fridays. She sometimes drank too much. She said things like Delightful. She told Paul everything made her so, so happy.

Weeks, days, months, hours. She no longer knows how time passes, or cares. She feels far, very far away from everything, as if a part of her—whatever that part may be—is floating high above everything, separate from her body, her flesh. Paul comes and goes. Mostly, he stays on the other side of the wall. If she listens hard enough, she can almost hear him breathe.

Rebecca calls to talk about her engagements, and her lawyer friend and life in the city. She does not mention the brain, nor does she question whether her mother has, after all these years, found God. She doesn't dare say, *How are things, really?* She sends her love, as always, before hanging up.

Others come and go, too. The nurse visits, bringing more flowers. Sylvia Walker stops by, her coiffed hair smelling of hair spray and vanilla, her nails perfectly manicured and painted pink. Martha Forbes brings oranges and green, bitter apples, swollen pears, which, left uneaten, will turn brown and rot. Laura Mulhaney shakes the globe and watches as the iridescent snow falls. Then, when others have gathered around the bed, Laura stands at the window and complains of infestation. Doesn't Paul know they have spray to kill these things? she asks. She goes next door to see him. She is gone.

Her neighbor, Gladys, tells her to look for signs. Angels, she whispers. And sometimes parents, or an aunt or uncle, too. But there aren't any angels, or deceased relatives, only ants. They crawl up Gladys's arm and sit on her shoulder. Angels, she hears herself say, lying. She is certain she hears the small sound of laughter.

Sometime later, after everyone has left, Paul comes in to see her. Those silver lights about him. She has come to think of him as a giant fish.

You're quite right, he says. You always seem to be right, so I shouldn't find it surprising. Yes, he says, more to himself than to her. *Of course* I'm tired.

PERHAPS, ALL IN ALL, she's lived a fraudulent life. Maybe only time and not love held her and Paul together. Perhaps she floated through—through marriage, through Rebecca's tender gums, through the parties. Perhaps the Mulhaneys, the Forbeses, the Walkers despised her, after all. The wives certainly did. Didn't the women always flock to Paul, gravitate toward his sweet, supposedly innocent flirtations? Who knows what happened when people disappeared into bathrooms and empty hallways. Who knows what happened in this very room, atop fur-collared coats. Perhaps Friday cocktails, like Paul's uproarious laughter and affairs, only served to choke out the slow, crawling silence at the edge of their lives. But there it is, anyway and finally: They are all older. They are all, frankly, *old*. And Darley and his betrayals are, finally, the least of her problems. It's not one person who has forsaken her but something infinitely more frightening—her own body, time, the world itself.

And these details betray her, too, her own thoughts. They assault her, they overwhelm her and fit no pattern or meaning. One quick breath. One slow smile. Her mother's folded hands. A cracked egg, a bloody shell. Paul's silver-rimmed glasses. Iridescent snow, and the turning of a ring over and over. How is it possible that none of these things seems greater than the others? Perhaps in the end, there is too much commonality, after all.

Perhaps in the end, the ants, the angels, are all the same, weighted evenly. She wants to translate and uncover *everything*—the gestures, the complicated looks and layers of irony, the words, the spaces and silences in them. Such negative spaces.

She's been tardy in telling Paul all these things she's kept to herself, all these things she's wondered.

All these ants. It happens every spring. *Every spring.* At least, she thinks, there aren't roaches. The ants crawl from the window, attach themselves to the blankets, climb over her. There are hundreds, thousands, millions of ants.

She says, So soon?

Deo volente, they say. *Vocatus atque non vocatus deus aderit.*

Bidden or unbidden, God is present. She hears the sound of laughter, which rises in the air. She presses down on the dispenser. More and more ants cover her body. She opens her mouth for them, she closes her eyes. On her tongue, the ants feel so light.

Darley, she whispers from under everything, come quickly.

He is in the other room. She is certain she hears him breathing. She is certain she hears the slow working of air in and out of his lungs. She presses and presses again. Darley, she says. Come quickly. *I have so much to confess.*

SAVE MY SOUL

⊤ he story goes like this: Wednesday afternoon my neighbor, Mr. Gun-Metal, stops by my house. I should already
have a premonition, like this will be the beginning of the end,
but I don't yet, of course, because I am stupidly optimistic in my
own way, which, according to my husband, is not optimistic at
all.

With Gun-Metal, there is first a breach of boundaries that I
try to ignore: I didn't even invite him over—I am a stickler for
calling ahead, advanced planning, that sort of thing; I would
never be the type of person to *just stop by*. But here he is in my
kitchen, sitting across from me at the table, staring at me with
those gun-metal eyes. He rakes his hand over his crew cut, then
down to the sharp line of his jaw. It's midafternoon, my husband
is working and will be late, and my neighbor has already dipped

into a bottle of wine that cost me twenty-three dollars and that he says he doesn't even like. This is the setup, the basic scenario.

Today he tells me a story about a cow, which starts off innocently enough. I am happy to hear about cows, because I am weird that way; I like the occasional odd topic of conversation. And I grew up on a farm and have all sorts of cow stories that aren't really stories so much as vignettes—milking cows, chasing cows, birthing cows, that sort of thing.

She was an old cow, he tells me, setting the tone. She must have been hungry, he says; her ribs showed through, and the flies buzzed around her. She probably escaped from pasture to search for food. Came walking down the highway and into our neighborhood, he says. The nearest farm is, what, about three miles south? Can you believe she didn't get hit by a semi? That would have been a bloody mess.

I can believe it, I say, taking the cow's side. After all, cows aren't nearly as stupid as people think. Well, maybe they *are* stupid—you've probably heard all the bovine jokes—but they're hypersensitive, which makes them cautious. What color was she? I ask next.

You and cows, he says. What gives? And anyway, what does it matter?

Details, I say. It's about details.

That's not the point, he explains, as if he has this down.

Okay, I tell him. I'm beginning to feel a little tipsy, which generally makes me gregarious and *better* with people, but today it's hard to conceal my disappointment. I wanted to know the cow's color, and possibly also its breed. There are all sorts of cows, I want to say: red Angus and Butlers, Herefords and shorthorns, Texas longhorns, *et cetera*.

I let this all slide. So what is the point, then? I ask.

The point is, within seconds everyone in our neighborhood had out their guns, he says. Except you, you probably don't own a weapon; you probably don't have a single weapon in this house. I could kill you now if I wanted, he adds.

I have a butcher knife, I say, even though I've only ever used it to cut watermelon.

You know what you are? he asks. He doesn't wait for an answer. Says, You're a passive Yankee tree-hugger.

But why? I ask. Not about me being a tree-hugger and passive—both are mostly true—but about the guns, as in, *Why pull a gun on a cow?* What would be the point, I might ask. It's not as if the cow is going to rob your house or car. And *why,* because this is always my first question, and it's never a good question with which to start anything.

Why? he asks. What do you mean, *why?*

Why get out a gun as a first response? Why get out a gun at all? Was it like a cow militia, or something?

Maybe, he says. Regardless, you don't want to know the outcome.

Oh, I say. I think I really don't like where this is going.

Want to know who pulled the trigger?

No, I tell him. I don't.

I did, he tells me.

That's a surprise. So, I ask, what did the cow ever do to you, to warrant murder? The whole thing pains me, but I listen anyway. This is semi-true: It's a semi-true story.

He leans back in the chair, crosses his arms, and stretches his legs. Wouldn't get off my lawn, he says, as if the point were obvious. That cow was on my private property and eating my zoysia. He asks: Do you know how much I pay for zoysia? Do you know how much I pay for privacy these days?

I do, actually, because I am an insanely private person. Still, to kill a cow because it's eating grass? And what were my other gun-ready neighbors thinking, as they watched this massacre take place?

I look at Gun-Metal sternly. This is all very unsettling, I say.

He grins, rubs his hand over his jaw. You're easy to unsettle, he tells me.

I say nothing.

For the record, Mr. Gun-Metal and I aren't friends. I don't know why he stops by my house unannounced. I actually don't know much about my neighbor, either, short of the one story he likes to tell: He was a combat soldier and won a Purple Heart for pulling an injured man out of a Humvee after an explosion ripped the vehicle apart. He and his injured buddy hid in the upland region for several days, waiting to be rescued. His friend suffered from shell shock, so my neighbor held a gun to him the entire time, saying, *You make a sound, I swear I'll put a bullet in your head, fucker.*

He's looking at me. He pours another glass of wine.

So then? I say, though I don't want to know, not really.

So, nothing, he says, shrugging, and this is why I realize things are truly going to hell. There is no sense of consequence, no sense of an arc, no enlightened moment of change.

Nothing, he says again. *End of story.*

AUGUST HERE is a lot like July, which is a lot like June: balmy, ridiculously hot. I hate monotony. Everything is mostly brown or a blanched, brittle green, and a brush fire ignited today, several counties over from where we live, set on purpose by someone with a love of fire or with a gripe against trees, or both. The fire has been burning uncontrollably, sweeping across the hills and valleys, which are plentiful here. From the Home Depot, I can see the irritable smoke billowing in the distance like a fall-out cloud. Brush fires aren't typically common where I live, but we've been in a drought for what seems like thirty years. Everything is blanched and brittle, easy to ignite.

Most of the people at Home Depot are pleasantly benign enough, like those visitors to Disney World: They are dressed in colorful, tacky shorts and tank tops that make their tanned arms look flabby, and really the only thing they are missing is frozen, chocolate-covered bananas in their hands. Even though it's ninety-five degrees, even though it's more than sticky-humid, I wear jeans and long sleeves and sweat in brute defiance. I hold out my desperate hopefulness for cooler weather. Today, people mill about, picking out pampas grass and dahlias and primrose—*primrose,* such a fussy name and milky smell. People emerge from exits with mulch and fertilizer, and most of them smile. I always think: Everyone looks good at a distance, everyone.

My husband, aka Post-it Man, aka Harry, is a tall, wiry person. He's thirty-nine—three years older than I—and he has short blond hair, square glasses, and a sloped nose. At Home Depot we take on a divide-and-conquer mentality with tasks: He will seek out hostas, while I get cleaning supplies. I am wary about the hostas, and I say so. These days our garden isn't much of a garden at all. I tell him the ground won't keep anything past a week, but Harry tells me to think happy thoughts, like Tinkerbell. Then he kisses me before parting and I feel slightly condescended to, because even though my husband is smart, he's not smart enough to cover up the fact that he's having an affair. He works at an office—an office that sells staples and other office supplies. Harry practically lives in one of those tiny cubicles, one laden with sticky notes that have pithy sayings on them like, *Go to heaven for the climate, hell for the company.* I've often wondered if this statement is an indictment against corporate America, but most likely he put it up there to impress Boop. She likes to think of heaven and hell a lot; she's a heaven-and-hell sort of girl.

Tinkerbell, I say, absently now. I make a fluttering motion with my arms and then pull down the rim of my *Life Is Good* cap because de-Nile is not just a river in Egypt. Then I walk to aisle six, which is near to God and filled with cleaning fluids that we buy in bulk. I admit to my fondness for Clorox cleanup wipes. My husband has told me this—that I am *Clorox Clean Compulsive.*

I suppose this is his way of being cruel.

1. Passive tree-hugging people do not do well with confrontation.
2. I am a passive tree-hugging person.
3. I do not do well with confrontation.

Can I live with an affair, I wonder, toss it up to something that will pass? And after it passes, will it create in me renewal, a feeling of love's costly though resilient worth? I do not know the answer to this, but I do know the following: Right now I'd like to scream at Harry and pop him a good one, right in the nose, and I'd like to take a butter knife to Boop's heart and extract it slowly. Very slowly.

I GET SIDETRACKED at the Home Depot so easily, which is obvious and nothing new. I bypass the cleaning aisle when I see all the lumber. As with my bleach fascination, I also hold a strange devotion toward wood, all kinds—cypress and white pine and ash and birch and cherry and poplar. If I come back in another life, I'd like to be the sort of person who builds things. Or maybe I'll just say *Screw it* and come back as a lumberjack, increase my carbon debt, and go with the flow.

Usually people in this aisle are so into planning some major home renovation they barely bother to talk. Today, though, a husband and wife argue over stupid choices. The woman, a short-statured blonde in L.L. Bean, says, God, I hate you, Clyde. I can't *be-lieve* you'd prefer cherry over mahogany for the kitchen. Are you dim? she asks. She purses her lips. Her eyebrows furrowed, and her husband, well, he's standing there with a *Fuck you, chickie-babe* look.

I want to say, can't we all get along? Isn't Earth the right place for love? What I end up realizing, however, is that kitchen renovations must sometimes be a last-ditch effort to save a marriage. Like babies, but something you can later sell.

I hate when I overhear arguments because, as is often the case, other people's woes and heartaches often cause me to dwell more incessantly upon my own, and I find that too much introspection is bad. Thinking too long, feeling too much—neither of these things does me any good. So I concentrate on wood instead and my karmic future as a lumberjack. I slide a piece of balsa out from its holding frame and run my hand over the smooth surface in an admiring way, as if I'm stroking a lover.

A skinny kid in an orange smock catches me in this act, red-handed. He asks me if I need any help.

Well, I say. I'd like to build a house.

He grins. By yourself?

Okay, so what? I ask. It's true I am five feet tall with a small frame and dainty features, the kind of woman who surprises people by speaking more loudly than they might originally expect. But I have the crooked nose of my ancestors, and let me tell you something: *They* were a people who knew how to get a thing or two done. Anyway, I really would like to build a house.

A house, I repeat, as if he is stupid.

That's balsa wood, he says, and points in an accusing way.

Yes, and? I ask. I think, Here is a boy, a freckled-faced boy who, at eighteen, thinks he knows something about me and my capabilities. I wonder what *he'll* end up doing with his life that's so tremendously interesting. I think at this rate of interrogation he's likely to be a lawyer or go into marketing, like, welcome to *those* crowds.

Seriously, he says. Do you belong in this aisle?

I object to that, I say. Strike the question from the record.

THE PERSON I SUSPECT my husband's having an affair with is his cubicle neighbor. I call her Betty Boop behind her back, not only because she has implants and big blue eyes and cropped blond hair but also because there's something about her—about the situation with my husband—that, on a good day, I find vaguely cartoonish. They think they are very sly, have worked it out so that we are all "friends." Originally, back when he was courting her six months ago, my husband said he thought Boop and I would really hit it off. As if. And he said he had met and liked her husband, Mr. Narcolepsy, but I don't know why anyone would like Boop's husband, because he's really such a bore at the dinner table. You can be talking about metaphysics or the nutritional value of a pastry crust or infanticide—it hardly matters—one, two, three, he's down for the count and snoring. It's all so blatant, this affair situation, which is the one reason I hold out hope that maybe I'm misunderstanding, maybe I'm blowing things out of proportion and my husband and Boop aren't fucking at all. I'd like to be optimistic here: My husband and I have been married eight years, and that's eight years that should be worth something.

Later, while my husband plants hostas and sweats in the melting sun, Boop calls. I can go for a week or two without hearing from her, and then I suspect she and my husband are meeting in the hour after work ends, the one hour that is always unaccounted for.

Hi, Jen, she says. I've just missed you so much.

Hi, you, I say back. And I add: I bet!

Because I refuse to let her be the reason that my marriage ends, Boop and I plan another get-together, and then we make small talk for a few minutes, about her dog, China—I hate small dogs, and China is a Chihuahua, the worst kind of small dog— and about her husband, who fell asleep in church while standing up. Like that's a surprise, I say. But Boop is genuinely unsettled. People in the congregation said maybe the Spirit possesses him, she tells me. She adds, I don't know how to feel about that, I just don't. I asked him if he remembers anything after he comes through, and he tells me it's always the same dream, that he's falling, and right before he hits the ground, a force pushes him back up suddenly, into the air, and he's saved. Now, *usually* that happens when someone is nudging him awake, but now I think maybe there's more to it, like God is trying to speak through him.

Wow, I say, because I can hardly pretend to care.

Is Harry there? she asks then, too innocently. There's an important work file I need to talk to him about.

This is code, I suspect, for, *I really need a fuck.* Really? I ask. Working on the weekend?

I labor, she says, while other people just sit around.

I know what Boop probably thinks, that she labors and works in her cubicle and fucks my husband while I do nothing with my time; I hardly even cook dinner. Truly, I have been lazier than lazy of late. She's asked many times what exactly it *is* that I do, but I've been depressed about my job, and anyway it's difficult to explain. Not like I'm a spy or anything—it's not that glamorous, or even secretive. It's just hard to put into words, and words are one of the few mediums we have as humans; you can see how I'm screwed. I'm a writer, actually, and when I tell people that, they usually tell me they are, too. Okay, I tell them, shrugging. Why not?

Anyway, when my lack of a "real" job description doesn't make her happy, Boop openly questions why I haven't fulfilled my moral obligation of having children. I think she wishes I were fatter because she herself has something of a bottom, that round sort of plumpness that goes beyond the word *curvy.* All that space, that big house, and for what? she once asked me. Not even a cat to scoop up after.

So maybe I'll get a cat, I had told her. What's it to you?

After he gets off the phone with Boop, my husband says, Important account. She (meaning Boop) needs to meet to discuss the financials.

I lean back in the kitchen chair, regard him, and make light of the situation so that I don't cry. You sell paper clips, I tell him. How important can it be?

Paper clips, he tells me, hold a lot of things together. You'd be surprised.

You know what holds the economy together? I ask. Besides marriages? Walmart, I say. I'm thinking of getting a job there. A *real* job. At the Walmart. What do you think?

He grabs his car keys and scans the kitchen as if he's forgetting something, like us.

Hello! I say. I'd like to discuss job possibilities, new career starts, spiritual vocations. I pull out a chair. Take a load off for five minutes, I tell him.

No, he says. I don't have time to open that can of worms. But I think the blue smock would make you look sulky, he tells me. Besides, those people would eat you alive.

I consider this. Do you think, really? I ask, not about people—that is true: All those needs, all those long lines, all the senseless waiting. And shopping at all is a little like marriage, in that whatever you get never satisfies you completely. Still, the smock statement is a shocker because I think, somewhat conceitedly, that I could pull it off. Why not?

Walmart is another reason why we're up to our eyeballs in carbon debt, I remind him. I've calculated our personal impact on the environment, and it's not good.

So what else is new? he asks, but he is distracted because Boop is waiting, and now, despite myself, I do cry.

Jen, he says, and he stares at me too long. Are you okay?

I nod. Sure, why wouldn't I be?

He says nothing, fiddles with the keys.

Well, I say. Give Boop a big wet sloppy kiss for me.

He winces, and I suppose I am the one who is now being cruel.

I *DO* ACTUALLY HAVE a job. Mostly it involves sitting around all day, often for weeks at a time, and dreaming up weird narrative juxtapositions, which is exactly the charge that most people level against me when they say I have no job at all. Sometimes when I am bored with my job and my thoughts and myself I sit around and drink or watch reality television or, when I'm feeling old-school, play Pac-Man on my computer or watch Disney flicks. When I'm feeling new-school, I sit around and social-network all day, checking the feed and then checking it again, so that I can obsess about nothing at all until such nothingness eats away at the fringes of my life. Anyway, what I'm saying is that I am a person with a serious abundance of anxiety, which is also why I take walks regularly to get away from the downloadable entropy of my life.

There are about twenty houses in the neighborhood, sprawled out on winding roads that are lined with tall, straight pin oaks and long-leaf pines. A large lake reflects the evening light. Birds and frogs chatter, and geese float along the water's surface. Our house is a large three-story Victorian with balconies on each floor and dome-shaped windows that give the impression of eyes staring outward at the world. What could be better? my neighbors ask. Mr. Gun-Metal, who lives across the street from me, has said it's a veritable palace, though he then added that a Victorian, in these parts, is totally out of place.

Today, I bring in my neighbor Laurie's mail because she's on vacation. My neighbors often find chores for me to do. For them. It's a win-win scenario, they tell me, because it gets me out of my house and into another's. Here, I hold keys, so many keys it is almost its own occupation. I am like the janitorial custodian of the hood. I check to see if stoves have been left on, if garage doors absentmindedly remain open. I retrieve mail for vacationing couples, water the dying hydrangeas and wilted roses. I walk Labradors and Boxers, scrub algae from goldfish tanks, drop pellet after pellet into tanks that house hermit crabs. It's always a strange experience to be in another person's house when they are absent. What if I rummaged? Went through their pantries? Tried on their lingerie? Found all their sex toys and arranged them in a provocative manner? What if I were nosy and hunted around for their bank statements? Checked on their state of affairs? I don't do any of these things, of course. I do what I need to and get out. But the thought that I *could* do all this is alarming; the thought that there are no limits when no one is watching unsettles me, makes me distrust myself. A part of me would like to snoop. A part of me thinks there's probably a lot of good material in each home, there's probably a lot of deep, dark secrets and stories.

THE NEXT DAY, I watch the news after my husband leaves for work. Of course the fires are all the rage. Driven by recent winds, they burn uncontrollably. On television, entire forests incinerate before my eyes, animals flee and take cover. Three counties over there are evacuations taking place, declarations of emergency. It's always the same. One moment things can seem optimistically fine and tranquil—everything plunking along at a good pace, everyone happy, everything ordered—and then suddenly something happens and everything changes, something breaks or explodes or ignites, something fails to take hold, or someone dies. Disaster often strikes, sometimes in a big way, that's true, but more often, I think it's the little things that ruin us.

The phone rings. I'm dying, my father says.

When I hear the distance that six hundred miles can make, I want to get out my *Life Is Good* cap again, or think happy thoughts or wade in the murky waters of denial. Why, hello to you, too, I say. Because between my father and me, I am usually the chipper one.

You're home entirely too much, he tells me. I always expected that I'd die alone. Now I think when it happens I can phone you and at least that base is covered—at least I'll hear some voice calling out from the other end of the tunnel.

I'd come over right away, I tell him.

Yep, you'd be there in ten, he says jokingly—even though I haven't been home in over a year, and my father has never once visited my house. At his age travel is difficult. This saddens me because I'd like to know what my father thinks about my house. He is astute about things. I've often wondered how the space would feel to him, if he'd think it inviting or cold, if he'd sense that, in it, my husband and I occupy separate rooms—my office, his office, my workout space, his den. I would also like to know if my father would think it's a good house, in terms of floor plan and foundation, if it is a structure that can withstand the wear and tear of time.

The fires are on the news, he says. Even here in the cold country.

They're a few counties over, I say. I don't smell any smoke.

Don't be dense, he tells me. You don't have to smell smoke for there to be flames.

All right, I tell him. So, what's new with you?

Other than I'm dying?

I thought you were going to die last week, I tell him.

It's a process, he explains.

You're not dying, I say.

You always say that, he tells me. It makes me worry about you. Before I die, he adds, I'd like to understand what you do. The most I can surmise is that you sit around and think about things. Where's the *action* in that? By your age, he tells me, I had already built two houses.

I know, I say. You've mentioned that before.

Of course, he says, you work hard all your life and the bank gets everything anyway, the company goes belly up. Not for you, though, because I don't know if you work at all, so you wouldn't ever have to consider an actual pension. Your mother says I'm not supposed to pick on you. I'm not supposed to tell you I'm dying, either. She says you're too sensitive about things and blow everything out of proportion.

Oh? I say, and wonder if it's true—maybe it's just me. I *do* have a thing for weird juxtapositions. Once, when I was a young girl of maybe nine or ten, my father drove me and my mother to the coal region, to see the house in which he grew up. It was a real shithole of a house—a simple wooden structure with uneven clapboards and a rickety foundation. It was a real shithole of a town, too, though it wasn't as bad as the ghost town three towns over. Anyway, we were talking about the general decline of the area when a couple of boys came running down the street. They were chasing a calico kitten, pelting it with stones. My father ran the boys off. The kitten had a cut over its eye, the flesh split open like a blood orange. I wanted to take the animal home, but my mother wouldn't allow it. Later, I wrote a story about a cat that got trapped in an old house and died, all while a neighbor boy tried to get it out and save it—it was one of my "dark" tales.

Maybe I *am* too sensitive, I say now, to my father. Anyway, as for what I do, I'm thinking about getting a job at the Walmart.

I decide, secretly, that's something you don't have to explain.
People *understand* the Walmart.

You wouldn't last a day working there, he says, surprising
me. My father worked blue-collar jobs all his life. He even dug
graves, like in *Hamlet,* but never once found a skull to teach him
anything. He tells me, simply: You're not cut out for Walmart.

What am I cut out for, then? I ask.

No offense, honey, he tells me, but I've never been able to
figure that out. Anyway, I only called to tell you I'm practically
a goner.

Okay, I tell him. Goodbye. Call me back tomorrow or the
next day, if you're still breathing.

Will do, kid, he says. Keep an eye on the smoke.

I will, I say.

My father is very matter-of-fact about things.

We are very matter-of-fact together.

IT'S A FAMILIAR SCENARIO, one everyone has played out.
If I were trapped in a burning building, as well as my husband,
my father, and a fluffy little kitten, who would I save, my husband wants to know, and in what order?

Well, I say. We should really add Boop and Mr. Narcolepsy
to this scenario, too.

Why? he asks.

To make the choice of who to sacrifice first easier, I explain.

Right, he says, and smiles tensely.

It's evening and the news has been on for hours. Outside and
in, we pretend everything is tranquil, the quiet supper, the geese
floating along on the lake, the moon that is already rising. But
the news tells us otherwise, and it's hard sometimes to reconcile

the disparity. I break asparagus, throw the tips into a pot for steaming. The smell of swordfish fills the kitchen. My husband is of course doing the majority of the cooking.

A part of me would like to say I'd save the kitten first. And already I know I'd probably leave Boop to the flames. Mr. Narcolepsy can sleep through anything, so I don't worry very much about him. Between my husband and father it's difficult, because my husband is having an affair and my father and I aren't that close, but at least he's alarmingly honest. Finally, I'd hate to think I'd be the type of person to only think about self-preservation, but there you go: Maybe, if it came down to a real life-or-death situation, instinct would take over and I'd simply save myself.

My husband glances up from whisking a bowl of tahini, lime, and dill. Well? he asks. You're stalling.

I've never been involved in a life-or-death scenario, I tell him. Once, maybe. Once when I was younger. This is actually a true story. I worked at a prison to pay for my college tuition. It was a cold day in December, and a light snow fell. I was walking downtown on my lunch break, minding my own business, when a man jumped out the ninth floor of an old, historic hotel. First I heard a sound, a *swoosh,* and I thought that snow had perhaps released from an awning. For a moment, it was all very confusing, the sound, the odd feeling it gave me. But when I looked up I saw a man, free-falling through the air, coming down fast. I often think about that flight, and his inevitable fall. When he leapt from that great height, did the man have a brief moment when it seemed he might soar? Be somehow miraculously saved? Did he think the ground would wait, that it wouldn't swell up to greet him in all its hard, concrete dimensions, that he could hang in the air forever?

He landed, of course. Hard, so close to me that blood spattered on my high heels and stockings. It was the first time I'd ever heard so many bones breaking, all at once. No one this close up looks beautiful. Still, I bent over to help, reached for him. Sir, sir, I said, in a ridiculous way, as if he'd absentmindedly dropped a handkerchief and I was calling to him after having retrieved it. The blood pooled around him. The man lifted his head. I think about this moment so often. Before he died, did he see the face of a girl who, though squeamish, was desperate to help? Did he feel connection at the thought that someone— anyone—might reach for him? Sense that the world is not such a bad place after all? Did he regret everything?

My husband taps on the bowl. You're stalling, he says. This is a life-or-death scenario.

In life-or-death scenarios there are never really good options, I comment. Someone always ends up dead. Someone is bound to be lost in the flames. Boop, probably. As you say, there are sacrifices.

He says, You're tough. He leans over, kisses me gently. You know, he says, Boop has nothing on you, really.

Then, when his face changes, when he looks pensive, I add, Well, obviously, you'd be the first person I'd save.

THE NEXT DAY, Mr. Gun-Metal stops by. Eventually there are always complications to the basic scenario. For example: I'm starting to notice he only comes over when my husband is at work. Also, when I open the door, a smoky haze hangs in the distance and there is a distinct odor of burning wood. I can almost hear the cracking noise the oaks make before their trunks

split and fall, but I know that, at this distance, I am only imagining the sounds things make when they are falling.

He hands me a bottle of wine.

Are you flirting with me? I ask.

Believe it or not, he says, I don't even think you're pretty.

Oh, I say, disappointed.

Frankly, he adds, you have a very ugly nose.

I like my nose, I say. It's a character-building nose.

If you say so, he tells me.

In the kitchen, we sit in silence because neither Gun-Metal
nor I is terribly good at small talk. He pours me two glasses, as
if he's lazy and knows I drink quickly. Then he stares hard and
rakes his hand through his almost nonexistent hair. He tenses
his jaw.

And so? I ask.

Wasn't only a cow I killed, he says.

Oh? I say. Did you sacrifice a goat, too?

Killed a man once, he tells me, and suddenly everything
about the room, about our interaction, changes.

I clear my throat, stare at my hands. You're a combat soldier,
I remind him, as if he needs reminding. Lots of soldiers have
killed in the line of duty.

He looks at me intently. Wasn't like that, he tells me. And it
was after the war.

This is how it goes with Gun-Metal, then: Suddenly he is
talking about a night many years ago, and suddenly I am impli-
cated; I have to make a choice about whether I will sit here or
not and listen. I have to make a choice about whether or not I
think he's crazy. But here's the thing: Here's what makes me me,
that I would always listen to strangers when they disclose their

secrets, because I can't not listen—it's practically my job to gather up stories, like a spy gathers intelligence, except without all the snooping around.

He's looking at me now, with those flat metallic eyes.

Is this a confession? I try to joke.

On the street one night, he says. I was out on the West Coast, Seattle. It was a dark night, no moon. I hate those kinds of nights. There was a man walking. Some gangbanger, probably. He called me a motherfucker—just like that, called me a motherfucker!—and he shuffled around in his pocket. Probably had a gun. I still think that. And, anyway, I wasn't going to wait around to see. Pop, he says, pointing his index finger. End of that story.

I lean back in my chair. I know we're going to be here awhile. I think, somewhat absently, that I'll need a lot of wine, more than I have on hand, to hear this.

Sometimes, he tells me, I think I didn't care to wait and see, either. Just one less asshole to worry about. The thing is, he says, once you step across that line you can't go back, it's not about war anymore; it's about your soul.

Were you cleared of wrongdoing? I ask dumbly.

Would it matter? he asks. When there's two men standing there with guns, or even one man with a gun and one without, it's the one who's left that gets to tell the story.

You could have just told the truth, I say, though I'm unsure exactly what the truth is. You could have told them it was dark, you were confused, there was a fight, et cetera.

I might have, he says.

Did you? I ask. Did you tell?

I'm telling you, he says. Bet you want to know why, don't you? Bet that's the question floating around in that brain of yours. He grins then, crosses his arms. Because I could do it and I could walk away then, is why. Because shit just happens.

You're lying, I say.

He grins wider then, Gun-Metal does, which unsettles me even more. It's all a house of cards, he tells me. Truth and lies, combat and civilian life. *Civilian* life, he says again, as if he finds the entire notion amusing.

I CALL MY FATHER after my neighbor leaves. Hello, I say.

What's wrong? he asks.

Nothing, I tell him, even though I am shaking. Nothing at all, I repeat, as if I am in court and have been asked what exactly it was, as a witness, I saw happen.

Liar, he says. No offense, honey, but you couldn't tell a lie to save yourself, which is odd considering your line of "work."

I deflect. Anyway, I say. I've decided against working at the Walmart, because it smells funny, like plastic and popcorn, and that gives me the willies. Plus, I'm not sure I could greet people in a way that actually feels welcoming. So, I add, what's up with you?

I realized something about hell, my father says.

What about hell, I ask, thinking of Gun-Metal, whom I suddenly see burning up in flames, everything in him consumed by anger and hatred and fear. On the news there are burning forests, the fleeing animals running down hills. I think they are repeating the same coverage from before.

Hell, my father tells me, is repetition.

I agree.

I'm dying, he says.

I know you are, I tell him.

Now we're finally talking. You don't have to worry about me, he adds. I'm not afraid to die, you know. Try living for seventy years. That's the hard part.

WE PRAY.

We pray because of Boop and her husband, because they are over at our house and it's dinnertime and they both pray in public and in private, because they pray loudly and ask for the Lord's blessings. They are serious prayers. They proclaim their devotion to God, if not to each other, shouting it from the rooftops and flaming mountains and valleys. Since we last spoke, Mr. Narcolepsy has been asked to give an inspirational speech to his church congregation, on the subject of slumber and God. He zonked out halfway through it, and everyone was very impressed.

I'm not religious, Boop, if you want to know the truth, I say. I really hate holding everyone's hands at the table, I add, because I end up thinking about germs afterward.

It's Harry who gives me that look, the kind that says, We should be nice to guests, the kind of look that says, *Fuck you, Chickie babe.*

I mean, I continue, it's not that I don't appreciate your hard-core religious ideology. You Baptists really have that down. I wish there were some cult I could belong to, too, of true believerism, like the Temple of the Anxious or something like that, a place where people don't pray but sit around talking about how nervous everything makes them—public spaces, plastic cups, old-school paper versus electronics, that sort of thing. Then, at this temple, when one of us would get too old and die, we wouldn't go to heaven but would just come into another form, like a cow or something sacred and good.

Boop ignores this and folds her hands tightly, for once keeping them to herself. She prays for the sinners of this great big world. She prays for deliverance from the fires.

The brush fires? I ask, interrupting.

Hell, she tells me and scowls.

But hell is a very distant, abstract thing, and the brush fire is currently only one county away from us. The winds are blowing east, though, so we are supposed to be in the clear. Still, I think of all those poor people who have been displaced from their homes, and all the lost furniture and pictures and sentimental things. I tell Boop, Someone should wake Mr. Narcolepsy, because he misses everything, because he's fallen asleep with a fondue skewer in his hand. I'm worried he'll impale himself, I say.

Oh, she says, as if she hasn't noticed him there, slouched over so that his balding, shining head greets us in a sad, sort of empty way. He looks so innocent when he sleeps. I regard him, thinking that sleep like that must be a blissful thing, all in all.

You know, Boop says, I just can't believe you haven't *found* your home in God yet. The idea of a *cult*? she asks, indignantly.

My home in God. I think about this. I don't know if I ever felt at home, anywhere, really. Once, I thought my home was with Harry. Well, I say, feeling angrier than I usually do. I don't know about God, I tell her. I pick up two clean skewers and hand one to Boop and one to my husband. But I think I found the two *screwers!!!!!!!!!!!!!!!!!!!!!!*

Boop glares at my husband.

He frowns and shrugs at Boop apologetically. Maybe, my husband says, we should call it an early night.

1. Everything built must eventually collapse.
2. All houses are built.
3. All houses must eventually collapse.

I didn't want things to break apart. I wanted everything in my life to hold together—my marriage, my various houses. I wanted, in a way, happiness, a life free from disasters. But after Boop and her husband leave, and while Harry and I ready ourselves for bed, I realize something and say it. It's over, I say. You know that, don't you?

He stops brushing his teeth for a moment and regards me. Us? he says, in a flat, resigned way. I know.

I decide I can pick myself up, pick up the pieces and start over again. My father is right. Everything is repetition.

IT'S THE MIDDLE of the night when the house alarm sounds. The winds have changed direction; the fire is at our front door. Right, I know, like you couldn't have seen this coming, the flames, the smoke, the burning structure. But once it's here, I'm surprised by how quickly it consumes things, how it makes the wooden floors creak and crackle and buckle. The fire swoops up the steps, consumes the railings and furniture and spare bed on the second floor. It ignites my paperwork. It burns all my books, my Tolstoy and Dickens and Alexie and Russo, my Pynchon and DeLillo and Roth, my Updike. The photo albums burn to nothing, the newspapers and magazines. And then there's the noise fire makes when it mixes with wind, the howling of it as it tears through the rooms.

Our bedroom is on the third floor, and there is only one exit that's feasible: the balcony. Dressed in his pajamas, my husband motions me outside, where the smoke and flames billow up, around us. We climb up on the balcony. Across the street, Gun-Metal's house is already in flames—an inferno that reminds me not of hell but words. Sirens sound in the distance, the fire trucks traveling here, right now. There is no choice but to jump—jump or die, believe that the landing won't be entirely too hard, that there is such a thing as being saved. The heat pounds my back, singes the hairs on my arms. Beneath me, floorboards buckle. My feet burn. I look down into the smoke and flames and calculate my odds.

MORTY, EL MORTO

—————

Morty Langly awoke to find the December chill edging against his blanket. In the dawning light a heavy snow fell, the first snow of the season. He peered out the window to the cars parked along the eerily quiet street. The snowdrifts bunched up against the tires, a sight that surely meant reprieves were to come: Sister Deuteronomy's religion test postponed and Sister Agatha's obnoxious crooning of *The Canterbury Tales* ceased for a time, thank Jesus. For the past three days, the old nun had waddled to the front of the class, cleared her throat, and in a voice that belied her heft, begun, *"Wan that Aprill with his shoures soote"*; she then proceeded, as Aggie Tuft remarked, to massacre Middle English until the dismissal bell sounded. Aggie was what the boys in the eighth-grade class referred to as a *brainiac,* and so Morty supposed she was right about Sister Agatha's pronunciation, though each day he didn't think about the nun's language so much as what Sister Agatha must look like naked—her blubbery skin, her torpedo breasts.

Ice pinged against the glass. Morty writhed down, under the covers. He envisioned the Wife of Bath, her depiction brought to life in his textbook—her dress hiked up along her gartered thighs, her bosom thrust forward. Even the mole on her cheek was enough to give half the boys at Our Lady of Perpetual Help (aka Our Lady of Perpetual Misery) an erection, particularly those without access to *Playboy*s or those with parental locks on Internet porn. In gym, even Eric Brumble had recently confessed to working up quite a sweat over the lusty babe, though the boys also suspected that Sister Agatha had no intention of ever reading the Wife's tale, because at the end of each class she would inform them all that they would *begin again tomorrow,* and everyone soon discovered this only meant starting over at the prologue, with *Wan that Aprill . . . ,* the Wife's tale forever out of the boys' collective grasp.

The snow swirled and whipped around, and Morty's thoughts flitted about. He wanted to jiggle off. The act (THE act) seemed to necessitate blankets. It was difficult to be chaste at 6:37 in the morning, he realized, though he also reminded himself that if his mother could see him now, she'd surely be disappointed. Thinking this, he turned his attention to the image of the Virgin Mary taped up on his wall. She appeared in miniature, her face serene, her arms outstretched, as if to hold him. He might have said a prayer—there was a time he loved to pray; there was a time he loved to wonder about God and heaven—but instead he imagined the silk falling from the Virgin's shoulders, her fair skin and perfect, holy nipples. His hands fidgeted then and instead of folding them in supplication, Morty spit into his right palm and cupped his hand over his flesh. He hoped, in a vain, desperate way, that God was a late riser on snowy days, such as this, though he secretly feared it was possible that God and all the saints and mothers in heaven saw every small and large sin committed on earth. Jiggling off to the Virgin, he reasoned, was surely blasphemy of the highest order. And yet.

Ashamed, he closed his eyes and moved his hand, *faster, faster, faster,* until the friction heightened and guilt and pleasure tangled in complicated ways. His breath quickened. On the day of Judgment he'd be cast down to hell for all this, he just knew it, and there he'd suffer through fires, and there in hell would be countless nude virgins lying supine, legs spread, and every time Morty would look in any direction, some demon would thrust a poker into his side. Or worse! He moved faster and faster, aware of his breaths, aware of the cold and icy snow and the otherwise consuming silence. *Faster and faster and . . .*

He opened his eyes and waited for God to level His wrath, but ten minutes passed and Morty yawned, waiting. The alarm sounded, and he decided that, on that note, it was time to get out of bed.

"THE GIG IS CANCELED," Morty's father announced when, with cereal in hand, Morty sat down at the kitchen table. Morty Sr. was a big, hulking man, a man who because of his height tended toward a lumbering, awkward appearance even on those rare occasions when he wore a suit. Today he was dressed in jeans and a long-worn and faded flannel, which were his more typical attire. At the table, he brooded over his coffee cup as if it demanded considerable contemplation. He glanced up briefly. "I'm glad the gig is off," he said. "Aren't you? They're saying we're in for a blizzard."

"Heck, yes, I'm glad," Morty said. "Test today. Never a better time for the gig to be called off."

Morty Sr. nodded and sipped his coffee. *The gig* was a leftover phrase from when his father drove eighteen-wheelers across country, in those days when his father wore a perpetual smug grin for being the driver with the most miles under his belt. That was before Morty and his mother were in the car accident last winter, before his mother was killed, and before Morty stopped speaking for a month. After all that occurred, Morty Sr. quit his job so that he could work closer to home. "In case you need me," he had told Morty. Increasingly, neither spoke of Morty's mother and often the boy had difficulty remembering the simplest things: his mother's face when she told a story, or the sound of her voice at night when she'd crack open the door and ask Morty if he'd said his prayers. Memories reduced to fragments; even Morty sensed it. And it was the things you took for granted that often became the things you missed most.

These days both Morty and his father were under the auspices and good graces of the nuns at Our Lady of Perpetual Misery and of Father Bastian, especially, who had seen fit to give Morty's father a job at school and also waive Morty's tuition for a time. Both developments left Morty embarrassed beyond words, a humiliation that only intensified when his father was actually *seen* in the halls, sweeping or emptying trash, or when—on the two occasions his father was persuaded to receive penance, even though he had refused since the funeral to step foot in church—Father Bastian walked over to school and crammed himself into the janitorial closet, both men sitting on overturned buckets, Morty Sr.'s crying heard from behind the closed door.

Now he and his father sat in silence while Morty ate his cereal. It was the boy who finally spoke again.

"Yep," he said, and he drummed his fingers on the table. "A test."

Morty Sr. took another swig of coffee. "So what test didn't you study for, anyway?"

Morty shrugged. "Just religion."

"How do you test *that*?"

"The usual. You know, like the choirs of angels—seraphim and cherubim and thrones and stuff like that. If it's in the Bible, it's fair game. That's what Sister Deuteronomy says, 'Fact, not fiction, my little chickens.'"

His father rolled his eyes. "Great," he said. "A flipping fundamentalist." He looked at Morty for a moment too long, and Morty wondered what his father was thinking about. Still, Morty sensed that the conversation, such as it was, was over, even though generally speaking, the lucid hours of morning were the best time to talk to his father at all. Lately, trying to have any conversation with his father proved as difficult as trying to talk to heaven: full of impossible silences. He missed the days when his father would crack jokes about priests and rabbis and monks screwing in lightbulbs and his mother would slap him playfully and tell him to *stop,* or days when his mother would cook a large breakfast and they'd eat so much that she'd hold her belly. "Well," she'd say when she finally got up from the table. "I guess I'll try and stand for Jesus." And Morty's father would joke that she'd stand or fall, for sure. "All depends on what you believe," he'd say.

In Morty's house, a well-kept two-story duplex on the east side of town, there had often been, over the years, dissenting opinions regarding issues of faith and fate. His mother had come from a long line of God-fearing souls, those who attended mass not only every Sunday and Holy Day of Obligation but also the occasional Wednesday, hump-day, service. If his mother would have had her way, had it not caused the first fight of her and Morty Sr.'s marriage so long ago, she would have wanted her boy to be named Matthew or John, men who were in God's grace and names that ensured, in her Irish way of thinking, that young Morty would not only be blessed but also lucky. Morty's father, however, believed a person made his own fate. He'd descended from a long line of miners, those who worked the bowels of the earth and who were born with nothing and died with nothing. Morty Sr. often said he'd eluded *that* particular sentence by choosing to drive across the country. It was a job that, for him, was proof a man made his own fortune. Anyway, such disparate views collided in the birth of young Morty, to the point where the boy remained nameless for three days and even the nurses had privately waged bets on the outcome. Morty was finally given a name that was seen as a compromise by his parents, but one that proved to be a curse of grade school, ensuring that he'd spend years being dubbed *Morty the Morbid; Morty the Mortician; Hey, Morty, El Morto;* and for those with a less developed sense of word play, just *Mort-y,* said with a face. It was Aggie Tuft who first started the name-calling years before on the playground—smart-ass Aggie, whom Morty did not have a crush on and whom he only once imagined naked. It was a brief fantasy that triggered a sneezing fit during fourth-period algebra class.

LATER, THEY SHOVELED the steps and front walk and Morty watched as his father, red-faced, dug into the ice-crusted snow. When he stopped to rest, his father squinted blindly up at the sky and cursed under his breath. "Snow, Morty," he said. "Unlike your religion, you can test snow, test the roads, the tread on tires. I don't know what your mother was thinking taking you out that day."

"I know," Morty answered. He wiped his brow. He scraped the last of the snow from the bottom porch step, but a moment later it was dusted again. His jeans were soaked. The wind bit into him, and he pulled his skullcap over his ears.

His father waved him off. "I got the rest," he said. "No worries."

Morty nodded to his father before climbing the drifts in the yard. With every step his feet sunk deep into the snow. He walked unsteadily to the back of the house and retrieved his sled from the shed. He dragged it past the duplexes where dogs had already yellowed the snow around the shrubs and trees, past the brick houses that sprung up a few bocks later, and past the tree-lined streets that led to Main, where the large houses each had antique lamplights and wreaths hung on the doors. A plow drove by, scraping snow and ice and spewing salt out its back end. Morty smelled exhaust. Beyond that, the streets were still empty, the sidewalks slick in places, despite being salted.

"Morty, El Morto!"

He turned. Of course it was Aggie Tuft. She sprinted down the front steps of her house. Her plastic sled bounced behind her. Her checkered coat flipped open, and, under a red beret, her dark hair fluttered about. Before this moment, Morty was concentrating on the snow, how the cold hurt his lungs when he breathed, how the snow filled the sky, and how, each time he looked up, everything was so white it blinded him. Before this moment, he was trying to remember what his mother had worn the day of the accident; he was trying to remember what errand they had to run that seemed so pressing. But now as Aggie neared him, she blinked back snowflakes, and he thought only of how dark her lashes were, and how they made her blue irises more pronounced. Morty suddenly felt underdressed without Our Lady of Perpetual Misery's standard slacks and shirt. He pushed a piece of polyester fill back into the tear at his elbow and hoped Aggie wouldn't notice.

"What are you doing?" she asked.

"What do you think?"

She didn't answer. She ran from him instead. Her boots scrunched the snow, her own grip on the ground noticeably shaky. "Can't catch me, El Morto," she taunted, glancing back.

"Smartass!" But despite himself, Morty ran after her. He pulled his sled harder, ran faster. Sweat formed under his coat. The wind stung his face. When, a half-block later, he finally passed Aggie, he tapped her shoulder and grinned feverishly, revealing the gap between his teeth. He stopped at the intersection, even though the sign read WALK.

"Loser," he said, when, breathless, Aggie caught up to him. He looked away, determined to ignore her.

"I never said it was a race, *El Morto*."

"It never is when you lose it." He turned toward her then and noticed how her cheeks, which were pale even in the springtime, had bloomed berry splotches. He shifted his weight from one foot to the other. He tried to think of something to say, but what? "No religion test," he declared finally, though he seldom studied and still did well. "No Sister Agatha today, either."

"God, I wish she'd just *die*," Aggie moaned. "'*A Knyght ther was, and that a worthy man . . .*' She's like an assault on my *brain*."

Morty didn't believe Aggie's Middle English sounded any better than Sister Agatha's, really, but he let the point slide. When the light turned, they walked.

"That's just about the oldest wooden sled I've ever seen. In. My. Life," Aggie said. She brushed a strand of wet hair from her cheek. "My sled is brand new, 'state-of-the-art engineering,' my dad says. The circular shape decreases drag and makes it go faster, the plastic keeps it light and aerodynamic. My dad would know, of course, because *he's* an engineer."

It was this facetiousness that made Morty hate Aggie, and why last week, in Sister Biology's class, he'd thrown a frog at Aggie and then watched as its rubbery body landed directly in her lap, causing her to scream and making the class bubble up with laughter. Did he regret that action? Did he regret her tears, her yelling that it *wasn't funny*? When he heard her brag like this, he didn't regret any cruelty inflicted on Aggie Tuft, at all. This was true despite the fact that Sister Biology had chastised him, reminding Morty that every creature, large and small, was a creature of God, and she added that each frog cost the school four dollars and that was four dollars *he* wasn't paying.

"An engineer. So?" Morty hocked a loogie into the snow. He grinned, happy with both its speed and distance.

"Oh, really juvenile," Aggie said. "If I spit like that my dad would have an absolute conniption."

"You couldn't spit like that if you tried," Morty said. "And like your dad would care. Isn't he away all the time? I bet he never talks to you about *velocity* and *aerodynamics*. I bet you don't understand what any of that actually means."

Aggie shot him a look that was very similar to the one issued after the frog incident—indignant, the start of tears visible. Her face grew redder. "My *dad* works for NASA, I'll have you know. He does very important and highly classified experiments, ones that you and your dad couldn't even comprehend."

"Really? Well, you know what they say about engineers, don't you?"

"No, what do they say about engineers, *Mort-y*?" She made a face.

Morty had absolutely no idea what people said about engineers. He wanted to crack a joke about how they couldn't even change a lightbulb, but all he could think of was what his mother had said after meeting the Tufts at a school function: That Aggie's mother seemed like the type of woman who put up with a lot of shenanigans, and Aggie's father seemed exactly like the type of man who slept around a lot. "A nice man, but all that polish," she told Morty Sr., speaking not only of Mr. Tuft's hair but also of his demeanor. "Ssss-lick."

"I figured you wouldn't have a comeback," Aggie said. "You with your half wit."

"Oh, I do," Morty assured her. "Engineers are slick."

"Slick? *Slick?* What does that even mean?"

"Oh, I'd tell you. But I don't want to make you cry."

"Right, like your father does," Aggie said smugly.

Morty resisted the urge to punch her then. He would have tackled her if she were a boy, but he refrained. If she weren't a lady, he thought. Not that Aggie Tuft was a lady, mind you, by any stretch, but still. He reached down, scooped up snow, and packed it into a ball. He threw it at Aggie but she dodged it.

They crossed the street. At the school Aggie continued: "You know, even if I'd wait a year for you, you wouldn't have a *good* comeback. So typical of boys, really. If you'd spend more time thinking and less time playing with yourselves, your brains wouldn't freeze up on you all the time."

"Right," Morty said. "You don't know what you're even talking about."

Aggie raised her eyebrows. "Really? Oh, p-lease, like we all can't hear you. If any of you boys knew how to whisper in gym class it would be a miracle." They were approaching the church now, with its old stone exterior and wide steps, its large, beveled window that formed the image of the Virgin, etched in pink and blue glass. "A MIRACLE!" Aggie exclaimed. She held both arms up in the air.

"Indeed!" Father Bastian said when he stepped outside from the church's vestibule. He looked to Morty like an old Irish immigrant bundled up in his black coat, a fur derby hiding most of his thick white hair and bushy eyebrows. "It is beautiful," Father Bastian agreed. "And it makes me so proud that the students of Our Lady of Perpetual Help like to discuss miracles, even on their day off from school."

Aggie stopped long enough to *tsk* this. She brushed snow from her coat sleeves. "Not the kind of miracles that Jesus likes, that's for sure."

"Is that so?" Father Bastian asked.

"Trust me," Aggie said. She squinted at Morty and smiled. He shot her a dirty look. "Anyway, we were just saying . . . we were just talking about . . . *Morty* was just saying how he wishes school would be canceled tomorrow, too, so we could have a long weekend. I was telling him, Father, that I'd *hate* to miss Sister Agatha's English class."

Father Bastian nodded. He rocked back and forth slightly, as if he were considering the merits of Aggie's statement. He ran a gloved hand over his face. "And does Sister Agatha inspire *you* to such adoration, Morty?"

"I guess," Morty said. "In her own way."

"Well, I love the snow days, myself," Father Bastian replied, looking around in an amused, thoughtful way. "As for school tomorrow, I'll put in a word upstairs. But the nuns hold a lot of sway up there, too, and if Sister Agatha has it in mind to read from *The Canterbury Tales* tomorrow, I doubt even the heavens could stop her."

WHEN THEY ARRIVED at what the students at Our Lady of Perpetual Misery referred to as Camel Toe Hill, with its dimpled impression at the peak, Aggie didn't want to be bothered with Morty at all. She ran off when she saw her two best friends, the two Marias. They stood by the cemetery wall, talking. Both were blond and stocky, though one Maria now had breasts that Morty fantasized about grabbing whenever she walked by him. "Brand new," Morty heard Aggie say, and he caught the gist again of state-of-the-art engineering.

The snow pounded down, obliterating the line between the earth and sky. Morty climbed the hill. He headed toward the long line of trees that stretched over the hillcrest, interrupting the monotonous whiteness. He could barely make out the blurred shapes of other students as they ran in the distance. He heard muffled shouts, taunts, laughter. There were at least twenty students from Our Lady who hurtled down the hill, screaming as they whizzed by and veered off in various directions, toward the right, where the hill leveled out in a benign way, or toward the left, where the slope was steeper and the path longer, the walk back up the hill backbreaking and where, on the way down, you'd have to maneuver over several moguls before stalling out at the cemetery wall that rose between the convent and the rectory.

When he reached the summit, Morty blinked hard. He studied the terrain, trying to figure out how to best execute his run. Eric Brumble and John Warner called to him from the woods. When Morty turned, he saw them marching out of the brush. They were both flushed. Eric wore a peacoat and high boots. He punched at the air in a playful, defiant way. John followed, his face so obscured by a scarf that only his glasses were visible. Both grabbed the sleds they had abandoned under the tree. "I got bets on getting down first," Eric yelled, and he hopped on his racer. John followed suit, as did Morty. He cut a new path. The cold punched Morty as he picked up speed. The wind tunneled through his coat. He lowered his head to shield his face from the ice. Halfway down the hill he veered left, toward the cemetery wall. He hit one good bump, and two, and three. The sled lifted in the air, came down hard. He veered left again, toward the grassy area where icy yellow stalks pushed through the snow and cushioned his sled's speed. Victorious, Eric was already waiting at the bottom. John followed behind both boys. "I knew I'd win!" Eric exclaimed. "Beat your asses."

"Head start," Morty said. "Rematch!" Breathless, they ran up the hill and then raced down again. After more than an hour passed, Eric, bored and exhausted from the climb, started a snowball fight that sent all three boys scattering into the woods. They pummeled one another's backs and legs. They hit tree trunks. The wind loosened the snow from the branches and sent it swirling down around them.

Finally, Eric said, "Come on, Morty. There's more to do than this. I've got something for you to see."

"Show him, Eric," John said.

"I'll show him," Eric said, motioning. He led the way along a trail already thick with footprints. He snapped low twigs and branches. When they reached a dense area of brush, Eric pulled out a *Playboy* that he had stuffed inside his jacket. The pages were damp and wrinkled from the snow. John pushed his glasses higher on his nose and smacked his mittened hands together. Eric paged through the magazine, while Morty and John huddled close, staring at photographs of naked women. "Holy shit!" John mused. "I'd do that one."

"Hell, yeah," Eric agreed. He pointed out those women he thought had perfect bodies, and Morty, his heart racing, his cheeks flushed in an embarrassed way, agreed. The boys discussed *melons* and *puckers* and *fun bags, bare pussies* and *hairy monsters.* "I can't wait to do it," Eric said, though Morty sensed it would be a long time coming. He shivered, balled his fingers together for warmth. He noticed the snow, dirtied from his boots.

"Look at that one!" John exclaimed, stopping Eric's paging. "Oh yeah, I'd do that."

"Me, too," Morty said, though he was beginning to feel ashamed, dirty, even, like he did in gym class when all the boys measured themselves to see whose pecker was the longest. There were some things that were best left to the privacy of one's bedroom, he thought, and he wondered if, when he returned home, he should say a rosary or pray to the statue of the Holy Family that he had stored in the closet after his mother's funeral. His mother would be so disappointed in him if she could see him now, gawking over these women. Once, last year, when his jiggling off had begun in all its complicated rigor, she'd found some nude photographs that Morty had printed off the Web. "Morty," she'd said disappointedly. His mother was a modest woman, all in all, and she was sensitive about things pertaining to sex. She sat down on the edge of his bed and held the pages he'd printed. To his embarrassment, she leafed through them, and then she looked out the window for a long time and was silent. "I'll have to talk to your father about this when he gets back from his trip," she said finally. But before such a discussion could occur, she and Morty were in the accident—the icy roads, the metal guardrail. Thinking about this and studying the *Playboy*, something came over Morty unexpectedly, something confusing and sad.

"How about her, Morty?" Eric asked. He licked his lips suggestively.

"Ah, they aren't that great," Morty told him. "I've seen better."

"Sure you have," Eric said.

"Sure," John chimed in. "Whatever, *Mort-y*."

"I'd whack off to this brunette," Eric added. "Hey, bet I could get off faster than either of you could, to this hot tamale right here."

"I'd get off faster," John says. "My pecker is bigger than yours."

"The hell it is," Eric replied.

"Well, I'm not freezing my pecker off," Morty said. He wanted to leave. "My hands are numb. I'm heading home."

"Suit yourself," John told him.

"Wuss," Eric called.

Morty flipped them the bird and walked through the woods. He was thinking about the photographs, of course, and desperately wishing his erection away. When he reached the clearing and grabbed his sled, Aggie Tuft was there, standing, surveying the hill. The two Marias were gone. Morty called to her and she turned and waved him on.

"I was wondering where you were," she said. She pushed away hair that whipped in her face and hopped onto her sled. She sat, cross-legged, before catapulting herself forward. "Can't catch me, Morty!"

Morty ran after her, set his sled down, and leapt onto his racer. The waxed blades caught in the icy snow at first but quickly gained speed. He propelled himself toward Aggie. He thought, fleetingly, that her sled wasn't so fast, not as fast as his old wooden one. There was something about it all that thrilled him—the snow whipping about, the cold air, the knowledge that somewhere ahead of him Aggie was there, at first a blur against the whiteness but then gradually sharper in his line of vision as he neared, her red beret, her checkered coat.

Morty felt, at this point, not a terrible tension in his arms and legs but only the cold wind, the blades atop the ice. He gained more speed and approached Aggie's right. She turned. A flash of nervous, excited energy came across her face. He thought, I've got you now, and Aggie yelled to her own sled, "Faster, faster, faster." He reached out and pushed her, hard, as he might push Eric or John when they roughhoused. Her sled wobbled, and, off balance, she hit a mogul hard before she veered left again, not toward the grassy area at all. Her sled seemed to fly in the air and Aggie moved faster and faster, until it was obvious to Morty that she wouldn't be able to steer away from the cemetery wall, and he imagined the unevenness of the wall and the unyielding quality of it, and how he couldn't do anything to save Aggie from hitting the wall, hitting it hard, slamming into it and catapulting forward. Aggie was blurry again by now, lost in the whiteness, her dark hair whipping around her. Her red beret flew from her head as she disappeared over a bumpy crest, and then Morty heard her scream. He raced past the beret, and he swore for a moment it was a puddle of blood, blood and not wool, and that if he touched it, it wouldn't be soft, but warm and tacky. His muscles tensed. He felt as if his heart might explode in his chest. His eyes welled up, though Morty was a boy who seldom cried.

When he reached the bottom of the hill, he crawled to a stop. He dismounted and ran, breathless, to where Aggie was lying on the ground. Snow dusted her dark hair, making her appear suddenly older. A few feet away, her sled had smashed into the wall and now was upright, pushed against it. The remaining children from Our Lady were off at some distance—he could hear them somewhere in the swirls of whiteness, but when he went to call out for help, his mouth was too dry for him to yell. He fell to his knees. He pushed Aggie's shoulder. "Get up," he said, softly, lifting her arm, but it was heavy and fell as soon as he released it. He waited and felt his jaw tighten, and then he yelled again, "Get up!"

For a moment, everything seemed muted by the snow, except for his heart, which thumped wildly. He was aware of his shallow breath. His hand rested on Aggie. Her eyes suddenly flew open. She turned her head and laughed. She moved her legs in an amused way, writhing on the ground. "What a ride!" she yipped. She held her stomach. "Holy! I wiped out. I wiped out hard. I've never wiped out!"

Morty got up and spit on the ground. "That wasn't funny," he yelled. He clenched his fists.

Still laughing, but less so now, Aggie sat up. "Oh, *Morty*," she said. "But it *was* fun! I've never gone so fast. I beat you down the hill! I won!"

"You did that on purpose," he said. "To make me think—"

"Me? *You* almost killed me, pushing me like that!" She paused suddenly when Morty began to cry. She stood up and bit her bottom lip. "Morty?"

Morty was too flabbergasted to respond. He spit on the ground again. He wiped his face with his sleeve. His entire body was shaking.

Aggie brushed snow from her jeans and coat before coming closer to him. She looked around, but there was only whiteness, and children somewhere off in the distance, laughing, unaware of what had happened. She stared at Morty in an earnest way. "No one saw," she said. Then, before he realized what was about to happen, before he could think to say anything, Aggie stepped so close to him he could smell her strawberry shampoo. She kissed him on the mouth. Her lips were cold and soft and she kept them pressed to his. His heart swelled, and it was as if everything in that moment were perfect, every fear soothed, every hurt alleviated, every burden lifted. He felt light, deliriously happy. He wanted the kiss to last forever.

When Aggie stepped back, she smiled shyly, and Morty put his sleeve to his mouth. He watched as Aggie retrieved her sled and then ran to find her hat. She glanced back. "I'm sorry, Morty," she said. "I didn't mean to frighten you."

MORTY WALKED HOME, mindful of cars that moved slowly along the icy streets. There was so much he wanted to say, so much he wanted to talk about. How foolish he felt now, thinking of accidents and seeing blood. It wasn't like that day with his mother, the day Morty had cracked a joke and she'd turned her head at the wrong moment. It wasn't like that day at all. Nothing bad had happened. Aggie kissed him, and the kiss was wonderful. Was God behind that, too?

At the house, he took off his boots and left them next to his father's on the porch. Inside, he hung up his coat. In the living room, he found his father sleeping upright on the couch. Generally, after Morty Sr. had said his own personal contrition and after half the bottle of Jack was gone, he fell blissfully asleep each night. Morty pried the bottle from his father's hand and replaced the cap before returning it to the kitchen cupboard, next to the glasses. "Dad," he said, going back, nudging his father. He sat down next to him. "Are you okay?"

His father opened his eyes slightly and yawned. "Oh, Morty," he said. "You're such a good kid."

"Hard day?"

"The hardest."

"Because of the snow? Because of Mom?"

"Not now, Morty," his father said. He patted Morty's thigh.

"Dad," he said finally, "can we talk?"

"Tomorrow," his father said, drifting more. "We'll talk tomorrow."

Morty thought his father might say more but there was nothing else, just the dinging sound from the television game show on television.

He found the hoagie his father had made for him in the refrigerator, along with pop and chips, but he felt too sick to eat, and too confused to jiggle off again. He envisioned Aggie lying in the snow and then opening her eyes to look at him. He thought of the kiss again, and his chest tightened. After a while, Morty slipped on his coat and went back outside.

It was dark now, and colder, though the snow had stopped and the sky appeared clear and black, the moon low and full. Morty walked the ten blocks back toward the school, taking the same streets he did before, passing the duplexes and homes with lanterns and lit windows, the silhouettes of people sometimes visible through the curtains. He wondered about each house, what each was like inside. At Aggie Tuft's house, he stopped and looked for movement inside. One room to the side of the house was lit, and he imagined Aggie and her mother were having a late dinner—possibly her father was there, too, possibly Aggie was talking about the day. Would Aggie mention the kiss? Or was she sitting there, quietly, thinking about Morty, keeping the thrill of the secret close? Was it her first kiss? he wondered. After she pulled her lips from his, after she stepped back, she appeared prettier than Morty ever had imagined, and it was like his mother once said about love—that love can make everything seem perfect

He breathed in the cold until it hurt. A car drove slowly by. He resumed walking until he reached the church, where he stopped to look up at the image of the Virgin Mary, but she looked down, blankly, at him, and he couldn't think of one single prayer to utter. He slipped past the gate and entered the cemetery, past the first and second rows of stones and the maple tree and the sitting bench. In the distance, the lights of the rectory turned off, one by one, and he crouched down and wiped the heavy snow from his mother's headstone. He sat down in front of it, waiting for a sign; he didn't know what the sign would be, exactly, but he was certain when it came he would recognize it. Still, even as he wished this, it occured to him that maybe God didn't see anything, not his jiggling off or looking at *Playboys*, not an accident or a first kiss. Maybe heaven didn't care and

God and all the angels were blind; maybe heaven and God didn't exist at all. Maybe his father was right, that Morty's mother just died, and that was it.

He pulled his legs up and wrapped his arms around them to keep warm. His lips were numb, and his hands tingled with cold. Eventually, he heard a cough in the distance and glanced around to see Father Bastian walking toward him. The priest's gait was unmistakable, the careful way he placed his feet, as if he was worried he'd fall. When he neared, Morty said, "Hello, Father."

"Morty!" Father Bastian cried. He pressed his hand to his chest. In the moonlight his face appeared ghostly. "Are you trying to give me a heart attack, boy?"

"No," Morty said. "I was just sitting here."

Father Bastian exhaled and waited a moment, still feeling his chest. Then he said, "Well, if it hasn't happened yet, I guess I'm good for another day." He tucked his hands in his pockets and looked around. "Quiet night," he said. "You come here often?"

Morty shrugged.

"Nothing to be ashamed of," Father Bastian said. "I come here a lot, too. It's peaceful among the faithfully departed, and a good place to think."

"I guess," Morty replied.

Father Bastian regarded Morty in a sad way. "Something on your mind, Morty?"

"Never," Morty said. He pulled his legs closer, blew into his hands to warm them.

"I see." Father Bastian nodded at the gravestone. "Now, your mother was one of the faithful. She had a lot of faith. In people. In the world. The whole kit and caboodle, really."

"She did."

"The world lost a good soul when your mother passed."

"It did."

"Sometimes things just happen, you know, like accidents, and it's no one's fault. You do know that, don't you?"

"I guess." He rubbed his hands together again and shoved them in his pockets.

Father Bastian sighed. "Okay," he said. "If this is the way the conversation is going to go, then I need a smoke." He removed a pack of cigarettes from his inside coat pocket and then took out a piece of tin foil, which he formed into a cup. "Instant ashtray," he explained. "I don't like to leave a mess."

Morty looked around at the other headstones and he nodded. "Makes sense."

The priest rocked back and forth gently. "It's a deplorable habit, really, and I don't recommend smoking at all. I'd also ask that you don't mention it to the nuns at Our Lady of Misery. If they found out they'd pitch a collective fit. They really would."

"They do have tempers," Morty agreed.

"You don't know the half of it. I'll tell you, those nuns don't leave a man at peace. They want you to shovel their sidewalks in winter, and they want you to rake leaves in fall and clean the church van in summer and plant their gardens in spring. I'm sixty-five, Morty. Do I look like I can do all that anymore? When I die, and if the nuns from Our Lady are there—and they surely will be, with possibly the exception of Sister Agatha—I'm going to ask for a condo outside of heaven, because the nuns will probably see fit to find all sorts of jobs for me, even there. I got into this business to be a servant to *God,* not to clean out gutters."

"I didn't know," Morty said. He didn't want to be rude, but his teeth were chattering and he still hadn't received the sign he was looking for. He held his arms tighter and looked up at the old priest, wishing Father Bastian would leave, but the old man only stamped his cigarette out.

"So now that I've told you all my problems, anything you want to talk about? Because, you know, there's nothing I haven't heard before."

"I know," Morty said, though it was clear from his tone he didn't.

"So is it girl problems, then?" Father Bastian ventured.

Morty grimaced.

"I saw you and Aggie Tuft were talking it up quite a bit today."

"Women," Morty said.

"Don't you know it." Father Bastian pulled his coat collar tighter and looked around again, and Morty could tell the old priest was tired. "It's cold as anything," he said. "I think I have some hot chocolate, if you want, at the rectory. You could keep me company while I have a cup."

"I'm fine, thanks."

"Nothing on your mind?"

"Most days my brain is pretty empty."

"I doubt your brain is empty. I doubt that very much. Like I said, I could use the company myself, so the door's open if you change your mind. I'm like the Motel 6: I'll leave the light on."

"No problem."

"All right then. Goodnight." With that, Father Bastian turned and walked carefully, making his way back across the cemetery grounds. Eventually he disappeared into the darkness, and then, later, a few lights went on in the rectory, one by one. In the distance the building looked warm and inviting. Morty drew his legs closer, for warmth. He was soaked through—his jeans and coat still damp from the day. He shivered. Something small did come to him, looking off into the distance. It seemed to him there were two choices, at least, that he could make in that moment. He could sit there, freezing to death in the process, or he could get up and get a cup of cocoa, which was certain to make him feel better. The world might be large, and God and fate might both be unknowable, but at least there was in that moment a simple clarity. The thought of being inside and warm consoled him, so much that Morty stood up and ran after the priest. He ran so fast he surprised himself with his desire. He ran so fast he felt as though he might fall, toward the rectory and lights.

ACKNOWLEDGMENTS

Most of the stories in *Everyone but You* were written during or shortly after my MFA program, during the years 2003 through 2005. I'd like to express my thanks to Louise Crowley and Vermont College. Mary Grimm, Christopher Noel, Laurie Alberts, Victoria Redel, David Jauss, Douglas Glover, Ellen Lesser, and Abby Frucht all led excellent workshops and imparted much wisdom. The talented Beth Helms inspired me to love words and to try harder.

Dennis Foley, Peach Gazda, Paige Harlow, and Terri Sutton kept me sane during those killer ten-day residencies, during which time I missed both my husband and dog to inordinate degrees. They are true friends.

My best friend and husband, Phil, has read countless drafts of everything I've ever written and so by now has realized the great majority of my hopes, fears, and quirky hang-ups.

My agent, Denise Shannon, has believed in me and kept my spirits buoyant, and for that I owe her my gratitude.

My editors, copy editors, and publicists at Random House have provided invaluable input and taught me much about the publishing process. Jennifer Hershey, Jessie Waters, and Dennis Ambrose have my sincere thanks.

Finally, many thanks to the literary journals that published such early work, and to the Illinois Arts Council and Christopher Isherwood Foundation for their support of the arts.

ABOUT THE AUTHOR

Sandra Novack is the author of the novel *Precious*. Her short stories have appeared in *The Iowa Review, The Gettysburg Review, Gulf Coast, The Chattahoochee Review,* and elsewhere. Novack currently resides in Chicago with her husband, Phil.